# HENG MOUNTAIN

## MIKE ROBINSON

SilverWood

Published in 2016 by SilverWood Books

SilverWood Books Ltd
14 Small Street, Bristol, BS1 1DE, United Kingdom
www.silverwoodbooks.co.uk

ISBN 978-1-78132-463-9 (paperback)
ISBN 978-1-78132-502-5 (hardback)
ISBN 978-1-78132-464-6 (ebook)

British Library Cataloguing in Publication Data
A CIP catalogue record for this book is available from
the British Library

Set in Sabon by SilverWood Books
Printed on responsibly sourced paper

*To my parents, my wife, and my children*

# CONTENTS

# 1

## WHISPER OF A FIGHT

The wooden door swung open and crashed against the stone wall like a thunderstorm shuddering through the house. With the front door still trembling, Jun staggered into a room and yelled, "Father, where are you?"

His father did not answer him.

Minutes later, when Jun realised his father was not inside, he moved to the back of the house. When he reached the back door, he fell outside into a courtyard. "Father...the soldiers... they are coming..." Trying to catch his breath, he walked along a pebbled footpath which led him away from the house. At the end of the path, he found his father sitting in a stone chair.

His father had been resting in his idyllic rock garden with the evening sun as his only companion, and as Jun approached him, his father steadied himself in the chair and pushed himself up straight. He was still shaken by the echoes of 'father' bellowing throughout his house. Both men stared at each other, neither wanting to acknowledge the terrifying truth that had chased Jun to the village.

When Jun reached the seat, he fell at his father's feet and sighed, "I'm sorry for startling you. We must leave the village."

Shen, Jun's father, reached out and sighed, "Your face."
He touched the blood seeping from Jun's forehead.

"Father, we couldn't hold them, but we have rattled their

armour and now they are riding with the resentment of the devil towards us. We have little time." Jun's words sank his father deeper into his most trusted chair. With his father's eyes fixed on the bloody scars on his face, Jun said, "We fought with our bare hands and broken farming tools, but we were no match for the emperor's men."

"How many of our men have been killed?" Shen asked, with the fear of the entire village mirrored in his face.

"Too many," Jun replied. "Less than a hundred men returned with me."

Jun stood up and moved away. Shen said, "Why didn't you listen? How many children are crying now because you—"

"I know," Jun interrupted. "But I couldn't just lie down and let these barbaric invaders crush our freedom."

"I tried to tell you," Shen said. "I wanted to live in peace. They might have listened..."

"Father, stop!" Jun yelled. "How many countries have they ripped apart? They will treat us like dogs and feed us with dust."

Shen pushed himself up and stood behind Jun. He placed a hand on his son's shoulder and said, "I'm sorry, Jun. You wanted to protect the village."

"Do you really believe that, Father?"

"We all believe that," Shen said, turning Jun around to face him. Shen put a hand on Jun's face and said, "When you were a young boy, your mother whispered to you, every night when you were asleep, 'Listen to your heart and hold on to your dreams.' She would lie next to you for hours."

"You don't—"

"Yes, I do," Shen said. "As you got older, she'd kiss you every morning and yell, 'Search for *your* inner strength because it will be far greater than mine.' She wanted you to be strong and *still* listen to your heart. You did."

"Father, please..."

"Jun, before she passed away, even when she didn't have enough strength to speak, her loving eyes showed me how she wanted to protect her precious little boy. 'Empty worried thoughts from your mind.' She insisted that I keep telling you this."

"I'm not a child anymore, Father," Jun said. "You've never really understood me. I just wanted to protect our peaceful way of life."

"You're growing into a brave young man. I see so much of your mother in you. She would have done the same," Shen said as he wiped the blood from Jun's face. "And I know you better than you think, Jun. You would have fought with the bravery of a thousand men, but I must ask you to find more of the inner strength your mother prayed for."

"What do you mean?"

"Jun, we...we need to surrender to the soldiers. If we don't they will punish our people for a hundred years."

"Surrender?" Jun cried. "But we must run, hide and take the women and children away from the village. We need to find another way to send them—"

"I'm sorry," Shen interrupted. "How many more soldiers will the emperor send, and if we do not surrender, they will tear up our village and burn down every home here."

Jun walked past his father and fell on to the chair. "What have I done?"

Shen moved closer to Jun and said, "Rest for a while. I will speak to the other elders and ask them to ride with me. We need to talk to the emperor's men before they reach the village." He then followed the path back to the house.

Jun tilted his head back and felt the warmth of the sun on his battle-scarred face. His heart jumped as he felt his freedom being dragged out of his body by the northern invaders.

When Shen walked out of the front of the house, he stopped and smiled at three villagers who were following the tears of the returning rebels to the centre of the village.

One villager smiled back at him and said, "Shen, the elders are going to the water well. We will wait for you there." He gestured to Shen to follow him to the well. "Tell Jun to hurry. We must send word to the other villages and tell them we need more men to fight."

Shen watched more villagers wander aimlessly past his house. He closed his eyes and thought of the children crying for their fathers. With his troubled eyes barely open, he moved back inside the house. He stepped into the courtyard, and just before he reached the end of the footpath, he caught a glimpse of Jun wiping away a tear with his bloodied hands.

Hearing his father's footsteps, Jun rubbed his eyes and tried to hide his tears of defeat. Shen stopped walking; the only time he remembered seeing Jun cry was when he had kissed his mother for the last time.

Shen moved closer to Jun and said, "Please come with me. You are the one person they need to see alive, and the only soul who can give them hope. I can't do this alone."

Jun couldn't look at his father. He stared at a miniature waterfall in the corner of the courtyard and watched the water trickling over pebbles and into a pond filled with gigantic goldfish.

"Father, for generations your family has helped to build every home in this village. My mother's family planted every tree around it. How can you surrender our history to them?"

"I'm not, Jun," Shen pleaded. "Your mother used to say, 'Sometimes you will need to give a feast of food to get the crumbs on the plate. And when you've licked many plates, you will have eaten a banquet.' She was right: one day you will eat like an emperor."

Jun sat as rigid as the stone chair. "I wish I understood my mother's wisdom. I'm sorry for failing both of you."

"You've not failed us. Your mother said you would find your own destiny and walk taller than any man. She also said that one day you would be guided by a guardian of light." Shen moved closer to the fishpond and placed his hand under the running waterfall. "She put the fish in the pond to help you understand her."

"Understand her? How?"

"She created this pond for you because she wanted you to see the world through her eyes. The still water is her mind, the fish her innermost thoughts and the water trickling over the waterfall is everything she experienced in her life."

"I wish she was here now."

"She is," Shen said. "Look how calm the pond is. The last thing I remember her saying to me, while we watched you sleep, was, 'He will lead our people to a brighter future, but he will need to travel to the corners of Asia to believe it.'"

"I remember so little about her, but I remember her telling me how she travelled to every river in the province to find those fish." Jun smiled. "Fish that glow at night."

"Yes, she did," Shen said, smiling and closing his eyes. He filled his mind with a picture of Jun's mother diving into an icy river to catch one fish which was bigger than both of her hands. Opening his eyes, he walked back to Jun and said, "Please speak to them. They will listen to you." He tried to pull Jun out of the chair. "They still believe in you. If you tell them we must surrender, they will. If we don't, many more children will cry for their fathers, and…"

Shen was hit with a vision of the Manchu leader revelling in his latest conquest. He let go of Jun when he saw rebels

13

hanging along the roads to the emperor's palace.

"What is it, Father?" Jun asked.

Shen covered his face with his hands, trying to shield his vision from Jun. The image filled his mind of a hundred executions, which thrilled the Manchu leader, as the peasants of the province were crippled by famine. Filling with despair, Shen shuddered at the thought of the Manchu leader's deadly message to the Hunan people who had dared to fight back against him.

The Manchu soldiers had never lost a battle. Their malicious mantra had been screamed across all of Asia throughout the seventeenth century. Their leader, Narchi, had ordered his men to cripple territories and communities. Many countries fell without a single drop of Manchu blood seeping into his fresh land.

Narchi was fierce and unforgiving. He lavished himself with the wealth from the defeated countries, and this was the essence of his latest invasion. His soldiers absorbed his brutal demeanour and breezed south through China's provinces like a river bursting its banks. However, when they reached the city of Beijing they collided with the Great Wall of China.

From east to west, the Great Wall swept across China's desert dunes and magnificent mountains. Ten men deep and twenty high, the wall had protected the southern territories for a thousand years, and the ruling Ming Dynasty for three hundred years. When the Manchu soldiers marched to the city, Emperor Ming ordered his men to stand guard on top of the wall and to watch, as their enemy peppered the wall with their spears.

For three weeks, the wall held firm. When the Manchu soldiers had thrown their last spear, Emperor Ming ordered his men to send their cannonballs hurtling through the evening sky. Thousands of Manchus were killed and their leader was days away from defeat until a Ming general betrayed the ruling emperor.

General Taan had fallen from grace with Emperor Ming for his brutal treatment of the peasants of Beijing. The emperor had sent him to the desert, but Taan believed he was worthy of much more than a command post built in the sand, and his embarrassment fuelled his hunger to help the Manchus. When the northern invaders were ready to retreat, he rode back to the capital to speak with the Manchu leader. With a taste of defeat on his lips, Narchi accepted the general's offer of a traitorous allegiance.

One night, with Emperor Ming's soldiers resting in their barracks, Taan carried out Narchi's plan and rode with six hundred men to the iron gates holding the Manchu soldiers out of Beijing. Fooling the guards at the gates, he said, "His Majesty has brought me back to help protect the city. He has ordered me to guard the gates."

The soldiers standing on the wall opened the gates, and General Taan and his most loyal men rode into the city. As soon as his men were on top of the wall, Taan ordered them to wear pale ribbons tied to their backs as a sign of betrayal to the emperor.

That night, General Taan gave the order to his men to open the gates, and the Manchu soldiers charged into the capital like wild horses running through an open plain. Taan hid on top of the wall as the Manchu soldiers hunted for the emperor's men. He peeped over the wall and watched the Ming soldiers being slaughtered on his night of betrayal: he had opened the gates to the city for the promise of his own province and the autonomy of an army of two thousand men. When the city had fallen, General Taan rode through the streets of Beijing as if he was the ruling emperor.

After Narchi's deadly dream had been delivered, he seized the banished emperor's palace in the centre of Beijing. With spring blooming throughout the city, he stomped through the palace gardens like a spoilt child splashing in a sea of sapphire flowers. For a month, he bathed in his tranquil surroundings.

One morning while Narchi was resting on his throne, he half-heartedly ordered, "General Taan, I want you to march south and complete my conquest."

"Of course, Narchi. I will order my men to ride in the morning."

"I'm giving you the Hunan province," Narchi said, agitated because the general had called him 'Narchi' in front of his advisors. "And as *your* emperor, I want you to reap the wealth of the province in *my* name and spare no one who stands in *my* way."

The traitorous general accepted his emperor's gift: a province in the south with little food to feed its own people.

Within a year of General Taan opening the gates, Narchi fulfilled his desire to declare himself the ruling emperor of Asia. He persecuted the people of Beijing, poor and noble, and they accepted their new enforced emperor without a whisper of a fight. With General Taan's men joining the Manchu soldiers, the peasants of Beijing lost their only hope of fighting back. When he marched his men into the Hunan province, the Hunan peasants' loyalty to the expelled emperor was tested by every tear in the villages Taan and his men tormented.

Within weeks of storming into the Hunan province, General Taan ordered his men to seize a derelict stately home, on a hill overlooking the region. He arrogantly showered himself with the little wealth of the land and sat for hours, gazing through broken windows which were as wide as the gates of the Great Wall. He laughed at the farmers below as they ploughed their fields until they dropped to the ground, trying to feed him.

Taan filled his expanding suit of armour, but lost his appetite to satisfy the emperor's order to complete the invasion. One day, when he had drunk the day dry with his last jug of wine given to him as a trophy by the emperor, he ordered a young lieutenant to come to the dining room.

"Take…theee hundred men…to the borders of this dill and dairy province and bring me something to dink," he slurred, clasping on to the table in front of him.

The lieutenant marched south with his men, and when they reached a valley north of Jun's village, they encountered their first ripple of resistance.

Jun and his oldest friend, Ling, had rallied the villagers to fight back against the soldiers. They had set traps for the emperor's men, who stumbled into the ambushes. The two young leaders then led the rebels to become a constant chink in the soldiers' armour.

After weeks of terrorising the soldiers, the rebels diverted the lieutenant and his men to a weakened bridge and waited patiently for the soldiers to march over the bridge. The lieutenant walked behind his men, and when the soldiers were nearly over, Jun gave the order to blow away the rotten stilts holding up the bridge. With a puff of gunpowder, most of the Manchu soldiers fell into the water and floated along the river to hell.

With only ten men left to lead, the lieutenant scrambled back to General Taan quicker than the general could drink a jug of wine. When he arrived at the general's stately home, he followed the crisp scent of crushed grapes as he sobbed, "General…our men…they've been taken…by a brittle bridge."

He found General Taan lying drunk on the floor and threw himself down next to him, bemoaning, "I bravely ran with the surviving men to the barracks, but hundreds of peasant farmers followed us, laughing at the emperor. They ordered us to go back to him."

Two of the twenty 'peasant farmers' that had chased the lieutenant back to the general had been Jun and Ling.

Twitching and trying to sober up, the general steadied himself as he listened to the tormented lieutenant as he grovelled on his knees in front of him. The lieutenant blamed the weakened bridge for the loss of his men and pleaded, "General, please give me more men to send these pathetic peasants down the river. If you don't, they promised to send us back to the emperor."

The general wobbled to his feet and then fell sharply on to the table. He rolled along it, sending the porcelain jugs, which were as red as the wine they had held, crashing to the floor.

Hours later, after the general had sobered up, he sent the order for every soldier in the province to ride to the barracks. Within two weeks of the lieutenant running back to the general, fifteen hundred men were beating their armour for the rebels' blood in the village below General Taan's home. Taan had ordered the rest of his men to guard him and his stately home.

One morning, Taan strolled with a purpose in front of the soldiers and shouted, "We've lost good men to these peasants." With his every step, his men banged their fists on their armour, until he stopped halfway along the line of enthusiastic soldiers. "Men we will honour by ripping these rebels apart." His face changed to the colour of the porcelain jugs broken on the dining room floor. He turned

to face the soldiers and stuttered with rage, "Bring…me…
back…their…leader!"

"Sir, I will ride to the village near the fallen bridge. My
men will drag the elders behind their horses until one of them
cries out the rebel leader's name."

"This is your last chance, Lieutenant," General Taan
snarled. "Do not come back without their leader."

The lieutenant saluted him and rode out of the barracks.
The soldiers beat their drums with every step to the village.

Jun, Ling and a small band of rebels tried to hold back the
soldiers, but the lieutenant's men marched harder than ever.
They tore up the ground beneath their feet and crushed any
resistance they encountered. The young rebel leaders had no
choice but to succumb to the wounds of the surviving rebels
and retreat to their homes.

Jun's village was the hub of the Hunan province, surrounded
by dirt track roads flowing towards the neighbouring villages.
South of the village was an emerald forest, deeper than any
ocean; to the east a lake as vast as the city of Beijing. The
trails to the west were now bursting with menace marching
towards the village: the lieutenant and his men were only
days away from it.

Jun had held dying rebels on the battlefield and seen the
hunger for more blood in the soldiers' eyes, and this was
the image chasing him back to his home. While his father
was pleading with him to talk to the villagers, four children
had climbed on to the stone walls of the water well in the
centre of the village. Frightened by the sight of the wounded
rebels resting against the well, the children stood patiently
on top, desperate to catch a glimmer of hope from Jun.
Within an hour of Jun finding his father, the entire village had
surrounded the well.

19

One of the children cried, "I can't see Jun. Where is he?"

"Is it true?" Another child screamed as she was pulled up on to the well. "Are the soldiers coming?"

The well had stood for two hundred years and the village had been built around it, with circular houses spinning away from it like wooden whirlwinds drifting out of sight. At the base of the well, men, women and children helped to bathe the beaten bodies of the rebels in the crystal-clear water. The villagers looked upon the well as a sign of hope and prosperity, and with the fear of the soldiers having drawn them there, they stood waiting for Jun to come out of the house.

Inside the courtyard, Shen pleaded with Jun.

"You must talk to them now. We are running out of time." Shen had shaken his vision of Narchi from his mind and was walking towards the house.

"Will they listen?" Jun asked, walking behind his father.

"To you? Yes, of course they will." Shen turned to face his son. "But before you speak to them, I need to give you something. Wait here."

Shen left Jun in front of a metal cage and returned with his hands full of meat. He opened the cage and guided a black eagle, with wings the width of the well, out of the gate. He put the meat on the ground for the bird and then walked inside its silver shelter.

"What are you doing, Father?" Jun asked.

Shen did not reply. He moved a clay slab along the ground, pulled out a wooden puzzle box and walked out of the cage.

"My puzzle box," Jun said. "Why is it hidden in the cage?"

"Jun, our people have hunted for centuries with eagles

20

and hawks. We follow their might and wisdom." Shen stroked the bird's feathers. "When I made this puzzle box for you, you tried for days to open it. You never gave up, just like the hunting eagles." Shen slid the pieces of wood around to open the box. He pulled out a white cotton cloth and passed it to Jun.

Jun sighed as he went to wipe the blood from his brow.

"No, Jun." His father pulled back his hand. "This is a map. I'm sure it will guide you to a safe place. Your mother said it leads to a path of greatness."

"Greatness?" Jun repeated, stretching the cloth as wide as the bird's claws. "I can't follow any path. I must go with the other men."

"You can't give yourself to the Manchu leader." Shen's stern tone startled the eagle. "You need to protect this map."

"Why, Father? Is it going to stop the soldiers from destroying our village?"

"Jun, please. Your mother told me that there is another map, and when you join them together, they will show a path to a heavenly place."

"I can't order the men to surrender and then run from the soldiers." Jun followed his father into the house. "What about the men who gave their lives for our freedom?"

"If you do not protect the map, their children will never taste freedom. I will tell them why you had to go. You must take this map with you and leave the village."

Holding the cotton map, Jun asked, "Where is the other piece?"

"I don't know, but I believe you will find it." Shen moved closer to Jun and brought his hands together, covering the map. "Many people in our province were given powerful teachings to protect, secrets they cannot share with their loved ones, but now is the time for me to share mine with you."

Jun stared at his father's eyes, looked deep inside his father's soul, and then said, "I will protect this map, Father…" He sighed. "My mother…she spoke of these secrets and I will not fail her again." Jun remembered the legends of the teachings, and accepted that he had to order the village to surrender.

Shen let go of Jun's hand, and Jun followed him to the front door. "Your map will lead us to peace," Shen said, stepping out of the house, "but first we must speak to our friends."

Shen helped Jun towards the well until Jun was grabbed by two villagers who shielded him from the caring hands swaying towards him. The villagers offered words of comfort, falling at Jun's feet. Jun held his head down, not wanting to show the dried blood peeling off his face, and when he reached the well, silence wiped away the tears of the villagers who were desperate to hear him bring calm to the village. The children standing on top of the well helped Jun up on to the stone walls.

Jun drew in a deep breath and shouted, "Please listen." Jun scanned the village, looking for his friend, Ling. "The women and children will need to stay in their homes. Men, wait here by the well. The elders are going to ride to the soldiers and surrender."

Several villagers screamed.

"No, Jun, no!"

"We can't show them any weakness. They will never let us live in peace," one of the village elders cried.

"I am sorry," Jun muttered, sinking back on to the wooden pillars of the well. The children pushed him back on to his feet. "A thousand men will die trying to defeat the Manchu soldiers. We tried to send them back to the hell on earth they call home, but more of them come each day."

For an hour, Jun fought a war of words with his people.

Although he was stronger than any man standing before him, he couldn't find the words to warn them that if they didn't surrender, their homes would soon become the latest battleground for the northern invaders. A wave of voices knocked Jun off the well. He landed on the ground like one of the fallen rebels.

Every man, woman and child stood silent, until a solitary voice shouted, "Listen to me! Jun has been fighting with my words and not his own."

Jun looked at his father.

"He has tried to defeat the Manchu soldiers – but lost many bloody battles – so we must help him fight with his inner strength and to find another way to send them back for good. We must do this for the future of our children."

Jun smiled back at Shen as he recalled how his father had prayed for peace every night as he paced the pebbled paths swirling away from the well. Jun thought of the night when he told his father the Manchu soldiers had marched into the city of Beijing, and how his father had pleaded with him not to fight. But now, after bathing the wounds of the rebels, their broken spirits had heaved Shen into the battle.

Shen walked among the fresh tears of his friends and yelled, "Now is the time for a greater wisdom." As Shen spoke, Jun hobbled towards the entrance of the village, sealed by a wall of wooden blockades. "And this will help to replace our broken weapons."

Jun walked towards the barricades and stopped at a broken cart abandoned by refugees from a neighbouring village. With the villagers drifting towards him, he pulled his bruised and weakened body up on to the cart and looked back to them. Standing taller than ever, Jun opened his arms as if to wrap them around his friends and held on to their hopes and fears.

Inhaling the history of the village, Jun yelled, "These magnificent landscapes have embraced more than a thousand years of mystical knowledge: secrets only the bravest souls dared to find." He could feel his mother beside him. "We are the guardians of these secrets, and they shall not fall into unforgiving hands."

Jun's words drew the villagers closer to him. "For generations, the legends of these secrets have been whispered along the hidden trails of our province. One of these legends states that a crystal spirit will hold all of China's secrets together, but they must be kept from darkened souls. We must fight to protect this prophecy."

"We will fight with you!" was the cry from the men of the village.

A few seconds later, with his mother's wisdom spiralling up inside him, Jun yelled, "I will... I will lead you to the Emerald Forest where we will build traps big enough to swallow the emperor's palace!" Jun's words spun around the village like a hawk searching for its latest prey. As the village erupted with cries for the soldiers' blood, Jun scanned it, looking for Ling.

When Ling had retreated to the village, he had run to his family home where he had found his parents kneeling in a room at the side of the house. The elderly couple, who had cared for Ling and brought him up as their own son, were praying for his safe return. When Ling charged into the sunroom, he was startled by the glittering evening sunlight being reflected around the room. Dazed, he rubbed his eyes in disbelief and fell on his knees next to a sword placed between his parents.

Ling stretched forward to touch the sword. "Where did you get it?"

"Ling, this sword is older than our village. It will split a tree in two and send evil to the ground," his mother replied.

"How long have you had it? And why did you hide it from me?"

"The sword is blessed," his father said. "It's yours."

"Mine? Who gave it to you?"

"Someone who said we would know when to give it to you."

"Give it to me!" Ling yelled, reaching for the sword. "What was his name?"

"I don't know his name," his father said. "We only met him once."

"It's beautiful."

"Ling, we've been blessed with you, and this is our gift to you."

Ling's parents sat and watched him swirling the sword around his head. After a few minutes, he stopped spinning and squeezed the wooden shaft of the sword with one hand. With the other hand, he stroked the metal blade. His fingers tingled along the perfectly formed edge. With the sword glowing in the sun, he brushed the delicate symbols engraved on it.

Ling scrutinised the markings on the sword as he moved over to a table sheltered from the sun. "What are these symbols?"

"We don't know," his mother said. "But we believe one day you will find out and fulfil the sacred teachings of this sword."

"I know nothing about this sword."

"We were entrusted with it on the first day we held you. It belongs to your family and you are its rightful guardian."

Ling placed the sword on the table and held hands with his parents. He said, "I will always remember what you've done for me, and I promise our people will remember my family name."

"One more thing, before you go," his mother said, her eyes puffing with sadness. "In your hands, the sword holds extraordinary powers. It's not just for drawing blood. You must remember this."

"I will," Ling promised as he picked up the sword. "I must find Jun and show him this. He has lost the will for battle and this sword might convince him to fight again." He kissed his mother and ran out of the house.

When Ling reached the well, Jun was pulling himself up on the abandoned cart. Ling couldn't see him over the villagers, so he pushed his sacred weapon into the ground, leapt on to the well and listened to his friend's battle cry. With Jun's words pulling the villagers towards him, Ling remembered the first day they had met.

At the age of eight, Jun had begged Ling's parents to let him help them harvest their farm because their crops were being destroyed by the hottest summer for a hundred years. Like many of the families in the village, Ling's parents were days from losing everything, so they warmly accepted the young boy's help.

With his plough taller than him, Jun battled through the crops and pulled out barley with his bare hands. His determination to save the farm was his way of thanking Ling's parents for giving what they could spare to help his mother when she was dying from the famine. Every year after his first harvest, Jun helped Ling and his family with the farm until he grew stronger than any oxen grazing on it.

Now Jun spotted Ling standing on top of the well, and shouted, "China has always had unwanted observers, but none more so than the murdering Manchu tribe."

Ling held his sword high so Jun could see it. Jun yelled, "Their leader is a tyrant who thrills himself with aspirations of a total invasion. We have little to give them, but the lure of riches has brought the soldiers to our province. Their leader has a burning hunger to take our history and our sacred teaching from us, and our destiny is to stop them."

The two young rebel leaders smiled at each other across the village. With the roar of the villagers bellowing in between them, they willingly accepted that their fight with the emperor had just begun. With cries of 'freedom' circling around the village, the rebellion was brought back to life: a rebellion soon to perturb the imposturous persecutor.

Jun's battle cry was bellowed across the Hunan province. Like a calling from the woods themselves, his words of war drew peasant farmers from every village to the Emerald Forest. His promise to his father to protect the sacred map, and the powers of Ling's sword, would send the young men on a journey to find and protect China's most precious secrets.

# 2

## ARMY OF ARROGANCE

The next morning, Ling ordered twenty men to round up the horses surrounding the village.

Jun helped the villagers to gather up their farming tools and placed them near the water well. He hobbled through the village, yelling, "I have sent word to every village in the province to join us in the Emerald Forest. Many villagers will follow us there, and we will lure the lieutenant into a battle that will be yelled around the palace walls."

Later that evening, the men were ready to march to the Emerald Forest. They stood at the entrance to the village and hugged their loved ones tighter than ever. The rebels held on to their families' prayers for their safe return, then twenty jumped on to their horses while the others lined up behind.

Jun stood next to a chariot which his father had built many years before and thanked his father for believing in him once more. He also promised to protect Ling, and then climbed into the chariot and laid down on the crumbling pieces of wood holding it together. Ling kissed his mother goodbye, and his father helped him on to his horse, which was ready to pull the chariot.

Sitting on his horse, Ling turned back to Jun. "Don't worry, Jun, the wagon will hold until we reach the forest."

Jun smiled as Ling held his sword high above his head,

then Ling turned to face the elders, women and children who were staying in the village.

"We'll try to send the lieutenant and his men back to the general, but some of us will not return. Please take care of the children who will be waiting by the well for their fathers. Take them into your homes, cherish them as your own."

Ling rode out of the village, surrounded by the rebels on horses. The other rebels marched behind and followed the trail to the forest.

After four days of resting, Jun was woken by an army of men bellowing his name. He lifted his head and stared at the hundreds of rebels trailing the chariot. With a weak wave of his hand, Jun acknowledged them, and with their passion for freedom cheering his every move, Ling galloped faster with every roar. Jun stopped waving his hand and held on to the chariot when his body bashed harder against it.

Ten days after leaving the village, the rebel army reached the Emerald Forest. Riding on his horse, Ling raised his sword to signal to the rebels to wait before they entered the woods. The convoy stood still, captivated by the forest's beauty. Jun pushed himself up in the chariot and his eyes followed the forest as far as he could see.

Resting on the edge of the woods, the rebels listened to the rustling of tall trees as they filled themselves with memories of when they used to live in peace. Ling ordered two rebels to hide Jun's chariot in the woods, and the remaining rebels marched into the forest, slowly moving in between tree trunks under the blanket of emerald leaves floating high above them.

"Look, Jun, look!" one of the rebels said with his eyes floating over the wispier shades of green flourishing from every season. "They remind me of this," he added as he unravelled a patchwork blanket from around his waist. "It's my son's. He wouldn't let me leave our home until I was protected by it."

Jun and the rebels nearby smiled at him as he held the blanket to his face, soothing his senses for a second. He then wrapped the comforting shield around him.

As they travelled through the darkening woods, Ling ordered the rebels to rest on a cushion of fallen bark from maple trees towering into the sky. After walking for many days, some of the rebels from Jun's village fell to the ground, still suffering from injuries from their many battles with the emperor's men. Once they were inside the sanctuary of the woods, the others collected leaves for them to sleep on.

Later, when most of the rebels were asleep, an older man, who had travelled from the southern mountain range to the forest, foraged for flowers. He searched through the night, gathering leaves to create herbal remedies to heal the injured rebels' wounds. Within days of absorbing the plants' potions, Jun and the wounded rebels had the strength to help build weapons for their fight with the lieutenant's men. No one saw the old man again.

Just days after the rebels had marched out of their villages, the lieutenant and his men barged through the barriers protecting them. In every village, the soldiers wasted no time in following the lieutenant's orders: "Shake their homes until the rebel leader tumbles out of his hut." The soldiers turned every house upside down, but they only found the village elders, women and children hiding inside.

While the soldiers tormented the villages in the province, the young lieutenant laughed at the frightened children as they peered through the windows of their homes. "Your fathers are scurrying like rats to the forest, just like the men from other villages!"

"Or maybe they are digging burrows to hide in, sir!"

The lieutenant and his men continued to torture the villagers, and the elders let the soldiers believe their laughter. "The men have fled to the forest!"

Inside the woods, the rebels were willingly chopping up fallen trees with their blunt farming tools. Their hearts and minds had been woken by Jun's prophecy for peace, which had walked with them for weeks. Soon they were ready to form a human wall of resistance against the emperor's men.

One morning, Jun and Ling welcomed more rebels at the edge of the woods. "Follow the trail into the forest," Jun ordered them. "You'll be greeted by the sight of our people building weapons to send the Manchu soldiers back to their emperor!"

One of the new recruits said, "Jun, there are more rebels coming."

"Yes, we know," Ling said, annoyed that the rebel had ignored him. "Soon we will have men from every village in the province."

"We've heard that the lieutenant and his men are laughing at us," replied the rebel. "They are running through the villages and shouting, 'Where are the men? Are they wandering to the woods like sheep following their peasant shepherd?'"

"We will fight like tigers," Ling yelled. "And the lieutenant's laughter will roar back to the general in defeat."

A few minutes later, Jun yelled to Ling, "Look, there! Hundreds of men are coming." The lieutenant's army of arrogance was sending more rebels to join the young rebel leaders.

"I thought you were ready to run from the emperor's men," Ling laughed. "But I'm glad I was wrong."

"My father brought me here," Jun said.

"Yes he did, but your passion for freedom is calling them into the woods."

"They're not coming here because of me. They are leaving their families behind because they want to protect their land."

Jun walked towards one rebel and welcomed him to the forest, but the rebels behind him walked past him. Ling had pulled his sword out of his coat and the rebels, captivated by its splendour, walked over to him.

Jun moved closer to Ling. "The legends embedded around your sword are pulling the villagers from their homes." He acknowledged the sparkling weapon. "Apparently they state that the sword will win more battles than me."

"Don't be jealous, my friend," Ling replied, pointing the sword at Jun. "This sword might save your life one day."

"It may." Jun laughed, lifting a crumbling branch off the ground. "But for now I'll worship this." He held the branch above his head, but it broke in two. Their laughter reached the rebels in the heart of the forest.

They walked back into the woods, then Ling asked, "Where do you think the sword came from?"

"My father never spoke of the sword."

"Never?"

"Maybe he didn't know of it," Jun suggested. "What did your parents tell you?"

"They said, it was the right time to give it to me and I should remember its *mysterious* powers."

"Really...and what might they be?"

"I don't know, but my mother was adamant it has them. What do you think?" Ling asked, hoping the legends were true.

"I think the soldiers will be here soon, so let's pray they witness its powers." Jun laughed again. "My father did say the village had protected many of the province's secrets, so if you believe in his wisdom, the sword will one day send back the emperor's men." Jun half-smiled at Ling. He moved closer to him and, not wanting to be outdone by his friend, Jun whispered, "My father gave me something to protect. It's a map drawn on the purest pale cotton."

"What? A map? Why didn't you tell me before?"

"I forgot. I needed to rest…"

"Rest?" Ling snapped. "I didn't rest for a day, an hour or a minute. I led the rebels here while you were sleeping in the cart."

"Yes, I know," Jun said. "I didn't think it was important." He pulled the map out of his pocket. "My father said there is another map, and when they become one the path shown will lead me to a heavenly place."

"A heavenly place?" Ling laughed, holding the cotton map up to the sun. "That will help us. Who has the other piece?"

"I don't know, but my parents believed I would find it."

"Where is it?"

"I don't know." Jun sighed. "But I know I need to find the rebels whom I ordered to carve out spears from the trees. The lieutenant and his men will soon be upon us."

Jun took the map and walked with greater determination into the woods. Ling followed behind him, saying, "It's beautiful, the map, but it's not a sparkling sword of secrets."

Ling swung the sword above his head, and Jun glared at his friend. With his stomach spinning faster than the sword, he thought, Why were his parents given the sword? Jun shook the resentment from his mind and said, "No, it's not, but it was a gift from my mother."

Ling stopped waving the sword when his friend's eyes reflected more than just the emerald leaves sparkling with the midday sun. "If your parents said it would lead you somewhere, then it will." For a moment Ling remembered the wisdom of Jun's mother. "Your mother said you'd lead our people to peace."

"Who told you that?"

"My parents."

"She must have been talking about you, little Ling. You have the sword, so you must be the chosen one."

Ling walked behind Jun for a while and smiled back at the rebels as they hid crossbows and shields, created from the forest, along the trails in the woods. As Ling caught up with Jun, he agreed. "I'll lead the archers on to the plain, ready for the soldiers as they march to the forest."

Jun walked ahead of Ling and said, "All right, I'll organise the rebels that will charge on foot, and the men with horses. I will make sure they stay hidden in the woods."

When Jun reached the towering trees in the heart of the forest, one of the rebels resting there cried, "We are ready to fight!"

Jun stopped and waited for Ling to come. Jun held on to Ling's arm and pulled him closer. "We must not fail them. Their families are depending on us too."

"Don't worry, Jun, my archers will pin every Manchu soldier to the ground with their arrows."

"I will hold you to your word, Ling, but we must also use our inner strength. We should always hold our family's wisdom and not take their blessings for granted—"

"You are right again, brother," Ling interrupted, patting Jun on the back with the sword and smirking. "Don't forget you are blessed with me too!"

"*Blessed* with you?" Jun laughed. "We will see, little Ling. You may end up being a curse, but for now I need your help to train the rebels," he added, pointing to archers sharpening their arrows.

"My men will remind you of your blessings."

"Don't be too keen to go into battle with the emperor's men. Remember what my father told us," Jun said, trying to cool Ling's enthusiasm for the battle ahead. "He said we must fight with wisdom, and not just with weapons."

Ling walked over to the archers and ordered them to gather wood to build barricades on the plain.

Jun ran to the rebels chopping up trees in the forest and yelled, "The archers will break the soldiers' ranks in two." He then ran deeper into the forest where lines of horsemen blended into tree trunks as wide as three men. "We can't fight them on the plains, but we must fool them into believing we want to."

As the weeks passed, Ling organised his small group of archers to build barricades on the plains flowing away from the forest. He was meticulous in his planning and placed each of the timber barricades thirty steps in front of the last.

"We will use these barricades to guide some of the soldiers into the forest where they will fall into our traps. We will send the other soldiers to the trees – the rebels there are ready to launch the spears."

Days later, on a hot summer's afternoon, Jun ran to Ling's barricade and crouched down next to him.

"I want you to hold the soldiers on the plain. You will need to split the soldiers' ranks in two and fool them into the many traps waiting for them in the woods." Jun pointed to the forest. "You must send the other sol—"

"I have already given my men their orders," Ling interrupted, his face as red as the midday sun. "What if we can't split them?"

"You will," Jun snapped back. "Just send them into the woods." He pushed himself out of the barricade without waiting for a response.

Jun ran to the traps in the forest and fell against a tree with a huge hornets' nest bulging and buzzing from its branches. The wasps swooped down towards Jun, who jumped to his feet and ran along the trail to the traps. With rattled wasps circling around him, he changed direction and ran to the only pond in the woods.

When he reached the pond, he leapt into the water and sat on the bottom. The water just covered his face as he held his breath and waited for the wasps to pass. A minute later, he surfaced and dragged himself out of the murky water. He walked over to rebels crafting spears and, waving a wasp from his face, studied the spears, which were big enough to split a tree trunk. When he reached the rebels, he helped them to stretch a crossbow between the trunks and positioned a spear to face the imminent enemy.

Concerned the hot summer days had weakened his friend, Ling followed Jun into the woods. When he spotted him, he tripped over a branch and fell to the ground, startled at the sight of the weapons Jun and his men had created. Ling walked over to Jun and stood in front of two trees linked by hundreds of small branches, twisted together to form a bow. He leant back against the bow and laughed.

"This crossbow reminds me of our childhood battles."

Jun gave his friend a fragile smile.

"We made crossbows like this, stuck between the fences on our farm, strong enough to launch the cattle into the barn!"

Jun continued to pull back spears and point them towards the plain. "That's where I got the idea from."

Ling laughed again. "Just make sure you don't launch any wandering cattle across the plain. We may run out of food!"

"You will see, Ling," Jun snarled. "These spears will be the most deadly weapons in the woods. I have sharpened each one of those." He pointed to a pile of spears taller than Ling. "They are made from the finest fallen branches in the forest. These crossbows will send them through the soldiers' armour. Then we will see who is laughing." Jun's frown sank deeper than the splinters in his hands.

As the days passed, Jun struggled to galvanise the rebels with his battle plans. With their mouths drying like the pond in the forest, the sweltering summer heat had scorched their will to fight. Jun walked along the trails in the woods, trying to stop the rebels' spirits from dwindling, and shouted his father's words of wisdom.

When he reached the other side of the forest, he ordered a group of rebels to dig a deep trap and to load it with spikes, ready for the enemy. Later that day, Jun helped two rebels to create pyres, with branches tied together and packed with leaves of the different shades of the forest.

"Make a trail to the traps," Jun ordered. "If the battle last until night, when I give you the command, I want you to light up the forest and guide the lieutenant's men towards them."

Once the rebels had hidden the small bundles of leaves in the woods, Jun walked to the barricades that were cracking under the heat of the azure sky. When he walked out of the forest, he held his hands over his eyes, shielding them from the white-hot sun reflecting off the barren plain.

He stopped at one barricade and rested on it. Ling popped his head out and said, "We can't hold out much longer."

"There is no other choice," Jun said. Ling handed him a damp cloth, and he patted his lips with it.

"What are the soldiers waiting for? They can't stay in the villages forever."

"Maybe they don't want to fight."

"The emperor's men will not run away from a battle!"

Ling came out of the barricade and threw his arrows on the ground.

"Ling, I was teasing you." Jun picked up the arrows, but Ling snatched them back.

"For weeks, my men put their heads to the ground, waiting to hear the slightest rumble from the soldiers. Now, after sweltering in the barricades, they are lying on the floor with little desire to fight." The heat was meddling with Ling's temper. "Soon, we will be out of food and then they won't need to march to the forest, we will starve to death."

"We must be strong. Many of the rebels fear for the families they've left behind." Jun offered the cloth to Ling, who refused to take it. "I know some of the men believe, more than ever, that the soldiers are punishing the village elders, while we hide in the forest."

"We are not hiding," Ling said, throwing the arrows into the barricade, "but we are living like animals, eating bugs and berries."

"Ling, they will come. Look at those men," Jun said, pointing to three men wandering through the woods. "They can hardly stand up. That's what the lieutenant has been waiting for."

Later that night, as an auburn sun drifted over the trees and sank out of sight, the forest quietly darkened. As the midnight stars lit up the night sky, a faint drumming in the distance stirred the rebels in the barricades. Within minutes, voices, venomous like snakes chasing their prey, rang across the plain.

Ling ran from his barricade to find Jun, who was sleeping next to a giant crossbow in the woods.

"Can you hear them?" he said, shaking Jun awake. "The soldiers...they are marching across the plain."

"They are here?" Jun asked.

"Yes…there must be a thousand soldiers marching towards us."

"Go back to your post. They will fight in the morning."

"How can you be so sure?"

"They will," Jun said without looking at Ling. "We know how they fight."

"Jun, they are still marching!"

"Ling, the lieutenant will follow the general's orders. He would have ordered his archers to send their arrows for us, and when they have drawn enough blood to fill the pond in the forest, to charge into battle with their horsemen, sweeping aside the men still standing. This is how they have fought in every country they have invaded, and they can't do this at night."

Ling ignored Jun and ran back to his post to warn his men. He had witnessed the devil's drums before, and knew how fast the soldiers could march to the forest. He believed the drums would beat through the night, so he ran along the line of barricades and yelled, "Jun believes the soldiers will set up camp and rest until morning. But I don't. We must be ready to fight."

The Manchu soldiers continued to march towards the forest.

A rebel jumped out of a barricade and shouted over the beating drums, "Ling, go back to Jun and tell him they are coming now!"

Before Ling could reply, Jun ran out of the forest and scanned the plains, searching for the Manchu soldiers. "I can't see them. Where are they?"

Ling shouted a prayer. "Let the night stars light up their armour!"

Jun bellowed to the rebels in the wooden barricades closest to the soldiers, "Fire your arrows. We need to know how close they are."

The rebels sent their arrows up into the sky and then listened to them bouncing off the soldiers' armour.

Ling said, "They are close." He shouted, "Retreat! Retreat to the barricades behind you!"

The rebels leapt from their posts and ran from the advancing soldiers.

The lieutenant's men continued to pound their drums. They shouted the general's orders with every step: "Bring-me-back-their-leader. Bring-me-back-their-leader."

On the other side of the plain, the lieutenant laughed with his men. "You were right. They are hiding like rabbits in their burrows!"

But he was wrong to dismiss the general's order to go into battle at first light.

As the infantry marched to the forest, they dropped to their knees and made way for the archers. The archers sprang forward like the lieutenant's horse, which was pulling its reins out of his hands. The archers launched a blitz of arrows towards the rebels, and when they landed, they deepened the cracks in the crumbling ground.

Inside the barricades, Ling cried to his men, "Listen to the ground. Their arrows will fly further than ours, so they will be in our range soon."

Minutes later, he and his men huddled together, trying to protect themselves from the onslaught of arrows now crashing against their wooden shields. With each beat of the soldiers' drums, the arrows followed, splitting the rotten branches of the barricades.

"Ling, the sun has weakened the wood," one of his men shouted. "The barricades are crumbling around us."

Ling yelled, "Fire your arrows!"

His men sent their arrows high up into the sky, and they landed thirty feet in front of the barricades.

"No— Send them grass-high!"

The rebels squeezed their arrowheads through the peeling wood of the barricades and launched them towards the soldiers. The arrows whistled over the plain, cutting hundreds of soldiers to the ground like rotting trees falling in the forest. Puffs of desert dust popped up, blinding the lieutenant's archers, who tumbled over the fallen soldiers.

Jun stood at the edge of the forest and witnessed the blanket of dust drifting high into the night sky.

"The soldiers are falling. Send the horsemen to them!" He signalled to launch the rebel riders to the plain. The horsemen burst out of the forest like a stampede of wild animals and charged towards the soldiers, their man-sized spears pointing towards their enemy. The rebels breezed through the fallen soldiers and sent them deeper into the cracks of the ground. Behind the wall of dust, hundreds of soldiers ran back to their lieutenant.

Unable to see through the dust rising to the sky, the lieutenant laughed at the rebels' plight with his men, until the roar of the rebels pulled him to his senses. His horse twisted and turned towards the forest, dragging the lieutenant into battle.

The lieutenant yelled, "Charge! Charge to the peasant farmers!", not realising that most of his men were running past him and away from the woods. He rode to the barricades with a few hundred men, jumping over the soldiers dying on the ground.

With the dust settling, the lieutenant reached the barricades and yanked his horse back, stopping at the sight of the rebels hopping around the broken burrows and cheering their moonlit victory. He pulled his horse away from them and scurried back to his command post.

With every leap, Ling and the rebels shouted, "Freedom! Freedom!", until they spotted the lieutenant's men.

The soldiers continued to ride to the forest and charged at the rebels, but Ling and his archers sent their arrows hurtling towards them. When the dust had settled, the lieutenant turned back to face the battlefield, falling deeper on to his saddle at the sight of his men nailed to the ground by arrows and spears.

An hour later, when the lieutenant had retreated to his command post, he bellowed, "Get the horses ready, we are pulling the guns to the forest." The artillery guns were the size of a horse.

"But sir, the horses have pulled the guns for weeks," a soldier cried. "They need to rest."

The lieutenant screamed at his men, "If they can't pull them, then you will." The soldiers dragged the guns to the plain.

Three hours later, they reached the battlefield, with Ling and his men still dancing around the barricades. The lieutenant signalled to his men to launch a thunderous light towards the cheering rebels. Seconds later the barricades exploded, blasting many rebels to the night stars. The survivors drifted back to the forest with the cannon blasts ringing in their ears.

Ling, wounded and dazed, crawled into the woods. When he reached the forest, he fell to the ground and rolled on to his back. He muttered to the rebels near him, "Find Jun."

Two rebels ran over to Ling and dragged him deep into the forest.

With the rebels retreating, the lieutenant charged towards the forest with his cavalrymen. When they reached the woods, he bellowed, "Follow them, and do not let one farmer escape."

Minutes later, Ling sat up, confused and holding his drumming head. "Climb the trees," he ordered. "We must light the fires leading to the traps."

The rebels climbed up the trees, pulling Ling up with them. Once they were off the ground, they launched their burning arrows to light the fires.

Bursting into the woods like a flash of cannon fire, the lieutenant and his men rode along the glowing trails, believing they had been lit for the retreating rebels. Blinded by his hunger to find the rebel leader, the lieutenant ordered his men to split into two groups. They followed different paths, and moments later, the soldiers riding away from the lieutenant rode towards the crossbows. Jun had staggered back to the crossbows with his men, and they sent spears piercing through the woods, catapulting the soldiers off their horses.

The lieutenant charged along the other trail and then dropped in his saddle, ducking and dodging the trees that were now ablaze. With the forest on fire, he covered his eyes to protect them from the flames and galloped with his men towards the graves the rebels had dug for them. Minutes later, the young lieutenant tumbled into a trap and screamed until he hit the bottom. His men tried to leap across the deadly tombs, but one by one they fell.

Hours later, when the forest fires had burnt out, ghostly shadows hugged the trees; then marched along the trails and drifted out of the woods. Ling followed the spirits of the soldiers and wandered past hundreds of rebels lying silent on the ground. He stumbled out of the woods and found Jun kneeling next to a rebel. He was holding a patchwork blanket in his hands. Ling knelt next to Jun, and with the sun lighting up the plain, they prayed that their battles with the Manchu soldiers were over.

# 3

## HORNETS' NEST

Rumours of the rebellion had travelled back to the emperor's palace quicker than the hornets fleeing their burning nests. At first, the emperor was tickled by the talk of the Hunan rebels fighting back against him. Each day his advisors tried to warn him, but with a dismissive stroke of his hand, he sent them tumbling away.

The emperor sat on his throne, laughing. "No one has ever defeated my army, and a handful of peasants won't even dent their armour." He believed General Taan had crushed the rumours, but his advisors continued to tiptoe around him, recounting the tales of betrayal rumbling towards the palace walls.

The emperor's palace was in the heart of Beijing. The timber palace was surrounded by four stone walls, one with metal gates opened for the peasant farmers to pour the little wealth they had into his advisors' hands. Inside the walls, the gardens had been protected from the changing seasons, and blossomed throughout the year with petals covering the palace's garden paths. Chants of 'freedom' fluttered through the flowers, as the peasants teased the emperor's men guarding the palace walls, but each day his advisors listened to his screams of laughter becoming louder.

The peasants mocked the soldiers, shouting, "The traitorous general is running back to your emperor," but the emperor was ready to celebrate a rapid conquest.

One morning, as the palace walls protected the emperor's gardens from the autumn rainfall, one peasant cried, "Our freedom is coming. The rebels in the south have given it to us." The palace gates opened, and two soldiers ran out of the gates and pulled the peasant inside the palace grounds. They dragged him to the gallows while the pompous emperor sat amused on his throne.

Emperor Narchi was Asia's most powerful leader. He towered over his feeble advisors and was almost as wide as his golden throne. That day, he strolled into his bedroom and rested on a bed of riches until disturbed by a rumour stronger than himself.

One of his advisors had left a note on the bed: a warning to listen to the peasant cries of freedom swirling through the city.

Narchi stormed into the advisors' chamber and banged on every door. "Why are you entertaining these lies?" he growled. "You should be entertaining me!"

"But, Your Imperial Majesty..." One advisor tried to warn him of the battle in the forest from behind his closed door. "The peasants are saying—"

"Don't talk to me!" Narchi screamed, kicking the door open. "You are supposed to be one of my *wisest* advisors. You should know when not to talk!"

"But the soldiers on the palace walls are talking of the rebellion too," another advisor muttered from behind his door. "The children are shouting to them, they say the general is returning here, without an army of men."

The emperor stood in the middle of the room, his anger pushing the advisor to the wall without touching him. "All I want to hear is how many rebels are hanging along the roads to my palace," Narchi snarled. "General Taan, punishing the peasants for daring to fight back against me."

Later in the evening, with the emperor indulging in a banquet set for an army of men, whispers of the rebellion churned along the palace corridors. The gossip grew louder and the emperor's advisors darted off into the corners of the dining room, none of them wanting to witness the emperor learning of his first defeat from the general who had delivered it.

Silence followed General Taan as he strolled towards the dining room. He sat next to him, expecting Narchi to sympathise with the young lieutenant's failings. Taan ignored the emperor spitting his food out, ready to taste his general's bloodthirsty tales of the battle in the forest, and filled himself with the banquet. He nonchalantly nibbled at the emperor's favourite food, oblivious to the greater battle ahead.

Taan started to tell his host how the young lieutenant had marched into a trap, spurting out with his food when he said, "Narchi... I...bring you news of...an attack on our glorious army. One of my lieutenants marched a small patrol of men over a bridge and it collapsed. Then we heard peasants had pulled the bridge down and they tricked us into chasing them into a forest. The peasants ambushed the lieutenant and his men, but I know with a greater army I can crush these rebels for good."

"Is this true?" Narchi said, pushing his food aside. "Tell me, General – the rebels, how many men did *they* kill?"

"Narchi, the lieutenant—"

"I am your imperial commander. Speak to me as your leader!"

"I... I'm sorry, Your Majesty, the lieutenant failed us and we lost many men, but I will win back this province."

The general realised he had walked into a hornets' nest. He stopped eating the emperor's food.

"Win back the province?" Narchi yelled, bouncing food off the table. "How did your men get torn apart by these farmers? My glorious army, marching to their deaths! *You failed me!*"

"But Your Majesty, I was busy crushing hundreds of rebels throughout the Hunan province. I had no choice but to send my best lieutenant to the forest. I am sorry he—"

"You were crushing rebels? Don't lie," the emperor shrieked as the food bowls spun on the floor. "You were collecting taxes from the weak and weary for your own personal pleasure!"

"But you said I could reap all the—"

"Take this traitor to the tower. I will deal with him later." Narchi feathered his hand, pushing the general's tales away from him. Taan threw himself to the floor as the emperor's guards tried to grab hold of him.

"Have you forgotten what I did for you," he grovelled. "I brought you the most powerful throne in Asia!" The emperor's men dragged Taan across the room by his legs as he sobbed, "I opened the gates of the city to you, and if it weren't for me, you wouldn't be sitting there. How can *you* betray *me*? Please, Narchi…"

The emperor turned his back on the general and ignored his cries for forgiveness as his men dragged him out of the room.

Taan's cries filled the palace corridors until the soldiers threw him into a room at the top of the tower. The room was smaller than the emperor's throne, with a thin slit in one of the stone walls letting in a tiny line of light. On the other side of the square tower, Narchi had built a wooden stage with a plank leading to a maze of gallows where he hanged his most disloyal subjects.

Taan curled up into a ball, sobbed until the morning, and then his bloodshot eyes followed the ray of light etching around the room.

Back in the dining room, one of the emperor's most trusted advisors, Ru, said, "Some of the soldiers who fought against the rebels returned with the general. They are waiting outside the palace. We should talk to them. They can tell—"

"Bring them," Narchi snarled. "I want to know every detail."

The emperor stiffened on his throne. One after the other, the five soldiers stumbled into the grand hall. They bowed in front of the emperor, without their gaze lifting off the palace floor.

"Your emperor wants to know what happened in the Emerald Forest," Ru said as the soldiers trembled in silence. "How did the rebels defeat you?"

"They set traps in the forest for us," the bravest soldier muttered.

Narchi hurled himself out of his seat like one of the rebels' crossbows had catapulted him across the room and growled, "What can you tell me about their leader? Speak, or you will join your general."

"We failed you."

"*Yes… I…know.* Tell me something I don't know or you will sway from the gallows in the morning."

Narchi moved closer to the shivering line of soldiers.

"I don't know what to say to make it right for you, Your Majesty. We didn't see their leader, but I can tell you that the rebels are not soldiers," another soldier sobbed. "They are peasant farmers, but in the darkness of night, the lieutenant led hundreds of men into their traps."

"The rebels were no match for your superior army. The lieutenant was a fool, he should have waited until the morning," the braver soldier added.

The emperor scowled along the line of soldiers, while most of his advisors moved swiftly out of harm's way.

"Enough," he ordered. "Take them to their new command post...the tower!"

After the soldiers had been dragged out of the room, Ru moved closer to the emperor and stated, "Apparently the rebels ambushed the soldiers with crossbows and spears. They made them with their farming tools and showed tremendous courage. No army—"

The emperor barked, "Stop! Stop talking. Why are you telling me this?"

"Your Majesty, you wanted to know what had happened, and I—"

"I did not ask *you* anything. Interrupt me again and I will order you to hang the general!"

The emperor's aide quickly shuffled his tiny legs away from Narchi.

Over the next few days, Ru and the palace advisors talked of nothing else but the rebels' resistance. The soldiers' stories swirled around the palace grounds like an autumn breeze while the emperor sat on his throne and covered his pounding head to block out the tales of the rebels' bravery.

One afternoon, when the emperor was holding his troubled thoughts as he stared across the city from his private balcony, Ru crept up behind him and whispered, "Your Majesty, please accept our apologies for the general failing you." He stepped on to the balcony. "Wu was never one of us. He was a Ming general and betrayed his own people.

We should have advised you not to trust him."

"How could they defeat my glorious army?" the emperor asked in a pitiful voice.

"I'm not entirely sure," Ru said, jumping at his chance to talk more of the battle in the forest. "But we could speak to the soldiers again before you punish them. They were too frightened to talk to you before, but I am sure we can learn from this defeat."

"Do you believe we can learn something from those peasants?"

"Yes, I do, because the rebels lured the soldiers into an ambush and did not defeat our army on the battlefield."

"What's your point?"

"The rebels fought with bravery and planning that our generals could only dream of. They showed us that anyone can be a match for our great army, with a foolproof strategy."

Narchi and Ru walked back into the palace and the emperor threw himself on to his throne. He waved his hand at Ru to continue.

"The soldiers who returned here brought us back a message from the rebels."

"What message?" the emperor asked, gripping his gold-plated throne.

"They said they want to live in peace, but warned us that if we send our soldiers back to the province, they will unite again and drag us to the Great Wall." Ru paused for a moment and then stated, "They might even chase us back home."

Clenching his fists until his hands turned as pale as Ru's worried face, Narchi tried to shake a thought from his head. *My army, jeered back to the northern territories.* Narchi boiled with rage, and raised himself over the padded seat of his throne before confronting Ru with the defeat in the Emerald

Forest. When he had let off enough steam, he collapsed back on to his throne. With his arms and legs hanging in every direction, he whimpered, "What are we going to do, Ru?"

"Your Majesty, I will summon the palace advisors and generals to devise a master plan to crush these rebels." Ru had hoped to persuade the emperor to talk to the soldiers, but after having been lambasted with the general's failures, he deemed it prudent to gather the emperor's wisest followers instead.

"Don't be long," Narchi growled. "My patience has left me, just like the lieutenant's men."

Ru ran through the advisors' chambers, shouting, "One of you must come up with a plan tonight, to defeat the rebels or we will all join the general in the tower!"

The advisors and generals rummaged through their rooms, searching for their military papers. Later that night, they crammed into one of the advisors' rooms, dithering and stuttering as they tried to plan the rebels' downfall. For three hours, the generals yelled their difference at the advisors, and with time running out, Ru tried to get them to agree but without success, so he asked them to follow him to the grand hall.

Before they had a second to settle, the emperor barged into the hall, launching one of the doors into the centre of the room. Narchi stared at his obedient audience; none of them dared to look at him as he strutted over to his throne. He tried to entice the advisors to glance back at him; then bellowed, "Ru, what have you come up with to grind these rebels into their ancestors' earth?"

"Your Majesty, maybe we should talk to the soldiers again," Ru replied, hiding behind the oldest general in the room. "I'm sorry, but we needed more—"

"What?" Narchi screamed. "Are you telling me you

haven't come up with a plan to punish the peasants?"

Narchi exploded with rage, like a cannonball blasting the barren plain, and then wobbled to the dining room. His advisors followed him and witnessed him shrinking in front of them as he fell down at the dining table. Ru ran around the gigantic square table as quickly as his little legs could carry him, ordering the cooks to bring the emperor his favourite feast.

Minutes later, Ru shouted, "What are you doing? Hurry, hurry, bring His Majesty his food!"

Within seconds, a dozen cooks were busying themselves around the dining table with food from every corner of Asia flowing from the kitchen. The emperor sat still, staring at the banquet before him and muttering to himself, "I ask for wisdom and you bring me food."

A timid voice squeaked, "Your Majesty, forgive me, but… why don't you take away the rebels' farming tools?" One of the cooks had spoken without realising it.

"How dare you speak to the emperor!" Ru shouted at the shivering cook standing next to Narchi. "You will be punished for—"

"Be quiet, let him speak," the emperor snapped. "I will be dead by the time you fools come up with something, so I might as well take advice from a cook."

The emperor fluttered his rings at the cook to continue.

"I cannot produce your food without the pots to cook it in. If you take away their farming tools, they cannot build weapons to fight back against you."

Narchi glared for a moment at the pitiful servant who was crouching next to him expecting to be dragged to the tower, and then asked, "Do you have another course to dish up?"

"Yes, Your Majesty," the cook replied. Ru held his hands

over his face in anticipation of Narchi launching the food at the cook. "You cannot afford to show any sign of weakness, but if you send an army of men back to the Hunan province, they will surely be defeated."

Narchi snapped a piece of chicken apart as if it were a rebel lying in his hands. He mulled over the cook's advice, and when he had killed two more 'rebels' on his plate, he pushed himself away from the table. He strutted past his advisors and plonked himself on to his throne. The emperor's advisors rushed into the room and bowed in front him.

"We cannot let the rebels hold on to their victory. At daybreak, I want the palace grounds filled with peasants."

The dithering advisors looked up in shock.

Narchi screamed, "They will cheer my name louder than ever before. I will show these rebel farmers why I am their emperor. No one will ever defy me again."

The next morning, with the autumn leaves blowing around the peasants' feet as they walked into the palace grounds, the emperor sat on his throne, counting his political advisors entering the grand hall. One after the other, they quickly shuffled around the room and assembled themselves into what they believed was their order of importance. The most senior generals and advisors trundled to the front of the hall, while the men of faith hid at the back.

When the hall was full, the emperor moved to the balcony and positioned himself on a metal box filled with the most precious pieces of gold from the peasants below him, ready to address his people. He wanted to stand taller than ever, and appear to the peasants that he was growing in strength.

The emperor held his hand up with his palm facing the crowd, as if to calm their fears of the rebellion. He yelled, "My people, I promise to bring order back to the southern territories. My generals will not sleep until the rebel leader is swinging from the gallows!"

The peasants greeted Narchi's pledge with a few seconds of silence. Then the soldiers standing behind them slapped the peasants on their backs, shocking them into clapping slowly. With the emperor still waving from his balcony, one of the soldiers gave a peasant a gentle nip from his knife, and this had him cheering for the emperor, but no one else did.

Standing inside the palace, Narchi's advisors and generals waited for him to come back inside. The emperor gave one final wave to his subjects and then, with a smug smile, he strutted back to his throne. Narchi leaped on to the throne, dressed in his black military uniform, draped in medals from every victory, which dragged him deeper into the throne. There was one military medal missing: the battle of Hunan province.

"I want to punish the peasants so they will never challenge my rule again," the emperor said. Ru stood next to him, waiting for Narchi to dictate the main course of the cook's plan. "You failed me," Narchi growled. "And now I want you to enforce new laws and show me how loyal you are."

Not a murmur was muttered in the grand hall. Narchi's noblemen listened carefully to the emperor. Ru wrote down the new laws.

"First decree: no one in this land can hold, or use, any form of weaponry. The farmers can no longer use their farming tools, which could be used against me.

"Second decree: any rebel who fought against my army will be punished by hanging.

"Third decree: peasants who participate in or encourage any form of revolutionary activities against my rule will suffer the same fate as the captured rebels.

"Fourth decree: anyone who gives the rebels shelter will be my guest in the palace tower."

"We cannot capture every rebel." Ru tried to reason with the emperor while scribbling on his paper. "The rebels travelled back to their homes."

"Be quiet, Ru. If *you* do not understand my expectations of success, walk through the courtyard and ask General Taan for his advice. He is hanging around there, his neck stretched from the gallows, just waiting to give it." Narchi stood up. "All of you" he yelled, pointing to the advisors, "will be protected by a general and his men. They will help you enforce the pain that I am going to inflict on *my* people."

"But, Your Highness, who will stay here and take care of you?" Ru grovelled, not wanting to meet a rebel.

The emperor glared at the shivering advisor for a moment and then smirked. "You can stay here, Ru. I will need someone to tell me when the rebel leader is captured."

The generals and advisors flew out of the hall and scattered throughout the palace grounds. Within hours, the advisors had gathered their belongings, and the generals had marched their men to the gates of the city, ready for the order to deliver the emperor's new laws. Just before they marched out of the city, Narchi ordered Ru to tell his advisors to nail his demands to every school building in China, because he believed the schools were the heartbeats of the villages.

Six months after leaving the palace, the emperor's advisors had nailed his ruthless laws to hundreds of schools. The peasants pleaded as the soldiers confiscated their farming tools, but they were bullied into believing they had no choice but to surrender them. The soldiers warned the villagers that they would return if they resisted the emperor's rule. Within a year of the farming tools being destroyed, thousands of farms fell to the seasons and acres of crops died. The peasants who refused to surrender their farming tools to the soldiers, were hung along the roads to the palace.

The rebels, who had fought so bravely in the Emerald Forest, were now seen as the prophets of pain. As famine spread throughout China, women and children sobbed inside the schools, while Narchi ran through the palace gardens, exalting his brutality which had crushed the rebels' resistance. His soldiers laughed at the cries for food from the peasants lying at the palace gates.

Inside the palace, the holy men who stayed with Narchi feared he had underestimated the hatred he had created. They prayed that the emperor would not be haunted by the hardships he had delivered to all of the provinces of China, but despite months of worried prayers, none of them found the guidance to tell him of their concerns. Even if they had, the emperor was too absorbed in polishing his latest medal, engraved with *Hunan peasants*.

Months later, when the famine had taken the bite out of the rebels' resistance, with one final twist of his iron rule, the emperor ordered his son, General Wu, to the palace. Wu was half the size of his father, and his bald head was as shiny as the brass handles on the emperor's throne. He had tried to be as brave as Narchi, but when he entered the grand hall, he trembled like Ru, who was standing behind the emperor. General Wu walked up to his father and bowed before him. Concealing his concern of being summoned to the palace, he puffed out his chest to fill his armour and waited for the emperor to speak.

The emperor turned around to Ru, who was trying not to quiver from fear of the emperor's latest order, but then cried like the peasants outside the gates of the palace.

Narchi looked back to the general and said, "Wu, you are my younger son and I am mindful that I've not given you the opportunity to prove to our people, and me, that you are worthy of your medals."

"But Father, you ordered me to guard the gates to the city and I have—"

"Listen, Wu," Narchi interrupted. "I made you a general against my better judgement. You are not like your brother or me. We are warlords of our people, and now I want *you* to create your own legacy."

"Yes, Father," Wu said as his chest shrank and his head sank into his armour.

"The other generals have failed to capture the rebel leader, and I foolishly listened to a cook who warned me not to send an army to find him, so I want you to ride south, with Ru and a battalion of men, to hunt for their leader. When you return with him, your soldiers will chant your name along the trails to the palace."

Ru dropped to the floor at the thought of hunting for the rebel leader.

"I will bring him to you, Your Majesty," Wu promised, with less conviction than his father had deployed to deliver his orders.

"I know you will, Wu, but you must remember this: Ru has told me that this rebel is like no other soldier we have fought before."

Ru slithered around the throne like a snake in the Emerald Forest. He grabbed hold of the throne and pulled himself to his feet.

"Your Majesty…is it…safe for me to travel to the Hunan province?"

"Ru, I believe it was you who said we could learn so much from the rebel leader," replied the emperor.

"Yes, but…surely it would be better to send a holy advisor with the general," Ru pleaded, praying the emperor would send anyone but him to the province.

"You are my most loyal and trusted advisor, aren't you?"

"Ah…yes… I am, Your Majesty, but I can be more help to you by your side, and—"

"Ru, please." The emperor pushed himself off his throne. "Don't worry about me. I am pleased for your concern, but your wisdom will be invaluable to Wu in finding the rebel leader. Like you said, we can learn from his wisdom, and you are the best person to do that."

With his throat drying with fright, Ru could not answer.

"Wu, ride to the Hunan province and show them our strength. Parade their weakness and do not fail our family name. Find him and bring him here."

"I will, Father," Wu replied, and then kissed his father's hand. "Come with me, Ru. Let's ride to this province and capture this peasant for our glorious emperor."

Ru crawled behind Wu and followed him to the army of men waiting outside the palace grounds.

General Wu charged south, with Ru and a thousand cav-alrymen, and a burning desire to restore his family's name. When he reached the Hunan province, he showed no mercy to any tongue-tied peasant who held on to the rebel leader's name, but none of them uttered a word to his men, until they reached Jun's village.

# 4

## SILHOUETTE OF HOPE

Many refugees from the Hunan province fled to Jun's village and the fear of a thousand more families reached the barricades protecting the entrance to it. Jun tried to rally his village to fight against the emperor's men. He ran through the streets, begging them to fight, but they too had lost their will for another battle.

One afternoon, Jun ran to the barricades and greeted more people from the neighbouring villages. As he ran past Ling, he asked, "How many men will fight with us?"

"They won't." Ling sighed. He turned back to Jun. "Many of them have already given their farming tools to the general's men." Ling tried to catch his breath from running back from another village. He added, "And they don't have the strength to fight. They are running out of food."

"I don't have the strength to fight, but I won't lie down and give my soul to the Manchu soldiers."

"Nor me, but we cannot stay here. Without food, our people will soon fight amongst themselves, and when the soldiers come here, it will not be safe for us to stay."

"Safe?" Jun repeated. "What do you mean? My family has helped to protect this village for generations. The soldiers don't know who we are. We don't need to run from our own people."

"Our people are dying. I've been to the other villages and seen families begging for food," Ling said with great sadness. "Some of them believe the battle in the forest has brought them this punishment."

"But we were—"

"I know, fighting for their freedom." Ling moved closer to Jun. "They're not concerned with fighting for their freedom anymore. They fear for their children."

"But we can persuade them to gather food from the forest and bring it back here," Jun said.

"The villagers believe the soldiers will return their farming tools when the rebel leader is captured."

Jun shuddered at the image of his own people fighting against him. "Come quickly, to my father's house. He will know what to do."

When Jun and Ling reached Shen's home, Jun ran inside and shouted his father's name. Ling followed him inside the house and into the courtyard.

Shen sat up and said, "This is like a nightmare, over and over. I can remember the last time you came running into the house calling my name." Jun and Ling stood in front of him. "They are coming again, aren't they?"

"Yes, and we need your help again."

Ling added, "Most of the Hunan people have given their farming tools to the soldiers. They'll curse the rebellion soon, they're fighting a greater battle with the famine."

"Both of you have grown into brave young men," Shen said to them warmly. "Jun, I asked you to do this once before, but now I need to ask both of you."

"What is it, Shen?" Ling said, with more determination than ever to fight. "We will do anything—"

"Yes, we will," Jun interrupted.

"Is it my sword, Shen? Does it have special powers?" Ling asked, pulling his sword out of his belt.

"No," Shen sighed. "I know nothing about your sword, but I know you need to run to the forest and hide. Rest there and then travel south as far as you can."

"No, Father, we cannot run!" Jun yelled. "You asked me before, and—"

"But Shen, we started the rebellion. You can't ask us—"

"The rebellion is over," Shen said as he stood up. "If you stay here, you'll be found by the soldiers, or worse, given to them by your own people." He beckoned Jun and Ling to follow him to the house. "The general will drag you both to the palace and our people will be slaves for a lifetime. Thousands will die. Unless you run, we will not live to fight another day and will lose our history forever."

"Father, how can you ask me to leave again?" Jun said. "I believed in your wisdom, and—"

"Yes you did, but now you need to believe in yours." Shen sighed. "This will give hope to our people. Without it we have nothing."

"But I—"

"Jun, you must leave now," Shen insisted. "Bring peace back to us."

Shen hugged his son and then Ling. They stood silent for a moment, and then Jun and Ling ran out of the house. An hour later, with tears shed in every house in the village, Jun and Ling left and travelled to the Emerald Forest.

Days later, as the evening sun settled over the village, General Wu, Ru and the soldiers breezed in. The soldiers pulled the young men out of their homes and towards the water well. Within minutes, the soldiers had tied the men to their horses and dragged them around the well. Ru begged the general to stop, but Wu continued to wave the soldiers past him as he bellowed at the women crying nearby to tell him the rebel leader's name.

Three hours later, the soldiers had stopped dragging the men and let them bathe their burns in a rainstorm. The villagers had held on to the rebel leader's name. Steaming with rage, Wu ordered his men to torch the village school and to bring the elders to the well.

An hour later, with the rain dampening the fire in the school, the general yelled at his men, "Whip the elders until they talk." But even after fifty lashes, the general failed to whip a word from the elders.

"Wu, please...stop," Ru begged. "They're going to take his name to their ancestors." He tried to pull one soldier away from an elder, but the soldier pushed him to the muddy ground.

"Why won't you tell me?" Wu growled at the weary men being held up by the water well.

Just as the general was about to whip an elder, Shen, who was drifting in and out of consciousness, opened his mouth to speak.

"You!" Wu shouted, pointing the whip at him. "Tell me where the rebel leader is. If you don't, you can rot there and watch me draw a map to the palace on her face!" Wu grabbed a child crying by the well and brought her to Shen. "Where is he?" He pushed the knife against the little girl's face. Her tears dripped over the jagged blade.

Shen tried to find the strength to speak. "He...is..." He sighed. "South."

"South, where?" screamed the general.

"To...the forest..." Shen closed his eyes and slumped back against the well.

"What's his name?" Wu asked.

"Jun…" Shen said, sacrificing his son's name to protect the little girl.

The general opened Shen's weeping eyes with his thumbs and asked, "What is your name?"

"Shen…please don't hurt the children."

"If I find you are lying, old man, I will come back to the village and kill you myself. Take me to the forest," Wu growled. He then ordered his men to grab every piece of food in the village. "How many rebels are we hunting?"

"Two."

"T…t…twooo?" Wu yelled, skipping around the well. "Oh, I see, your rebel leader does not fight with an army of rebels anymore."

The soldiers dragged Shen up on to a horse, and he wobbled from side to side, trying to sit upright, as the general laughed at him and mounted his horse.

A few days later, they reached the open plain before the Emerald Forest. They pulled up their horses at the sight of cannon craters cut into the ground and filled with lashings of rain.

Wu shielded his eyes from the rainstorm to see the forest. He shouted to Shen, "Where is the trail into the woods?"

"Ride around those craters and follow that path." Shen pointed to an opening in the woods. "You should follow this trail to the tall trees. If they're not hiding there, then they are travelling south, but I don't know what village they are travelling to." Shen collapsed into his saddle, as Wu's joy of finding the rebel leader's trail lifted his spirits enough for him to ignore the downpour of rain.

Jun and Ling had rested in the forest for a few days and then rode further south. With the rainy season dampening their belief in another day to fight the emperor's men, they rode along a stone-filled path to the southern valley. After days of travelling through the valley, they had to walk their horses through open marshland. With each step, their feet were drowning in a slimy, muddy sea.

"Look, over there!" Jun shouted to Ling. He pointed to a strip of mud hovering over the water, gradually sinking into the soggy wilderness. They trudged over to the strip, reaching the other side of the marshland as night fell. Then, suddenly, they spotted soggy footsteps sunk into the ground before them.

"They're not footprints of the emperor's men," Ling said. "Most of them are too small."

Jun moved over to the footprints and placed his feet next to them. "There must be at least forty people travelling in front of us," he said. Jun and Ling leapt on to their horses and, with the rain pouring over the footprints, followed them towards a cluster of trees sprouting through the swamp.

They plunged over to the trees, and just before they reached the nearest of them, a voice cried, "We've been waiting for you."

Jun and Ling dived off their horses into the boggy swamp. A few seconds later, Jun lifted his head off the muddy ground and yelled, "Who are you? What do you want?"

"We're rebels, like you, and we want to fight again with the emperor's men," another voice cried from behind the trees.

Flapping in the murky water, Ling cried, "How do we know we can trust you?"

"We've come from the provinces in the north and won many battles with the emperor's men. We've travelled for hundreds of miles to fight with you," one of the rebels said, wading through the swamp towards them. "The villagers in the north are giving their farming tools to the soldiers because they don't have the strength to fight back."

The swell of water washed the dirt from the rebel's face.

"You are a—"

"Woman?" the rebel interrupted.

"How… Why?" Ling yelled, falling back into the water. "Are there any more women?"

"Yes, we all are."

"And you are waiting for us?" Jun asked.

"Yes, Jun. We had to cover our faces with dirt so we could fight with the men."

"How do you know my name?" Jun asked as he moved closer to the female rebel.

"My name is Ling," Ling grunted, pushing himself out of the water, not wanting to be ignored.

"Yes, Ling, we've heard of you too," the female rebel joked, as she stood drenched in front of them. "My name is Mea. I'm their leader." She turned around and pointed to the rebels appearing from behind the trees. Mea was smaller than Ling, but as sturdy and strong as Jun. "We've come to protect both of you."

"Protect *us*?" Ling laughed. "We don't need women to do that. And we don't need any help from the northern traitors who opened the gates to hell."

"Are you going to fight against the emperor's men alone?" laughed Mea.

"No, we are not," Jun said, glaring at Ling.

"Good," Mea said. "We are peaceful people, but when the soldiers killed our men for fighting for their farming tools, we wanted to fight for the children lying dead in their schools."

"I'm sorry," Jun said.

"We began tormenting the Manchu men once we had nothing to stay in our homes for," Mea said, turning to Jun. "We wanted to fight, so we came to your village, just after you left, and your father told us that you were travelling to the Emerald Forest."

"My father?" Jun asked, praying that he was safe.

"Yes, Shen. He told me that the general and his men were marching to the village, so he sent us to the forest, but we couldn't find you there, so we kept on moving."

"You are welcome to join us," Jun said. "Where should we travel to?" Ling glared at him for accepting Mea's help.

"South – that's what you father said, Jun," Mea replied, moving closer to Ling. "He said the soldiers will not march forever."

"That's helpful," Ling grumbled.

"Is that *your* sword?" Mea asked.

"Yes," Ling said, surprised at Mea's interest. "What do you know about it?"

"Me?" Mea laughed. "I've been raised on the legends of a sacred sword – it was created in the northern territories. It could be yours." She smiled at Jun and beckoned him to follow her to a shelter of mud huts hidden among the trees.

After sheltering for the night, Jun and Ling followed the female rebels further south. As they passed through villages, more peasants joined them. To begin with, the villagers gave them shelter from the sleet now falling and as much food as they could spare, but as the weeks passed and famine spread further south, they closed their doors on the rebels.

General Wu continued his pursuit of the rebel leader. He rode through the Emerald Forest, trekked through the southern valley and sailed over the swamp. His men whipped the peasants they passed into pointing the general towards the trails of retreating rebels. By the time Wu and his men had reached the southern mountain range, they were only days away from capturing Jun.

With the winter winds whistling around their gaunt faces, the rebels were weakening. They prayed for a miracle to halt the soldiers who were marching closer to them each day. When they climbed to the top of a valley, their hearts fell as they turned back to the villages below and watched the houses burning in the distance as the general and his men punished the villagers who had helped them.

With his body aching from the cold and the loss of the villagers' homes, Jun's thoughts followed the winds to his home.

"Will we see our families again?" he asked Ling.

"Yes," Ling replied with conviction. "They've given too much for us not to, but if we stop now, all the pain they have suffered will be crushed under the soldiers' horses."

"What about our village?"

"Jun," Ling snapped, "as soon as the soldiers marched into our village, it would never be our home again."

"Yes, I know, but—"

"Please don't. We must dig traps on this trail," Ling said, believing the traps that had killed the soldiers in the Emerald Forest would save them again.

Later, with little strength and bare, bruised hands, the rebels dug out traps in between a flurry of fir trees their trail weaved through. The trees were sprouting cones on their top branches, like tiny owls protecting themselves from the cold, and Ling ordered some of the rebels to cover the traps with branches and cones to hide them from their pursuers.

Just before they had finished digging the traps, Jun told Ling, "When the traps are ready, you should hide your sword in a fallen branch."

"Yes, I will hide it and make a walking stick. We will need it, because even if the soldiers fall into these traps, we won't stop them, but it will just give us a few more days of freedom and a chance to find a safe place to hide."

By the time the rebels had finished digging their traps,

many of them could taste more than the fresh snow whipping their lips. They felt betrayed by their countrymen, and as the soldiers continued to hunt for them, they were losing the courage to go on. With little food and the bitterness of winter biting more with each frozen sunrise, the rebels' bravery was breaking with every shiver of their bodies.

A few days later, when the general and his men reached the fir trees, they stopped when they heard screams of 'help' further along the trail.

"Who is it?" General Wu snapped at Ru.

"Ah… I don't know, General, perhaps…we should send the men over there," Ru replied, shaking in his saddle, and not just from the cold.

One of the general's lieutenants shouted, "I will go, sir."

Wu dismounted his horse and ordered, "Be quick. We cannot give the rebels a day's rest."

The lieutenant marched his men through a blanket of snow towards the voices crying for help. When the general had lost sight of the soldiers, an avalanche of laughter came rushing back to him.

"Why are you laughing?" Wu shouted, annoyed with the lieutenant and his men.

"Peasants lying in a trench dug for us," was the distant reply. The general ordered his men to follow him towards the cries of laughter. The lieutenant stopped laughing when the general reached the trap.

Standing on the edge of the trap, Wu chuckled at the six men lying on top of each other. The peasants begged for help, but the general laughed louder at them.

"Dress them as rebels," he ordered to his men. General Wu wanted to seize his chance to show the villagers nearby that he was strong and unforgiving. He ordered his men to punish the peasants painfully and publically, barking, "Hang them from the trees, high above the ground, and let the peasants see our emperor's orders. Cut into the trees, *If you help the retreating rebels, you will suffer the same fate as these.*"

The soldiers continued to hunt for the rebels through the hardening snowstorms. Without fear of failure or concern for the blistering winds circling around them, they ploughed through the terrifying terrain. Wu ordered his men to ride on with the emperor's words.

"My father ordered us, to the last man, to hunt these rebels wherever they may fall and bring him back their bodies." Head down and focused on the rebels' frozen tracks, Wu shook the doubt from his head. He could not fail his father.

"General," Ru chattered through his helmet, "the season is against us."

Wu yanked his horse closer to Ru and said, "One of the peasants who fell into their trap told me that there are hundreds of rebels retreating. We cannot give them a day to start another rebellion. We must ride through the night until we've found every last one of them."

"But Wu," Ru persisted, "we don't know where the next village is."

"I won't accept any of them escaping me. Neither will your emperor." The general's fiery determination was enough to warm the soldiers' spirits for a while, but hours later their armour was creaking with the cold.

Meanwhile, one morning, Jun and the rebels had reached a forest as bare as the barren valley. The rebels were weakening with every step and they were no longer concerned with losing a battle with the emperor's men – they were losing their fight against hunger.

With the fear of hunger wrapped around them, stronger

than the torn clothes scarcely protecting them from the cold, the rebels wandered in between the trees. Suddenly, Jun whispered to them to stop, when disturbed by a deer rummaging for food.

"I'll catch it," Mea said, stomping towards it, but she fell on the snow and only got within a tree's length of the deer. Ling ran after it, but soon he too fell to the ground in defeat while the other rebels could only rest against the trees.

"Look...there," a rebel yelled, jumping to his feet. He pointed to an eagle sweeping down through the bare trees. Ling searched for the eagle and then watched it circling above the deer. The eagle swiftly swept down, but the deer had darted away from danger.

The eagle circled for a while and waited until the deer had stopped, sniffing for food again in the snow, and then without a flap of its wings, it glided down behind the deer and landed on its back, dragging it to the ground.

"Ling, your sword!" shouted Mea. Ling ran to the deer and steered his sword in between the eagle's claws.

Mea crawled over to Ling and helped him drag the deer into the trees, back to the other rebels. Laughing with Ling, Mea yelled, "I could eat all of this myself."

Later, when the deer was roasting over a fire, Mea walked over to Jun and asked, "What is it, Jun?"

Jun curled up against a tree, shielding his face from Mea. "The eagle – it's my father's. It has come to find me."

"Oh...come to help us find food?" Mea asked, kneeling down next to him.

"An eagle will only seek a new master when it...does not have one." Jun sighed, a tear dropping into the snow.

Mea leant against him, held him tight and sighed, "Your father... I'm sorry."

Ling watched Mea holding Jun. Then, he walked over to

them and said, "I'm sorry, Jun. I should have realised...your father." He sat next to Jun. "He may be safe and...have sent the eagle to you."

Later that night, with a dusting of snow falling on them, the rebels sat on the fallen trees they had dragged around the fire. With the deer crackling over a fire and the snow inside the ring of rebels melting away, one whispered, "Listen...can you hear something?"

"Where?" Jun asked as he stood up and moved away from the fire.

"There...a man, he's coming towards us," the rebel replied, pointing to a lone traveller approaching on a sturdy black horse. The man dismounted and walked over to them.

Ling shared a glance with Jun; then asked the man, "What do you want?"

"Do you want food?" Jun asked.

"No." The traveller laughed. "You will need it more than me."

Ling stood up, moved closer to Jun and snarled, "Who are you?"

The traveller stepped over the fallen trees and stood in front of the fire. "My name is Dao. I saw the smoke drifting over the trees and followed it here. I thought it might be you. I want to help – please, let me take some men to divert the soldiers along a forgotten trail. I will send them searching for empty footprints."

"What?" Ling yelled.

"Listen, some of the soldiers will perish, but those who survive will fall days behind you."

Startled by Dao's request, Jun replied with caution. "I'll give you ten rebels..." He paused for a moment as he did not want to tell Dao about the female rebels. "But when you've distracted the soldiers, you must lead them to a safe village."

"How do we know we can trust him?" Ling said. "Some of the rebels have said there is a bounty on our bodies."

"We can," Jun said, watching Dao talk to the rebels. "There is something familiar about him…"

"Yes, there is," Dao said. "I helped you in the Emerald Forest. My herbal potions brought you back to life."

"It was you?" Ling said.

Jun smiled and walked behind ten rebels resting on the trees, tapping each one of them on the shoulder. He then approached Dao and said, "These men are all brave souls. Please guide them to safety."

The rebels stood and embraced Jun as friends.

"I will do all I can," Dao said, "but you must fulfil a promise to me: to never give up the fight with the emperor's men and…to always protect our children."

Jun nodded purposefully, smiled at his friends and said, "We will meet again." He glanced at Dao and asked, "Where should we go?"

"Follow those trees." Dao pointed to a line of bare trees with brittle branches leaning towards the east. "They will lead you to a river – it's frozen, but it will lead you to the base of the southern mountain range. The trail will become narrower with every step. You will need to leave your horses in the woods, but if you follow this path it will lead you to a place of warmth and safety."

Dao mounted his horse and led the ten rebels out of the woods. Over the next few days, and when they were safely away from the other rebels, they trod footprints into the snow for the general and his men to follow. When they had set their last footprint and trekked back along their steps, Dao fulfilled his promise to Jun and guided the rebels to his village.

Back in the woods, the rebels had licked the last bone of the deer and set their horses free, and in the morning, they set off to find the river. They trekked through the snow, and when they reached the frozen river, they followed it to the mountain range.

After weeks of walking alongside the river, Ling asked Jun, "What are we doing? We haven't eaten for days."

"We must keep moving," Jun said.

Where is the river taking us? Ling wondered. He said, "The eagle has stopped finding us food."

"I believe we are following a path of destiny."

"Destiny won't feed us," Ling snapped back. "Our people should have helped us. We tried to protect them."

"You can't blame them. Many of them have lost loved ones because of the emperor's laws." Jun stopped walking and stood next to Ling. "Like Mea, and the female rebels, we are peaceful people, forced to fight back because our people are suffering."

"We only needed a little food and shelter."

"We will follow the river," Jun said, hoping to pacify Ling. "The soldiers will follow the trail leading through the forest. If we believe Dao, this is the safest path to the mountain."

"Mountain?"

"We will surely find a safe place near the great mountain." Jun pushed forward, harder than his body could take, trying to stop Ling from holding him back.

After a few more days of trekking along the river, the rebels' resolve weakened, two of them becoming too weary to walk. Ling wanted to leave them behind, but Jun and Mea told them to rest on the ice, and then grabbed them by their clothes and pulled the two rebels along the frozen river. Each step sent a creak and crack scurrying over the frozen water below them.

Exhausted and hungry, Jun ordered the rebels to stop and rest for a while. He had noticed an opening in a cluster of rocks away from the river and went over, searching for food. Minutes later, he shouted, "I've found berries!"

When they had squeezed the last berry of its purple juice, Mea showed Jun an opening between two freshly covered snow peaks.

"Where does that path lead us?" Jun asked.

"To more food, hopefully," Mea said, smelling her frozen fingers, absorbing the essence of the fruit. "It might be the path to the mountain. The travelling man said we would be safe there."

"Or we will die, falling into his trap," Ling shouted. "You can't be certain he was the man who helped us in the forest."

"Mea is right, we should listen to her," Jun said.

"What, a woman?"

Mea's body stiffened slightly at the Ling's response.

Jun said, "Dao helped us once before and I'm sure he is helping us now. He wouldn't lie to us...he's a man of faith."

"What are you talking about?" Ling snapped.

"He was wearing holy beads on his wrist. I remember my father speaking of them and the prayers they hold. We must believe in him, he wanted to help us."

"I did not see these beads," grumbled Ling.

"We need to travel towards the mountain. Some of the rebels won't make it through many more nights. My father... he spoke of a village at the base of the mountain. It's our only hope."

With the blizzard whipping their weary legs, the rebels huddled together like a pack of animals sheltering from the cold. As night fell, they followed the river and picked up the path to the village. Crunching the snow with every exhausted step, they entered the village and walked towards the bright, flickering lights in the windows, each one darkening as they approached.

Swaying from side to side, battling for breath with each burst of snow, the rebels fell hard on the ground.

"What's that?"

"I can't see," Mea cried. "My eyes…they are frozen."

"There," a rebel muttered. "It's a light, swaying with the wind."

"Where?" Ling asked without looking up.

"There, I can see it." Jun pointed to a soft, distant glow, barely visible through the hardening snowstorm. He dug his hands into the snow and crawled towards the light. "It's an angel. Maybe she is coming for us…"

With his face bitten by the icy ground, Jun's thoughts froze on his father. His body warmed slightly as he recalled Shen's speech, which had inspired him to climb on to the abandoned cart. He whispered his mother's prayer.

"One day, a guardian of light will show you the way."

Jun dug deeper, searching for the inner strength to crawl towards the swaying light.

"Jun she *has* come for us," Mea cried.

Then, with his fingers fused together by the bitter winds, Jun tried to crawl to the light. "Follow the guardian of light," he sighed to the rebels next to him, but he did not have the strength to move. With hope for the rebels buried in the snow, Jun's eagle landed on his back and dragged him off the ground, pulling him to the silhouette of hope.

The rebels pushed themselves up, and with a feeling of abandonment and blistering pain, they followed the eagle through the village's darkened passageways. Hypnotised by an angelic figure beckoning them, they held on to each other and stumbled towards the light.

75

As they got closer, a soft voice called them in from the cold.

"Please – come inside. You can rest here."

Before the rebels had time to believe their frostbitten eyes, they were resting on the floor of a school with fires burning in every room. The young woman who had beckoned them inside had set the fires for them. She was a schoolteacher, in the only inhabited village near Heng Mountain.

General Wu and his men continued to pursue the rebels, unaware of the great mountain, but within two years of the rebels arriving in the village, the beauty and secrets of the mountain would be echoed across all of Asia.

# 5

## GUARDIAN ANGEL

Resting on the classroom floors, the rebels dared to dream that they had found a heavenly place near the mountain, warm and sheltered from the soldiers. Many of them drifted off to sleep.

"My name is Wan. You'll be safe here," the teacher whispered. "The soldiers will not reach our village until after the snowstorm has passed." Her gentle voice carried them to the top of the mountain.

With the rebels resting, Wan stoked the radiant log fires, sizzling and drawing the rebels closer. Now, the rebels prayed for more snow, hoping that a blizzard would engulf the mountain range and stop the soldiers' pursuit.

Within minutes of arriving at the school, Jun's and Ling's minds were also drifting to a safe hiding place on the mountain's peak. With their frostbitten faces thawing in front of the fires, images of their families waiting for them warmed their fragile bodies.

"My mother said a guardian of light would guide us." Jun couldn't take his eyes off Wan. "She is here."

"Go back to sleep," Ling said, lying next to Jun.

"Who's this guardian?" Mea asked, lying on the other side of Jun.

"No one, Mea, go to sleep," Jun said.

"I heard you say guardian of light," Mea stated, annoyed that Jun was more interested in looking at Wan.

Jun rolled over to face her and whispered, "Our people have feared, for generations, an invasion from the northern tribes of Asia. We always believed they would come and seek our most trusted knowledge. These secrets are too powerful to fall into their bloodthirsty hands, and the legends tell us that there are guardians who've dedicated their lives to protecting them."

Smiling back at Jun, Mea whispered in his ear, "In the northern territories, most of our secrets are hidden in sacred places, scattered throughout the provinces. But my people talk of a sword, with the power to bring a thousand men to the ground."

"Ling's sword?" Jun whispered so Ling would not hear him.

"So you want to talk now?" Mea smiled. "There are others, but I believe Ling is lying next to it. Our people have searched for hundreds of years, trying to find the sword." She placed a rug over Jun and asked, "How do we find one of your guardians?"

"Walking through a snowstorm," Jun muttered, falling asleep.

He closed his eyes with an image of his father, safe and welcoming him on the mountain's summit. Then, he thought of his childhood, when his father told him about the spiritual leaders who protected their province's secrets.

Shen had said, "Some of the guardians are innocent protectors of these teachings and haven't witnessed the knowledge entrusted to them yet." Jun felt his father's warmth when he remembered him saying, "The knowledge was passed to these guardians with the most delicate of disguises. This was to protect them and their secrets."

Jun fell into a deep dream of Wan being a guardian angel.

In the morning, Wan weaved in between the rebels resting in the classrooms and placed wood on the fires to keep them warm. Mea woke up when Wan walked into the classroom where she was lying, and watched as she stoked the fire.

"Thank you for helping us," Mea said. "You're the bravest woman in the province." She tried to stand up, but fell back on to the floor.

Wan walked over to Mea and helped her up. "You are still very weak. Please come with me, I have something for you." Mea followed Wan to the kitchen, and once inside, Wan said, "I've boiled water with leaves stored from my garden. It's cooled down now, you must try it. It will help you regain your strength."

"Thank you," Mea said with a warm smile. "We've walked for weeks without food. My ancestors will bless your people because they were waiting for me, even though I am far too young to join them."

"You *are* too young to join them," Wan laughed, stirring the water on the stove. "But I wasn't born in this village. I came here to see the beauty of the mountain before the Manchu invasion, but after staying in the village for two nights, I couldn't leave."

"Why?" Mea asked.

"There was no school."

"You *are* a guardian angel," Mea said, studying Wan's beauty.

"I wanted to stay and teach them the wonders of the world," Wan said as she gave Mea her medicine.

"What are they like, the villagers?"

"The village has grown from twelve families. They are all very close to each other. They named the village Sau because, like the name, they built the wooden huts with their bare hands."

Wan and Mea stood in the kitchen, talking for hours about how they had arrived at the school. Wan told her how Sau was built in between the river flowing from the great mountain and a forest falling from the mountain's peak, because the twelve families wanted to protect their homes from the severe seasons of the province.

The village was draped in colours from every religious pilgrim who passed through it as they travelled to the mountain. Every roof had been painted a different colour to show gratitude for the prayers of the pilgrims. In the spring, the red, white, black, green and yellow rooftops would sprout out of the snow, like the plants in Wan's garden.

The local people called the great mountain the Heavenly Mountain, because the mountain's peak towered into the sky, piercing the clouds like a gateway to the stars. When Wan agreed to teach the children of the village, she had asked the elders to build a school with the classrooms facing the mountain. Within days of the school opening, the children were sitting in the classrooms, dreaming of the mysteries of the mountain while Wan filled their minds with her stories.

For three days, the blizzard blew a barricade of snow against the school doors and locked them inside. Wan skipped along the corridors and laughed at the rebels dreaming of the mysteries held on the mountain.

"Our ancestors have brushed away your footprints with the storm."

But her spirits were soon to be brought back down from the mountain's peak.

One morning, Wan jumped over the rebels resting on the floor, desperate to see who was banging hard on the front door as icicles outside fell to the ground. Excited and expecting help from one of the villagers, she opened the door and let in a wall of snow.

The twelve village elders greeted Wan, shaking with the cold, having dug out a path to the school from their homes.

"Wan, you must send the rebels away. If the soldiers find out you are helping them, they will kill us all."

Wan climbed over the snow and out of the school. She whispered to the elders, "Please let them stay, for a little longer. They won't make it through another storm without food and rest."

One of the elders barked, "We cannot make them leave, but we will not help them in any way, and we will certainly not be giving them any of our food. There is barely enough for us to survive the winter."

"They are trying to free us from the emperor's men." Wan tried to hold back her tears. "Every village in the province has turned its back on them. How can we do the same?"

"Sorry, Wan," muttered an elder, without catching her eye. "We cannot help them. You must ask them to…"

Wan turned her back on the elders, who were still trying to convince her to ask the rebels to leave. She moved back inside the school and slammed the door. Jun and some of the rebels, who were sleeping on the classroom floor, woke up when the door slammed shut.

"Why is she crying?" a rebel asked Jun.

"I'm not sure," Jun replied as he walked to a window and watched the elders shaking their heads and walking away from the school. "But the elders look upset too." He crept into another classroom and knelt down next to Mea. "We cannot stay to long. The village elders will turn against Wan if we do."

Ling stood up and walked over to Mea and Jun. "What? Where else can we go? We will perish on the—"

"Be quiet, Wan is coming," Mea said as Wan walked past the classroom door and into the kitchen.

Leaving the classroom, Jun walked towards the kitchen, inhaling the warm scent of soup bubbling on the stove. He stepped inside and smiled, as Wan gathered as many soup bowls as she could carry from the crooked kitchen shelves.

"Wan."

She spun round with the bowls and dropped them on to the table, startled by Jun calling her name.

"So...rry," he said as he dived across the table, trying to catch the bowls.

"Jun... I've made soup," Wan said, helping him off the table. "Every vegetable from my garden is brewing in this pot." She stirred the pot, which was as big as the stove, then poured the boiling soup into a bowl and passed it to Jun.

He said, "Your kindness has shown us that what we've been fighting for is still alive in our province."

"You don't need to keep thanking me. You are all welcome here."

"Ah...it's h-hot," Jun gulped as he burnt his lips. Wan gave him some water to cool his mouth, while his tongue tasted the many vegetables in the soup. "Thank you for giving us shelter."

"You would have died in the storm." Trying not to laugh at Jun cooling his mouth by fanning his hand in front of it, she added, "We should thank you. Our people needed protecting. Please forgive the village elders, they are scared. I cannot offer you much, but I *can* give you shelter from the cold."

Wan waited for Jun to finish his soup and then walked out of the kitchen to fetch the other rebels. Mea, who was resting in a classroom, waited until Wan had passed her room and then followed her along the corridor.

"We can't stay here. The emperor's men will be here soon. We can't put you in any more danger."

Wan turned back to face Mea. "The snowstorm has hidden your tracks, so please let me help you for a few more days."

"But the village elders…"

"You must stay here for a while. Some of you will not make it through another blizzard without the strength to keep moving through it."

Mea laughed at Wan's persistence. "You are much stronger than you look."

Wan smiled; then walked towards the kitchen. "Please follow me," she shouted. "I've made soup for everyone, but some of you will need to wait to enjoy the tastiest soup in the province. There are only twenty bowls!" A tender smile from Wan lifted the rebels off the classroom floors; her humour led them all to the kitchen. "All of my vegetables are brewing on the stove and an eagle is pecking at my window for the little meat I have. What did I do to deserve this?"

Queuing along the corridor to the kitchen, the rebels waited patiently for the next available soup bowl. Mea agreed to take charge in the kitchen as Jun and Wan stepped into a classroom decorated with canvas paintings and paper drawings covering the wafer-thin walls.

"Where can we hide?" Jun asked, smelling the dried paint on the canvases.

"If you try to hide near the village or along the trails of the mountain range, the soldiers will find you."

"But where should we go?" Jun said, picking up a book more colourful than the drawings.

"That's mine," Wan said, taking it from him. "I can lead you to a safe place," she added, trying to distract Jun from the book. She smiled and pointed out of a window.

"The mountain?"

"Yes."

"How can you take us up there? Who will teach the children?"

"Please wait here," Wan said, walking out of the classroom and leaving Jun sniffing the fragrance of a jasmine flower following her, while he stared at the mountain. She returned holding a cloth in her hand. "This will guide you."

Her hand trembled as she passed the cloth to Jun.

"Where did you get this?"

"From someone I love dearly. You cannot tell a soul about it."

"It's a beautiful map...just like mine," Jun said, stretching the map out.

"Yours? Do you..." Wan closed the classroom door so no one could hear her, "have a map?"

Jun gave the map back to her and said, "Yes, my father gave it to me." He then rummaged through his coat's pockets, pulled his map out and passed it to Wan.

"Your father? What's his name?"

"Shen."

"Oh...it means 'spirit'."

"I remember him telling me that. He also said that I would find another piece to my map. Do you think it's yours?"

"I don't know, but you will need to use your intuition to be guided by mine." Wan moved the maps around each other. "They don't join together."

"They don't?" Jun sighed.

"No, but don't worry. Just follow the path shown on my map, and remember one thing..."

"What is it?"

"If the path you are travelling along becomes distant from you, choose another."

"Your wisdom is much older than your innocent face."

"Really?" Wan quipped, laughing as she passed the maps to Jun. "Your courage is far greater than the scars on your face."

"What I meant was...ah...you're wise for such a young woman."

"I have some more wise words for you," Wan said, her smile as wide as the maps she had passed to Jun. "The man who gave it to me said, 'This map will take *you* to a sacred place', but he then said it was not marked on it."

"What? A sacred place...not marked on it? What was he talking about?"

"Everything is true under the stars, Jun. Everything is true under the stars."

"Everything is *dark* under the stars." Jun laughed. "If the hiding place is not marked, how will I know what to look for?"

"That's what I said to him, but all he kept on saying was—"

"Everything is true under the stars," interrupted Jun.

"Yes, that's what he said. I'm sure you will work it out. If the map was easy to read, and it fell into the wrong hands, then we would all be in grave danger."

"Yes, we would."

"Before you came to the village, I was thinking of what might happen if didn't tell anyone about the map and the stars. Perhaps no one would have found the sacred place, but I believe your destiny is to find it, even though I have no idea what or where it is." Wan laughed again. With a growing belief in Jun, she stated, "One more thing – you will need to hide there until spring, or the soldiers will follow your footprints across the mountain."

*

85

Over the next few days, Wan discreetly asked her closest friends to help the rebels. She tapped on their doors and whispered, "Please help them. They are fighting for our people. They need food for their journey into the mountain range." Her friends gave what they could spare.

One morning, when Wan went to one of her friends' houses, her friend sighed, "Wan, please do not ask us for any more food. Please ask them to leave. The soldiers will punish us for helping them."

Wan fell down on the doorstep and held her head in her hands. Her heart was dragged to the ground with the thought of the rebels starving on the mountain. Crunching her way over the frozen snow, she staggered back to the school as the children peered out of their icy windows. She tried to shield her tears from them, but each child wiped away Wan's tears on their windows from inside their rooms. Believing the children were waving to her, she poked her hand out of her coat and waved back at them.

Later that day, Mea ran to find Wan in one of the classrooms. "Look! The children keep bringing us paintings."

"They are beautiful," Wan said, running her fingers over one of the paintings.

"Why are they painting butterflies for us?"

"They are for me. They want to remind me of who I am."

"Who *are* you?" Mea asked.

"They are all special children," Wan replied, taking two drawings and pinning one to the classroom wall. A tear trickled down her face and dropped on to the other painting in her hand, spreading the paint across the paper. "They are reminding me of who I am. My name, Wan, means soft, gentle and free as a butterfly."

"Really?"

"Yes, for generations my family has believed that we are

born into our name. One of the children in the school is called Shu, and every day she shows her kindness and generous nature. That's what her names means. Another child is named Wei, and he tries to be as strong as a giant. All the children here are growing into their given names. This is a gift from their parents – a gift that the children will not see until they are older."

"Does every name have a meaning?" Mea asked, like a child. "Do you know what my name means?"

"A plum." Wan laughed.

"Rotten fruit, I knew it!" Mea yelled, dropping the paintings on to the floor.

"You are like a beautiful fruit, firm on the outside and tender in the middle."

"What about Jun and Ling?" Mea asked picking up the paintings.

"Jun, a 'handsome leader'," Wan replied, blushing. She paused for a moment, and then sighed, "Ling means 'vibrant spirit', but I believe he is lost."

"Lost?"

"Sit down here," Wan said, pulling out a child's chair for Mea to sit on. "I teach the children what my father taught me at their age. I can still remember him saying, 'It's in your name – it's in your name, this will show you the path to follow!'"

"So why do you think Ling is lost?" Mea asked again.

"My father told me that our spirits will follow many paths and we should always be true to ourselves, even when our paths are troubled by others. You are doing this, Mea, because you are strong and willing to fight, but you are still full of kindness. Ling is a vibrant soul, but his anger is pushing him away from his path."

"I can see this," Mea said. "And Jun is a born leader?"

"Yes, he is, but only if he continues to follow a path of a leader."

"But he is...isn't he?"

"Yes, but in the months ahead, many people will try to drag him from his destiny. Your strength and kindness will be most valuable to him, because as my father used to say every day, 'You must walk your path alone, but chose wisely the people who walk beside you!'"

"What? How did he think of these mad ideas?" Mea stood up and pinned another drawing to the wall.

"From every step he walked...most of them alone!"

They looked at each other, trying not to laugh. Then Mea dropped a painting to the floor and said, "Can you hear that? The men...they're fighting. Quick, follow me."

Mea and Wan ran into another classroom where Jun and Ling were arguing, while some of the other rebels tried to separate them.

"We've only had a few days' rest!" Ling shouted.

"Ling, we cannot stay any longer. The soldiers will be here soon."

Wan moved between Jun and Ling, shouting, "You can't leave now, some of you do not have enough strength to leave the village, they need to rest."

"We will always remember your kindness," Jun said, moving away from her. He turned to face the rebels and said, "We leave today."

"But we need more food!" Ling yelled as he moved closer to Jun.

"We need nothing more than someone who believes in us. This will take us to the top of the mountain," Jun stated, smiling at Wan. She tried to find the words to keep Jun in the school for a while longer, but her mouth froze with a thought of him freezing to his death on the mountain.

Wan walked out of the classroom, and when she was halfway down the corridor, she ran to the back of the school. When she reached the door, she threw herself out into the garden. Slipping on the frozen snow, she fell headfirst on to the icy ground and cried out "No!" towards the mountain. Lying on the ground, she tilted her head towards the children flying past the school on their wooden sledges, and waited until the rest of them had gone before standing up. She brushed herself down, held her throbbing head, and walked through the garden and around to the front of the school.

Minutes later, with Jun and Ling still engaging in a war of words inside the school, the front door blew open and Wan came bouncing in.

"Our prayers have been answered!"

"What is it, Wan?" Mea cried.

"I knew they cared." Wan ran into a classroom with packages of food under her arms. "There are more parcels outside. They left as much food as they could spare. I knew they were proud of you and everything you've been fighting for."

Wan rushed back to the front door and brought more parcels inside. She gave one to Mea, who shrieked with excitement like the children playing outside in the snow. Jun and some of the rebels helped Wan to bring in the remaining food packages, while Ling walked out of the school and grabbed his own.

When Wan had given the last package to the rebels, Jun led her to the kitchen. Holding on to her, he said, "Thank you, Wan. I will never forget you."

"I have enjoyed your stories of you and Ling fighting on the farm," Wan whispered. "He looks up to you more than you know, just like the other rebels."

"He used to look up to me, but not anymore," Jun sighed. "But I will try to lead the others."

"The rebels will follow someone who is brave and strong," Wan said, her brown eyes bulging with sadness, "but some of them will be fooled into following their anger as this will hide their weakness. Promise me you will remember this."

"I promise, and I also promise to come back, not just to protect the village."

Jun opened his hands slowly and let go of Wan.

Later that day, with the sun breaking through the crisp, pastel clouds, Wan led the rebels towards the forest that swept up high into the mountain. Jun walked next to her, the silence of the afternoon frost only broken by the rebels' steps crushing the icy paths beneath them. After hiking for an hour, they reached the base of the mountain.

Wan pointed to an opening in the trees. "Heng Mountain has many glorious valleys and idyllic waterfalls. The mountain is more tranquil than any other, but its trails are not for weakened souls. The mountain has taken many lives, so please tread carefully. We *will* welcome you into our homes again... I hope that day comes soon."

"We will follow this path," shouted Jun, pointing to a gap between the trees, which was the width of a child.

"Are you sure, Jun?" Ling asked with an anxious frown, staring at the small opening.

"Yes, I am. We must follow this path and use our instincts to find somewhere to hide on the mountain."

"Instincts...they will help us," Ling snarled at Jun. "What we need is a miracle!"

Jun ignored him and marched the rebels to the trees.

Wan cried out, "I will pray every day for you!" Ling looked ahead, as the other rebels turned back to her. "If you find hunger, keep searching. When you lose the will to walk one more trail, keep moving. When all hope seems lost, keep believing."

"We will always remember what you have done for us. If you find yourself in danger, we will find you." Mea walked backwards for a moment, calling to Wan, then smiled at Jun as he led them all into the woods.

Wan stood at the base of the mountain until the last rebel drifted into the forest. She waited for a while before following the fresh footprints back to the village as an icy tear trickled down her gentle face. Wiping her eyes, she remembered the warmth of the elders' food parcels.

When she returned to the school, she found the twelve village elders waiting inside for her. One of them opened the front door and asked with a grimace, "Have they left for good?"

"Yes." Wan sighed. "Thank you for the food." She walked into a classroom with the elders following her. "You lifted their hearts high into the mountain."

"Food? What food?"

Wan stood stunned for a moment until she looked through the classroom window and watched a young boy, Wie, pulling another child, Shu, on his sledge. Shu had injured herself while sledging, and when an elder shouted at them to go back to their homes, the children just smiled warmly at Wan.

"The children..."

Wan fell into the elders' arms, realising that the children had used their sledges to bring their food to the school.

# 6

## MOUNTAIN'S RAGE

While Jun and the rebels had travelled to Wan's school, Dao fulfilled his promise to Jun and diverted General Wu and his men away from the rebels. Hundreds of soldiers perished on the mountain as they followed the general along the deadly trails set by Dao. Weeks later, when the general stumbled into a village north of Sau, the blizzard that had locked the rebels inside the school held them there for days.

After the blizzard, the general and his men trekked on foot to the southern mountain range. Without a footprint to follow, they travelled to a village the peasants had spoken of: a village at the base of Heng Mountain.

Days later, the general marched into Sau and within minutes of entering the village, he was ordering his men to drag the villagers out of their homes. With the peasants shivering in the cold, the soldiers threatened to warm them up by burning their homes if they didn't tell them where the rebels were hiding.

"Tell the general who's been helping the rebels!"

The soldiers ignored the villagers' pleas of innocence. They laughed at the villager who cried, "The rebels passed through the village without resting! We did not help them!"

"Bring the elders!" Wu yelled at his men.

The soldiers grabbed hold of the elders and dragged them to the general.

"Tell me, where are they? I won't rest until I've found them!"

No one answered him.

"All right, you don't know where they are." Wu smirked. "Lieutenant, put three of the elders outside the school. Take their shoes off. Let's see if their feet bursting with blisters will remind them of where the rebels are hiding."

An hour later, with their feet blistering on the frozen steps, none of the elders had uttered a word to the soldiers. Crying inside the school, Wan touched the children's drawings, trying not to run outside. Her heart was desperate to help the fragile men standing on the steps, her head kept her sitting in a classroom, weeping with worry for all the villagers.

Another hour passed, then, just before one of the elders took his last breath, Wan jumped up out of her seat, her heart beating like a captured animal, and ran out of the school trying to find the general. When she found him resting in a house, she flung herself at his feet.

"Please, sir, none of the elders wanted to help the rebels. The children gave them food to leave the village. I think the rebels scared them."

"The children – scared by the rebels, and gave them their food?" The general laughed at Wan's story. "Bring the other elders to me," he ordered one of his men. "I will show you how we punish people who betray the emperor!"

"No, please, General, I beg you!" Wan sobbed. "The elders asked them to pass through the village."

Ru, the emperor's advisor, moved closer to Wu and whispered, "General, we are many miles away from our territories. We will need the villagers' help to survive the winter."

Minutes later, incensed by Ru's advice, the general ordered his men to leave all the elders in front of the school. They crouched down next to each other, freezing and huddling like weary cattle on a farm, while the general sulked and strolled through the village.

"Where are they?" he bellowed at the peasants hiding from him, kicking the snow from his boots. "I will leave the elders outside the school until someone tells me where the rebels are hiding."

"General?" an elder croaked.

The general walked over to him. "Are you ready to talk?" he laughed at the shivering man.

"The children did not give the rebels their food," the elder explained. "The rebels stole it."

"Speak up!"

"No one helped them. They helped themselves to everything we had. They left the village for the mountain."

"The mountain!" Wu laughed. "No one would survive a week in the wilderness of the mountain." The general's men laughed at the elders quivering in the snow. "Don't worry. We will find their bodies on the mountain trails."

Wan stood on the top step of the entrance to the school and shouted to the general, "The great mountain will punish tyrants." Not wanting to give him any doubts as to where her loyalties lay, she added, "Heng Mountain's treacherous trails will take evil and unforgiving souls."

General Wu walked up the steps and stood in front of Wan. He studied her beauty and said, "Don't worry about us. We will follow their tracks in the snow and bring you back the thieves who stole from children." He then danced down the steps, shouting to his men, "We will rest for a while and then follow their trail up the mountain."

The general beckoned to his men to help the elders off the steps, but for one of them it was too late. "We will stay here for one night, and you will give my men everything you have."

Wu gave the order to his men, and the soldiers burst into every house in the village, searching for what little food the villagers had. Looking on, Wan told one of the elders that the soldiers epitomised Wu's name, 'brave and strong', more than Wu did, because she believed he was a coward. Blinded by their general's name, the soldiers' determination for glory did not help them find the food the villagers had hidden.

Frustrated with the lack of food, the general ordered his men to come back to the school and rest in the classrooms. With night falling and not one fire lit in the school, the classroom windows cracked with frozen lines etched across them like silky spiders' webs. The eye of a snowstorm settled over the village.

Wan almost apologised to the soldiers for not being able to light the fires. She said, "There are no more logs to burn. The children used them to build fortresses in the snow to protect them from the rebels, and...well...we have none left."

As the windows darkened with the storm, the soldiers covered themselves with books and drawings, fearing they would freeze to death, just as they imaged the rebels had perished on the mountain.

General Wu walked into the kitchen and watched Wan for a moment, studying her as she cleaned a perfectly clean table. "Did the rebels stay here?"

"No...no, General, not for one night," Wan stated, choosing her words carefully.

The general stared at her as she resisted the urge to smile. He waited until she had walked out of the room, then rubbed his hand over the table as he walked around it. He strolled out of the kitchen and into a classroom where fifty of his men were trying to rest.

"Search the school. I want to know if the rebels stayed here."

An hour later, the soldiers had found nothing to show the rebels had stayed in the school, and Wu reluctantly accepted Wan's story. He patrolled the corridors, tugging at his armour with irritation at the tales of the children giving their food to the rebels.

"Each one of you will wake up in the morning with the strength of two men and the speed of the winter winds. We will capture these cowards who run from us."

With snow falling hard in the village, the roof of the school groaned like Wu as he walked into a classroom and pushed two soldiers lying on the floor apart. The soldiers were sharing the only woollen rug in the school, but Wu grabbed it, wrapped it around him, and tried to rest for the night.

Later that night, the soldiers filled the room with their frosty breath, while Wu dreamt of praise from his father, Emperor Narchi, as he dragged the rebels along the palace walls. His dream began with him following their footprints in the morning to the summit of the mountain.

The next day, the soldiers slept until midday, because a blanket of snow covered the school windows, and the soldiers dreamt it was still night. Trapped inside their homes, many of the villagers feared the general's acceptance of their story would be blown away like the rebels' footprints.

Later, just before the general had realised it was the afternoon, some of the children dug holes in the snow and climbed out of their windows. They built snowmen and waited for him to explode at the sight of the snow covering the village. Holding their breath, they watched the general burrow his way out of the school, eager to march to the mountain. The children buried their heads in the snow as the general yelled to the sky.

"Noooo!" Wu screamed to the top of the mountain. An

avalanche of snow from the school roof fell on to his boiling head.

One after the other, some of the soldiers climbed out of the school, falling into the frozen ocean engulfing the village. Wu puffed his chest out and tried to wriggle free, looking like one of the children's snowmen.

After wading through the snow, the general's men turned around to face him and watched him slide down the school steps, with a white cloud, like a soft pillow, hugging the mountain's peak in the distance. Shaking the snow off him, Wu shrieked at his men in the classrooms to pull him back inside the school.

Once inside, Wu yelled, "The rebels would have died in the blizzard. Our mission now is to find their brittle bodies on the mountain, and to bring them back to the village. We will not tolerate any more resistance to our glorious emperor. We will show the peasants this when we pile the rebels' frozen bones in the middle of the village and build a fire bigger than the school."

General Wu ordered his men to clear a path out of the village, but the fresh blanket of snow held them there for five more days. When they had cleared enough snow to cover the mountain's peak, Wu ordered three hundred men to stay in the village with Ru.

"Ru, these men are now under *your* control," Wu said as he marched out of the village. "I believe the peasants helped the rebels, so you may need to use my men to stop them from warning the rebels about us."

"But General, *I* don't know how to fight the rebels!" Ru cried. "What if they come back here?"

"Be brave, Ru, be brave." Wu said. "Most of them would have died in the storm, so if they do come back you will be victorious!"

"General…please don't leave me here…"

Wu led his men out of the village. He turned back to Ru and shouted, "If they don't come back to the village, we will find their frozen statues and bring them back to you."

After a few days, the winter winds blew Wu's joyful spirits away. Moving slower by the day, most of his men wanted to be with Ru in the village. After travelling for three more days, one of them moaned, "Where are the rebels' trails?"

"Keep moving!" Wu barked, despite the increasing winds and no trails to follow.

The soldiers roamed along the mountain's snowy paths for a few more days, but with little food their bodies shook harder. With his mouth chattering from the cold, a soldier cried, "Sir, we won't be able to survive for much longer. Even if we find them, we won't have the strength to carry them back down the mountain."

"Why don't we take shelter in the forest?" another soldier cried, with little strength left to ask. "We might find food in the woods, or burnt-out fires leading us to the rebels."

"No one could travel through those trees!" Wu yelled, pointing to the woods.

"G… Gen…ral, please. We will die on the mountain if we do not return to the village."

The general's determination to live up to his name had closed his mind to the rebels travelling into what he called 'the impassable forest'. Exhausted, hungry and frozen to every bone in his body, Wu said, "The rebels could have waited for us to leave the village. We must go back."

"What about the emperor's orders?" another soldier muttered from under his ice-glazed helmet as he tried to protect his frostbitten face from the winds. He stuttered with the cold, "Sir…will he…forgive us?"

"We may never find out," muttered Wu.

As the soldiers scurried back down to Sau, they believed there was something far greater than the blizzard beating them down the mountain. Fearing the mountain would keep them from living long enough to face the emperor's rage, some of the soldiers threw themselves down the icy paths, body-sledging like schoolchildren. With every swirl of the bitter winds, the remaining soldiers drifted in and out of chilling hallucinations. They started to hear murmurs of warnings, teasing them with words of mystical secrets on the mountain.

"Our spirits will guide the rebels. Darkness will soon become light."

"Don't listen to the winds," Wu cried. "Our bodies are frozen, but do not let the cold take your minds."

The general tried to fight the whispers surrounding him, but soon he too was tumbling down the mountain faster than his men. He talked back to the whisperer, asking for the mountain's rage to spare him and to take the rebels, oblivious to how close he was to them.

Meanwhile, further up the mountain the rebels rested underneath a shelter of the trees marked on Wan's map. Jun had hidden the map from the rebels, but used it to guide them away from the mountain's most dangerous trails. The rebels followed a path along a tree-lined track that protected them from the snowstorm that held Wu and his men in Sau.

One morning, while resting against a large tree, Jun closed his eyes and searched inside himself for the warmth of a young woman that still radiated in his heart. He wrapped both maps around his hands, trying to keep Wan's words of wisdom and his mother's inner strength with him.

"Are you using your map to keep warm?" snarled Ling as he threw the branch he had used to hide his sword away from him, believing Jun was wrong to listen to Wan. "That's all it's good for."

Jun pushed himself off the tree. "We had to leave the village. The soldiers would have hanged Wan if they'd found us in the school."

"Yes, Wan. She is your only concern, and not a friend who has walked through every season with you."

Ignoring Ling, Jun moved away from him and studied every marking on Wan's map. His eyes settled on an opening delicately drawn near the edge of the forest. He followed the markings with an ice-blue finger, flowing over small trees and water running over rocks.

Jun walked back to the rebels. "We must find a stream."

"How much further do we have to travel?" Mea asked, staring at a small group of rebels lying in the trees behind her. "Some of them can't walk for much longer."

"I'm not sure, but we must find it before nightfall. The stream will take us out of the forest and we will have no shelter above us." Jun turned to Ling. "We have little food, but I sense we will find much more there."

"Your senses will surely feed us, Jun." Ling laughed. He stabbed his sword into the ground and yelled, "You're blinded by her beauty and you cannot see that you are leading us to hell."

"Don't say that, Ling. Stop!" Mea said, standing up. "We must not fight amongst ourselves. We need to find this stream. It may lead us to food."

"Food? What food?" Ling growled. "Even his eagle has given up on finding food and returned to his lady friend in the village."

Mea ignored him and said to Jun, "Follow the river. That's what the travelling man said, wasn't it?"

"Yes, it was. But I think he was talking about the river

flowing to Wan's village," Jun said, walking alongside a trickle of water seeping into the woods. Ling, Mea and the rebels followed him.

"Jun, this stream could flow from a lake or river," Mea said. "We may need to travel across to the other side of the mountain to find it."

"The blizzard has frozen both of your minds," Ling barked at Mea.

"We need to find the river," Mea snarled back at him. "Wan said if it doesn't feel right then we should take another path."

"Has she ever climbed this mountain?"

Mea stopped in her tracks and turned to face Ling. "She gave us a hope of finding a place to rest. A place where the soldiers won't find us, let's not forget that."

The rebels continued across the mountain and hours later, the trickle of water flowed into a river running through the woods. Jun and the rebels walked out of the woods and hiked along a path at the edge of the mountain, but as night fell, some of them had not realised that the trail alongside the river was narrowing.

Suddenly, a rebel fell off the ridge and pulled two others down with him, crashing into the trees further down the mountain, and coming to rest with a snapping of legs and arms. Within minutes, Jun and Ling had tied a rope to a rock and climbed down the ridge to help them.

"Jun, we will need to strap their legs together," Ling said.

"You've broken your arm," Jun said to the female rebel, putting his hand over her mouth and trying to stop her screams reaching the emperor's men. "I will carry her on my back and climb up the rope." Jun lifted the female rebel on to his shoulders. "Once you've strapped his leg," Jun pointed to one of the men who was biting his coat, trying not to yell, "tie him to the rope and we will pull him up. When he is safely on the path," Jun nodded towards the other rebel who was lying lifeless on the ground, "we'll pull him up."

Jun carried the female rebel, as she sobbed in silence, to the top of the ridge and placed her on the ground. He asked Mea to strap the woman's arm to her body, then moved to the edge of the path and asked Ling, "Have you tied the rope to him?"

"Yes, but be quick," Ling whispered. "Even if the general is on the other side of the mountain, he would have heard her screams."

Jun and Mea pulled the injured rebels and Ling to the top of the ridge. Once there, two of the female rebels bandaged the broken bones and asked the strongest men to carry them.

After walking for a few more hours, the moonlight was now reflecting on the icy water. Jun and the rebels followed the river as it became deeper, faster and veered down and into the mountain's core. Then, the rebels had no other choice but to follow the path down and away from the river only to be halted by a gorge of gigantic rocks.

As they got closer to the rock face, Jun ordered, "Mea, come with me." He tried to run to the gorge, but his legs stiffened and he stumbled towards the rock. "Can you hear it?" he said, trying to climb up the rock face. "It sounds like the rocks are falling into the river."

Ling stepped on to the rock, ready to climb up it. Mea pushed Jun up the rock face and they climbed to the top of the gorge. When they reached the top of the rock, the wonder of a raging waterfall hit them and pushed them back on to their heels. They gazed at the force of the waterfall, with icicles as wide as the rocks they had just climbed. Startled by their moonlit reflections twisting and turning in front of them, Jun and Mea fell to their knees.

With their names echoing around the gorge, Jun stood up and yelled to the rebels below, "Come and see the beautiful hiding place we were destined to find."

Ling climbed the rock as the other rebels pulled and pushed each other up it, and Jun yelled at the injured rebels waiting below, "We will pull you up soon. We need to find a cave for you to rest in. It will give you shelter from the cold."

When all the rebels had climbed down to the other side of the gorge, Mea and the female rebels looked for somewhere to light the fires but found nowhere to shield the smoke from them. With no fires set, Jun sat on a rock and held on to both maps, looking up at the moon which almost filled the night sky, and tried to remember what Wan had said to him.

"Everything is true under the stars."

He held Wan's map up to the moon, and with an instinctive force pulling his hands together, he placed his father's map on top of it. Startled because the maps become one, Jun tilted them towards the stars and gazed through the glittering patterns. With a squint of his eyes, he tried to understand the markings on the map, but failed to see what was in front of him. Walking towards the water, he put his hand just in front of his nose. He pointed to the waterfall, copying the image he had just seen on the maps.

"Look beyond the pointing finger!" Mea shouted to Jun as she squeezed out of a cave.

"What?"

"In the northern provinces, every parent tells their child to 'look beyond the pointing finger'. This means look past your nose, Jun!" Mea laughed as the female rebels all pointed at the waterfall. Without hesitation, Jun leapt into the icy water and swam towards the gushing water shield.

"Jun, wait!" Mea cried as he ducked under the waterfall. She rushed towards the edge of the water, holding her breath, waiting for Jun to reappear.

Minutes later, Jun shouted from behind the waterfall, "I have found an entrance to a cave. It's big enough for the general's army to sleep there. You can light as many fires as you want!"

The injured rebels fell to the ground like the roaring water, believing Jun had found them the safest shelter on the mountain. One rebel jumped into the water and swam towards the waterfall until the sheets of ice slowed him down. Desperate to see his heavenly resting place, the rebel flapped his arms through the layers of ice crushing against him until he reached Jun.

Ling stood at the edge of the water, staring at the rebel splashing in the water, and shouted at the female rebels, "Gather as many branches as you can. Let's hope the cave is big enough for the smoke to drift out of sight."

"Ling, you can use your sword to catch the fish," Mea cried, excited like a child at finding the enormous cave. "There might be enough fish to last us until spring." Ling did not answer.

Jun ordered two rebels to take off their coats, and to pack them with twigs and leaves and to swim with them over the icy water to the cave. Within minutes, the two rebels navigated the coats through the water dispersed by the icicles above and as soon as they reached the cave, Jun grabbed the leaves and twigs and set a fire ready for their midnight supper.

Later, as the smoke from the fire drifted towards the rolling water shield protecting them from the emperor's men, the rebels stared at the waterfall and gazed at the night sky above. They rested on their damp beds of thawing leaves while bursting from their banquet of fish. This was just like a dream – the sizzling smell of fish roasting over the fire sending them off into a deep sleep; a dream of food and warmth, a day they wanted to wake up in the morning and live again.

After resting for a week in their idyllic surroundings, Jun sat in a quiet corner of the cave and again placed the two maps together. A tiny step marked on the map, next to the finger drawn on it, caught his eye. He put the maps back into his coat and walked around the cave, looking for a step cut into the stone walls.

An hour later, he spotted a large rock on its own at the back of the cave. With the other rebels resting, Jun rolled the dark stone to the side and rubbed the surface of the rock face with his hand. The stone crumbled into clay, and within minutes he was digging as fast as he could push the clay behind him. Before he had time to wipe the clay from his eyes, he was lying in a tunnel with a dim light in the distance. He crawled along the passage until he pulled himself into the core of the mountain.

With freezing water oozing out of the rock, Jun counted the carved steps sticking out and leading to an opening in the rock face. The slippery steps spiralled high into the circular core of the mountain. Jun climbed up them until he reached the opening in the cave and crawled through the rock, and after a few minutes, to his amazement, he fell into a lush, green valley which had not been touched by the snowstorms.

With a smile wider than the core of the mountain, Jun listened to birds singing in the winter sun. The orange, white and purple birds swooped across the valley as he moved away from the cave and stumbled on to a perfectly formed path. He walked along the path, placing a foot on each stone, and when he spotted tiny clouds of smoke in the distance, puffing up into the sky, he dropped to the ground with his heart beating faster than the birds' tweets. His only thought was, The emperor's men are resting ahead...

Then, Jun crawled over pebbles leading to a tree the width of the clouds of smoke. He knelt behind the tree for a moment, searching for a spot to hide, and then rolled over to a steep grass bank. He lay on the bank, popped his head up and spotted hundreds of steps cut into the rock of the mountain in the distance. He rolled back down the bank. At the top of the steps there was a wall of trees shielding a holy temple. The triangular temple was high above the trees and sat on wooden stilts, with fires burning around it.

Pulling himself to the top of the bank, Jun scanned the horizon to see where the smoke was coming from. He caught a glimpse of a man in a bright red robe, swishing at the fires at the base of the temple. Studying the man, Jun felt his stomach tighten as he thought, He might be one of the emperor's men. What if he's setting a trap for us? Jun sank into the bank, realising he would need to come back with more rebels.

When he reached the cave behind the waterfall, he could hear the rebels' laughter and their determination to bring retribution on the emperor's men. Jun moved to the centre of the cave and, with the waterfall roaring behind him, waited for them to stop laughing.

"Jun, what's wrong? Why are you looking so serious?" Mea asked, bathing a rebel's frostbitten fingers in warm water.

"I have found the safe hiding place Wan wanted us to find."

"We know, Jun, we are resting here," laughed Mea, unaware of the holy temple Jun had found: a temple hidden in the mountain for centuries, with mystical knowledge and secrets the monks living there wanted no one to find.

# 7

## HOLY HIDING PLACE

Standing in the centre of the cave, Jun said, "Listen. I've found something."

"Yes, Jun. You found the cave," Mea said again.

"No, it's not the cave." Jun walked towards her without waiting for a response. "It's a passage at the back of the cave. It led me to the core of the mountain."

"What? How?"

"When I reached the core, I climbed up some steps which led me to a valley."

The rebels sat in silence with their mouths open, like the fish they were roasting.

"The valley is filled with flowers, and has birds singing in every tree."

"Birds singing? A valley flourishing in the winter?" Ling laughed. "What next, the emperor's men?"

"The valley lies within the mountain and is protected from the seasons," Jun said, glaring at him. "I walked through the valley for a while and stumbled upon a trail of steps leading to a temple. The temple looks almost impossible to reach because it sits high off the ground. It's surrounded by gigantic trees – trees wider than five men."

"Why didn't you take one of us with you?"

"We should go there now. Take me back with you!"

Jun waited for the rebels' excitement to dwindle, then said with great authority, "No, we must wait." He held up his hands to calm the rebels. "Do not let the valley's beauty fool you. The temple is almost impossible to reach, and—"

Ling jumped to his feet and stood next to Jun. "We can't stay here," he said, looking at the other rebels now listening to him. He ignored the injured rebels, and yelled, "Come on, let's go!"

Moving out of Ling's way, Jun cautiously stated, "A man dressed in a robe was lighting fires around the temple. It may be a trap. We cannot just charge towards the temple, we must make sure it's safe."

"Jun is right," Mea said, standing up. "The emperor's men may be inside."

"How did they reach the temple before us?" Ling snapped.

"Maybe from the other side of the mountain."

"You think you know everything, don't you?"

"No, I don't, but we cannot afford to make the wrong choices."

"Like walking along a path at the edge of the mountain." Ling smirked as he looked at the injured rebels.

"That path brought us here."

"I'll go back to the temple," Jun said, "with five rebels, and if we do not return in four days, block the tunnel to the cave. You will need to wait here until spring and then travel back down to Wan's village."

Ling, burning with resentment towards Jun, walked to the edge of the waterfall. Staring through the rumbling water, he thought of his childhood and the summer days on his farm: him trailing Jun around the village and listening to his friend's every word. Trying to blank out the pieces of their shared past holding their friendship together, Ling stood silent as Jun selected the rebels to go with him to the temple.

The next morning, Mea and the other four rebels Jun had chosen followed him through the passageway leading to the core of the mountain. When they reached the core, they looked up at the circular cave and the spiralling stone steps sticking out.

Just before they climbed the first step, Jun warned Mea, "Be careful. The steps are wet and some of them are brittle. They might crumble away when you stand on them."

"Thanks," Mea said, annoyed in case Jun thought she was heavier than the others.

"No... I meant...just be careful. We need to reach the opening to the valley."

Mea stomped up the steps behind Jun. "Is it a sacred temple?" she asked.

"Keep moving, Mea, we will find out soon enough."

The other rebels followed Jun and Mea into the hidden valley and along the path until they could see the steps leading to the temple. They rested on a grass bank, and Mea asked Jun, "Do you think they could be rebels signalling for us to find them?"

"I'm not sure, but do you remember what Wan said about following the right path? I feel I am being drawn to this temple."

"Yes, and I feel the same way, but I also remember what she said about when you can't walk another step!" Mea fell back down on to the grass. "How long will it take to climb those steps?"

Jun smiled and said, "I knew I should have asked Ling to come with me."

Mea laughed and then pushed herself up off the grass.

"When we get to the top, we will need to get into the temple grounds without being seen," Jun said.

"We will find a way," replied Mea, trying to find the will to climb the steps to the temple.

"Once we get through the trees, we will need to crawl to the gates of the temple to see if there are soldiers inside. If the monks are alone, we will still need their blessing to enter the temple." The Hunan people had always respected the holy men and their temples. "Come on, Mea, let's walk to the heavens!"

When the rebels had climbed up the last step, they stood in front of the line of trees shielding a stone wall that surrounded the temple grounds. Jun moved closer to the trees and realised that they were growing into each other, making it impossible to pass through them. He tried to squeeze through, twisting and turning in the slightest of gaps, but he could not reach the wall.

After an hour, Jun and the rebels walked further from the steps and tried to find another way to get to the wall. "There must be a way, but we cannot reach the branches to pull ourselves up."

"We've travelled so far and a wall of bark and beauty has stopped us," Mea said as she sat down and leant back against a tree. A few seconds later, she said, "Jun, look. Over there." She pointed to a tree next to her. "I can see an opening in the tree, and steps carved inside the trunk."

"Where?"

"Yes, they are steps," Mea repeated, pointing to them. "They will take us up the tree and on to the wall. We must be able to jump down into the temple grounds from there."

Within seconds, Mea was climbing up the tree. Jun laughed.

"Go on, Mea, don't wait for us. Lead us to the temple."

"Are you sure I won't get stuck?" Mea asked, smiling back down at Jun.

Jun and the rebels followed Mea up inside the tree, but as they climbed higher, the tree became narrower and the steps spiralled out of a hole in the trunk. With a mist of ash and smoke surrounding them from the temple fires, Jun whispered to Mea, "I can't see the steps. It's too dangerous. Remember what happened on the path at the edge of the mountain."

"I can't go back inside the tree now. We must keep moving up."

Feeling for the steps with her feet, Mea pushed herself up the tree. When she could not feel any more steps, she reached out to the wall and found holes cut into it to hang on to. She pushed herself through the branches and pulled herself up on to the top of the wall. Jun and the other rebels followed her every move until they too reached the top.

Minutes later, when the smoke had drifted slightly away from them, Jun and the rebels found themselves kneeling on the wall and staring at Mea, who was rubbing her eyes in disbelief. When Jun and the other rebels turned towards where she was facing, the last of the smoke drifted away, revealing the holy temple.

The temple had steep steps leading down to the fires burning in small metal drums, which were delicately positioned around the temple's base. Some of the fires had weakened while others were burning brighter than the ruddy leaves the rebels had just climbed through. While the temple's beauty drew them closer, a mist of ash came floating around them and shielded the temple from sight.

Jun whispered to Mea, "We cannot jump off the wall. It's much higher than I thought."

The smoke again drifted away from them. "Look down there. I can see steps sticking out of the wall," a rebel whispered.

Mea moved on her hands and knees to where the steps

began. When she reached them, she whispered, "These steps will take us down into the temple grounds. It's safe, follow me."

"Wait," Jun said. "What if there are soldiers inside?"

"It's too quiet, Jun, trust me."

When the rebels were safely down, they crept through a garden bursting with fertile vegetation. Jun caught up with Mea, and she whispered to him, "Look at those carrots. That one is the size of a rabbit."

Mea and Jun walked through the smoke to the end of the vegetable garden, with the other rebels behind them. As they got closer to the temple, the slightest of breezes again brushed the pale smoke away from them, and the rebels' eyes settled on two towering wooden doors at the top of the steps, protecting the temple.

Dazed by the fires reflecting off the temple, the rebels tried to focus their eyes on the giant doors made from the redwood trees they had just climbed. Then, they moved to the side of the temple and hid among a row of red rose bushes, taller than Jun.

"We should wait here," Jun whispered. "The holy man will come outside soon."

"Jun, many brave souls have given their lives trying to find one of the sacred temples," Mea said, peering through the bushes.

"Do you think the emperor's men are here?" one of the other rebels asked.

"No," Mea whispered. "I told you, the temple is too quiet. We would have heard them before now."

Jun said, "The legends of our people state there are more holy temples."

"Five," Mea said. "One hidden on each of the great mountains."

"I believe this is the Heavenly Temple," Jun said, smiling at Mea while she was pricked by the rose bushes. "I have always dreamt of finding this temple, and now maybe I have. This sacred temple, and the knowledge held inside is the foundation of our people's beliefs."

Sitting down in the camouflage of the rose bushes, Jun and the rebels waited for the temple doors to open. The radiant fires continued to reflect off the wooden doors and the stilts holding the temple off the stony ground. The temple's warmth reminded him of the school in Sau, and he prayed for Wan to feel his relief at finding her safe resting place.

"You are blushing again, Jun," Mea said, believing she knew of whom Jun was dreaming.

Jun opened his eyes and stuttered, "Yes...a holy...hiding place and...we need to get inside," trying to distract Mea from his thoughts.

Later that evening, as the rebels tried to rest among the thorns, the grand temple doors creaked. The rebels jumped to their feet, squeezed their heads through the bushes, and waited for the doors to open, but they didn't. Exhausted from travelling from the waterfall and being scratched by the rose bushes, Jun ordered Mea to keep watch while the other rebels rested.

With the comfort of lying on the lush leaves in the cave and then the excitement of finding the temple, the rebels had forgotten their hunger. Now it niggled at them throughout the night. Sensing none of them were sleeping, Jun warned, "We can only enter the temple with the monks' blessing. Women are not allowed in the temple."

Mea moved over to Jun, punching the bushes away from her. "So I cannot enter the temple? Why didn't you tell me before?"

"I needed your help. Ling is against me so I needed someone who believes in me."

"So you used me to get to the temple."

"No, I didn't use you," Jun said. "I needed your help because there could have been soldiers here. I knew I could trust you, and you can always trust me." Jun stretched his arm and touched Mea's face. "You can't enter the temple as a woman, so you will need to disguise yourself as a man again."

With the stroke of Jun's hand on her face, Mea blushed to the colour of the rose bushes and smiled.

Jun said to the rebels, "Try to rest. When a monk comes out, I will approach him and ask him if we can enter the temple. This will give Mea time to cover her face with dirt."

In the morning, with the sun sending hummingbirds flying through the valley and over the rebels, the temple doors creaked, cracked and swung open. A monk walked out of the temple, skipped down the steps and over to the fires. He fussed elegantly and purposefully over the waning fires, prodding them with a roll of crumpled paper and bringing them back to life.

Jun waited until the monk was closer and then launched himself from the bushes, scraping his arms against the thorns, and ran towards the monk. The holy man, startled at the sight of Jun rushing towards him, screamed and threw his lit papers high above his head. He then sprinted up the steps and back inside the temple, with Jun scurrying after him. The monk yelled to the others inside to close the doors behind him.

"Wait!" Jun cried, in hot pursuit of the monk. "I want to speak to you. Please don't be afraid."

Without waiting for a reply, Jun ran into the temple and

the wooden doors slammed shut behind him, locking him inside. He searched for another way out and ran further along the corridor, falling over his feet, shrinking down and hiding from the flurry of footsteps running towards him. Surrounded by a silhouette of towering shadows reflecting from the candlelight, Jun's stomach twisted with the thought of falling into the soldiers' trap. He curled up into a ball and waited for the general to speak.

One of the shaking shadows commanded, "Leave this sacred temple at once."

Jun stood up and walked over to the shadows. One of the holy men rasped, "Who dares to enter our holy place of worship?"

"Please, I'm sorry for scaring you. I mean you no harm," Jun said, lifting his arms to show he did not have a weapon. "I would like to speak to your leader."

"No, you cannot speak with him. No one gave you permission to come into the temple. You must leave now!"

"I found the temple by mistake," Jun said desperately. "We are being hunted by the emperor's men and...we just wanted to find a place to hide."

"You cannot stay here."

Jun stood in front of the monks' shadows, waiting for a response, but silence was his only answer. He bowed and turned back to the grand doors, asking the monks to open them. When he reached the doors, a gentle and commanding voice stopped him.

"I am the leader here. How did you find our temple?"

Jun turned back to face the leader, his mouth tightening with tension. "Please don't be afraid of us, Your Grace. We come in peace."

"Peace?" the leader replied with his voice trembling. "You charged into the temple like a wild animal."

"I'm sorry."

"Yes, well...so you are not alone."

Jun searched for the leader in between the shadows of the other monks. He talked to the smallest one. "No. Five more rebels are resting outside, but there are many more waiting for us to return to them. They are waiting in the cave hidden behind the waterfall."

"Is this how you found the path to the temple?" The leader moved closer to Jun and stood next to a candle on the corridor wall, showing his face. His beard flowed down to the middle of his chest and his shaven head reflected the candle. Jun was twice the size of him.

"Yes, we were seeking shelter from emperor's men. Three rebels are nursing broken bones and some are suffering from blisters from the cold. I stumbled across the passage, which led me to the valley. The smoke from the fires led me to the temple."

The leader asked, "What is your name?"

"My name is Jun, Your Grace. I've travelled from a small village near the Emerald Forest of the Hunan province. I led a rebellion against the emperor, and his men are now hunting me and the rebels who refuse to surrender to his rule. This temple is our last chance of freedom."

"Why are you refusing to surrender? The rebellion is over."

"The soldiers are taking away the farming tools from every village. Famine is sweeping across our land and many of my people are dying. The emperor is draining the little riches we have from us, and if we do not fight back against him, he will destroy the history of our province and our people. The rebels who've walked a thousand miles with me have sworn their loyalty to the Ming emperor, and we will fight another day against the Manchu soldiers."

"Please go to the courtyard," the leader said. "One of the monks will take you there. I need to think about what you are asking from us. My thoughts will be chirping in my head like a....ah..."

"Hummingbird?" laughed Jun.

"Yes, the birds... I, ah...could not think of anything."

Jun smiled back at the leader. He then walked out of the temple with the monk and into the courtyard at the back of the temple.

Later in the afternoon, the leader and eight of the monks were kneeling on the wooden floor of a prayer room. With their hands in front of them, they chanted their prayers for guidance, and with each prayer they sat up straight with their hands held together, then rolled back down to touch the wooden floor.

Kneeling on the ground, the leader asked the monks to leave the room. When they left, he listened to the many birds sweeping through the temple grounds while he wiped his sweating hands on his robe. Then he covered his face with his hands and searched for more wisdom from his ancestors. His head and heart gave him conflicting advice.

With his head spinning from his endless prayers, the leader walked out of the prayer room towards the courtyard. He found Jun resting on a wall and stopped in front of him.

"You've put us in an impossible position," he warned. "We are peaceful people too and cannot encourage war, but we also give help when needed. This is what my prayers have shown me."

Jun bowed his head to the leader. He said, "I am sorry, Your Grace. I shouldn't have entered the temple without your blessing. When I realised this was a sacred temple, I should have turned back."

"Yes, you should have," the leader said. "There are twenty

monks, and myself, in this temple and now that you are here, I must think about them, and about keeping the temple as a place of worship and peace. Leave the temple."

Jun fell off the stone wall.

"I will send the monks to you with my final decision."

Outside the temple, Mea and the rebels had been wrestling with the roses for hours, praying for Jun to convince the monks to let them stay, and that there were no soldiers waiting for him inside. When Jun returned to them and the temple doors closed behind him, Mea ran towards him.

"Jun, you're safe," she cried.

Another rebel yelled from inside the bushes, "Are there any soldiers inside?"

Mea hugged Jun and asked, "Have the monks agreed for us to enter the temple?"

Jun walked past Mea and the rebels to the vegetable garden. "The leader of the monks wants more time to pray. We will need to wait and respect his judgement. I could see the worry in his eyes."

That night inside the temple, kneeling on the floor in the prayer room, all the monks started their prayers. The leader stood in front of them, tapped a small cymbal with a tiny drumstick and hummed in tune with the cymbal.

The monks chanted, "Breathe for today. Touch others without anger. Listen to words truly spoken. Absorb the earth. Search for the compassion in all of life."

The monks' prayers held their beliefs together.

For two days, the leader and the monks prayed for guidance. Jun, Mea and the rebels sat patiently on the steps below the temple. They had eaten food from the vegetable garden and spent their days keeping the fires burning so the monks would not have to come outside the temple.

On the third morning, the temple gates opened and disturbed the rebels. Two monks walked out, and one of them smiled at Jun and gave him a warm gesture to come into the temple. Jun accepted with a nod of his head, but not before turning to Mea and checking she had disguised her face.

Jun and the rebels walked behind the monks through the grand doors and followed them to the back of the triangular temple. They passed a wooden statue of a chubby monk, smiling with each of his five heads. The statue had twelve arms, six each side, and each hand was holding an animal bigger than its hands.

When the monks and the rebels reached the back of the temple, they walked into the dining room and sat down at a table almost the length of the room. The rebels jumped on to their seats, like children on their first day of school, and sat nervously waiting for the leader.

The leader shuffled into the room with a tray of food and sat opposite the rebels.

"You've been fighting against evil with more courage than a tiger."

Jun and the rebels ogled the giant vegetables steaming in front of them.

"And because of this, I'm allowing you to stay here until you are stronger than an ox."

"Thank you, Your Grace." Jun laughed again at the leader's way with words. "We kept the fires burning for you, and we will help the monks to keep them going."

The leader smiled back at Jun, accepting his promise. "Yes, I'm sure you will, Jon. Please eat. You must be hungrier than a—"

"Horse, Your Grace."

"Ah, thank you, Jon," the leader said. "I can't remember anything anymore."

"My name is Jun."

"Jun...sorry. I will stitch your name on my robe. I have a memory like the fish beneath the waterfall." The rebels laughed with the leader. "My name is Bato, I think..." The leader introduced himself, to more laughter. "Please eat before I forget that I asked you to stay."

"Thank you," Jun said, filling his mouth with food.

"Now, Jun, we will try to help you, but please respect the holy temple and the monks who study here."

"Stud...y?"

"Yes, study."

"How do they do that?"

"With their eyes open," Bato said, smiling at Jun's inquisitiveness.

"I'm...sorry." Jun swallowed his food. "I meant to ask, *what* do they study, Your Grace?"

"Their studying is for them to find," Bato said. "If you walk around the temple with your eyes open, you will see their teachings."

After finishing their food, the rebels helped the monks to clear the table. Jun moved over to the other side of the table to sit closer to Bato.

"Can I travel back down to the cave and return with the remaining rebels?"

"No, Jun." The leader remembered his name. "I will only allow six rebels to come here at one time. You must tell the others this when you go back to the cave."

Jun thanked Bato, but he knew that Ling would not wait to come to the temple. He also feared Ling would lead some of the other rebels to feel the same way.

An hour later, the rebels had helped the monks wash their

plates, and then Bato asked some of the monks to show the rebels around the temple grounds. For the rest of the day, and night, Jun and the rebels watched the monks studying and praying inside the temple. When a monk showed the rebels to their room, they leaped on to the beds and fell asleep before the monk had closed the door.

Later the next day, Jun walked through the courtyard with Mea and the leader approached them.

"Jon, I have made medicine for you to help heal the injured rebels in the cave."

"It's Jun, Your Gra…" Jun remembered how long he had been away from the cave. "Thank you, I need to go." He turned to Mea. "I need to leave now! It's been four days since we left the cave."

"Do you want me to come with you?" Mea asked, in a deep voice.

"No, I need to speak with Ling, and you need to rest."

Jun ran out of the temple to the stone wall. He climbed the steps on the wall and jumped back down the tree, landing on branches to soften the fall. As he tumbled down the pebbled path, he heard 'four days' chanting inside his head. Then the chanting stopped with a vision of Ling blocking the passage to the cave.

With his head spinning, he fell down the path to the bottom and rolled towards Ling's feet, and those of a small group of rebels standing before him.

"Ling! Why did you come through the passage? I asked you to wait for me."

One of the rebels helped Jun to his feet. Ling growled, "Some of the men started to block the passage, but I told them to stop because I thought the soldiers had captured you. We came to help you."

"Never mind that now. The monks gave me some medicine to help heal the injured rebels. The leader stated he did not want more than six rebels staying in the temple. He said any more would distract the monks' prayers."

Ling did not greet Bato's request with a warm response. "Who are you to tell us whether we can enter the temple or not?"

Jun ushered Ling away from the other rebels. "I am not saying this, it's the leader of the monks."

Ling glared at him, unconvinced.

"You can go there in my place," Jun added quickly. "Tell the leader I sent you and I will come back to the temple soon."

Ling brushed past him without muttering a word, and Jun sensed he was losing his oldest friend. Staring at the floor, Jun caught his breath for a moment, then shouted to Ling, "Follow the path, then climb up the tree to the left of the path. You will need to climb on to the stone wall and find the steps down to the temple grounds."

Ling ran up the path to the temple without responding, and Jun led the other rebels back to the cave. When they reached the waterfall, he walked out of the cave and shivered with cold. He pulled out the two maps and placed them over each other. Studying the path on the map which had unlocked the passage to the sacred temple, Jun remembered his father's prophecy: "This map will lead our people to peace."

Jun held on to the maps, looked up to the sky and said, "Father, your wisdom has led us to the most beautiful valley in the province, with hummingbirds and monks praying for a peaceful life."

The monks' prayers were soon to be tested by the rebels staying in the temple.

# 8

## ELEMENTS OF LIFE

Without stopping to catch his breath, Ling ran to the top of the path. He dragged himself up the trees, tearing his body on the branches, and jumped on to the stone wall. When he reached the temple, with blood dripping from his head, he banged on the doors like his life depended on them opening.

"J...Jun has sent me." Ling breathed. "I need to...speak to your leader."

The temple doors opened. Bato walked out of the temple and stood in front of Ling.

"Jun has sent you? Why?"

Not fazed by Bato's question, but still out of breath, Ling replied, "I fought with Jun...against the emperor's men. No one has walked more with him, fought harder with him, and he trusts me like no other."

"He never spoke of you."

"Jun wanted to take care of the wounded rebels. He knew he could trust me to come here and take his place."

"I see," Bato said, stroking his beard. Ling wiped the blood from his forehead and held his breath in anticipation of praise from Bato. "Jun is a natural leader."

"What?"

"With so much trust in you, he could have asked you to take care of the rebels with the medicine I gave him. He needed to rest more than most, but he sent you to rest and learn from the monks. One day he will build an army of men."

Ling tried to stutter a response, but failed to find one. He brushed past Bato and walked inside the temple where the monks were busying themselves with gardening, cooking and physical exercises, each one dedicating his days to studying and prayers.

Days after arriving in the temple, Ling approached a monk and asked, "Why do you tend to your garden and then pray every day?"

"We are learning from our predecessors, and our journey is to improve on the teachings given to us," the monk replied, shuffling soil. "When we've learnt all the knowledge passed to us, we expand it, document it, and then pass it on to other monks."

"Why do you leave the fires burning?"

"We must first experience every part of the teachings given to us, and then we burn the teachings. The fires represent an element of life. This is why we keep them burning." The monk patted the soil around vegetables the size of his feet. "We follow a path of learning, and this journey will lead us to enlightenment."

"Why do you shave your heads?"

"To show we have given our wealth away, and that will never know a family life."

"But the leader has a beard," laughed Ling.

"After many years of prayers and dedication, we may, one day, be lucky enough to become the leader of the monks, and then we only shave our heads, and this shows—"

"Yes, yes," Ling interrupted, "what does it show?!"

"How many days...we have been the leader." The monk smiled.

Over the next few weeks, Ling, Mea and the other rebels trailed a different monk every day, absorbing knowledge until it was their time to leave the temple.

With the other rebels waiting outside to come into the temple, Mea ran to find Bato. She crossed paths with him in a corridor and asked in her deepest voice, "Your Grace, can Jun and the rebels left in the cave come here?"

Bato turned to face Mea. "I haven't completely lost my mind. I told Jun six rebels."

Mea sighed. "I am sorry for startling you, but I am going back to the cave with Ling today, and the rebels waiting outside are begging us to ask you…"

"What is it?" Bato asked, walking back to her.

"The winter is still upon us, and soon there won't be enough fish to feed us."

Bato did not reply. He bowed and walked to his prayer room: a room kept only for the leader's prayers, positioned in the centre of the temple.

Once inside the triangular room, he fell to his feet, closed his eyes and embraced a thousand years of wisdom flowing through the room. He prayed for guidance, filling with an instinct to protect the mountain's magical mysteries, but his faith was fighting against it. How can I let them starve? The thought vibrated through his body. How do I protect our secrets? This thought tingled in his head.

As the weeks passed, six rebels came and left the holy temple until Jun returned. When he entered the temple, a monk led him to Bato, who was pacing around the courtyard.

Jun said, "Your Grace, the rebels in the cave are fighting a battle they cannot win. We can't catch any more fish, and many will not survive until spring." Jun knelt before Bato and offered him his hand. "Please allow them to come to the temple. I promise they will not burden you."

"Jun…yes, Jun. I remembered his name," Bato muttered to himself. "You always place others before yourself. Sending your friend back to the temple was an act of someone born to lead. I knew I could trust you, and your judgement, from the first day we met, ah…whenever that was…"

"Thank you," Jun replied as Bato pulled him to his feet, humbled by the leader's faith in him.

Bato placed a hand on Jun's shoulders. "I have studied the rebels helping the monks with their daily duties, and this has opened my eyes and answered many of the questions inside my head. Send word to the other rebels to come here."

Jun ran to the rebels who were waiting in the courtyard. "Go to the cave," he said, patting each one on the back. "Bring every rebel here. Carry the injured, leave no one behind!"

When the rebels had left for the cave, Jun sat down in the centre of the courtyard, on a small wall surrounded by flowers from every province in China.

Bato walked over to him and asked, "Will they all respect the monks' prayers for peace?"

Jun tried to hide his concern about Ling, and the rebels listening to Ling. Not wanting to lie, but shielding the battles he had had with Ling in the cave, Jun said, "We will always remember your kindness."

Within weeks of Bato offering all the rebels food and shelter they were back to full health and settled into life inside the temple grounds. By the time spring had sprung life into everything on the mountain, the monks had taught some of the rebels to read and others to paint on the finest paper in the province. Like children learning in a school, childish excitement filled the rebels' days. For many, this was their first time in a school.

One afternoon, when Bato was walking around the temple grounds and talking to the rebels as they worked with the monks, Jun walked over to him and said, "We are learning many things from the monks. What *don't* they study?" He laughed.

"We can learn from everything around us, Jun," Bato said. He ushered Jun away from the other rebels. "But there are teachings here I do not want the rebels to learn."

"What are they? Why can't we learn them?"

"These teachings cannot be taken out of the temple."

That night, Ling noticed twelve monks going into a circular stone building at the side of the temple grounds. He was desperate to find out what they were doing, and ordered his band of rebels to follow him to the stone room. Once there, they sat outside, waiting for the monks to come out.

Mea spotted Ling and the rebels waiting outside the room and asked, "Why are you sitting here? The monks need your help to prepare the food for supper."

"We are resting," Ling said.

"We are also waiting for one of the twelve monks to—"

Ling slapped some sense into his most loyal rebel.

"I can see why this one looks up to you," Mea said, laughing at Ling's choice of followers. "And he's the bright one."

The rebels sitting next to Ling laughed with Mea.

"Come on, tell me," Mea said.

"Did you see the twelve monks going inside the stone building?" Ling said, not interested if she had.

"No, Ling, I didn't."

"Well, we are going to find out what they are doing in there," Ling said, with a smile like a young boy telling on his best friend.

"You need to help the monks in the kitchen. They are waiting for you."

"No, we don't, but we do need to tell the leader that women are staying in his temple. You won't be laughing then," Ling shouted as she ran from the stone room and went to find Jun.

A few minutes later, she found him inside the temple. "What are the monks doing inside the stone building? Ling and his men are waiting outside."

"I don't know, but we should not disturb them."

Two nights later, some of the rebels were running around the stone room, fascinated by what the monks were doing inside. Jun tried to curb their excitement.

"Please help the monks prepare the evening meal," he shouted, but the rebels continued to circle the stone building. Jun rushed to Ling and pleaded, "Ling, please stop them. They must help the monks. We promised..."

Ling pushed Jun away and snapped, "I don't care about the other monks. I want to know what they are doing inside the stone room." He peered through small windows in the stone walls, but inside the monks had placed their robes over them.

Jun ran to the monks and requested a prayer with Bato. The leader agreed to meet with Jun, but he wanted to speak with him inside the stone building. Later that night, with Bato's blessing, Jun walked past the rebels circling the stone room and moved inside. Trembling with excitement, Jun sat next to Bato. With his eyes spinning around the room, Jun watched the twelve monks dashing around it, believing they were making a fool of him.

Jun blurted out, "Your Grace, the monks...they are... what *are* they doing?"

"Jun," Bato said in a stern voice, "you are witnessing the monks studying animal movement."

Frowning with confusion, Jun said, "They are moving like animals?"

"Yes. Each of the monks tests an animal's movement against another monk."

"They are fighting!" Jun jumped up and tried to copy some of the monk's moves.

Bato did not match his excitement. Thinking for a moment, he chose his words wisely. "The monks are studying animal movement. Each of the animal systems has unique positions and postures. The monks' movements reflect the characteristics of each of the animals they are studying. Now we must leave them."

"No, we can't leave now. I need to know who created these fighting systems."

"They were not created as such, and they are certainly not for fighting against one another."

"But—"

"Listen." Bato ushered Jun away from the monks. "We study animal movement for exercise and meditation.

"I know. I've seen the monks moving like this, but on their own while praying inside the temple. Now they are fighting against each other."

Realising he had little choice but to tell Jun more about the animal systems, Bato said, "The monks practise the moves on their own. It's a way of remembering their systems. We've been meditating like this since the first holy temple was built in China, but now their meditating has evolved into this." Bato turned to face the monks and opened his hands towards them. He and Jun both stood still, observing the twelve monks challenging each other with different animal moves, and Bato closed his eyes and prayed that this information would appease Jun's hunger for more knowledge of the animal systems.

"Twelve animal systems, so each monk trains in just one

system," Jun said, with his mind spinning around the stone room quicker than the monks. "If we learnt these fighting systems, we could defeat the emperor's men and win back our—"

"Stop yelling," Bato said, concerned that the rebels sitting outside would hear Jun. "We do not study them for combat. I trust you, Jun, and as I said before, I trust your judgement." Bato pondered for a moment while watching Jun jumping and kicking like the monks. "I will let you, and you alone, observe the animal systems. This may help you, when you return to your village, to protect your people. However, I ask you not to tell anyone else about these systems or where you saw them. This is important."

Jun cooled his excitement for the animal fighting systems burning inside him, realising he had to keep Bato's faith in him.

The following night, Jun stood inside the stone building, nailed to a wall with the wonder of the monks' skills. While the twelve monks trained in the room, he watched their every move, keeping his eyes glued to them pulling, pushing and kicking at each other. The monks smiled at Jun's jaw dropping, when he realised they were studying something as threatening as a dynamic combat system.

While Jun was inside, Bato asked Ling and his followers to move away from the stone room and to help the other monks with their daily duties. He patrolled the grounds of the temple, trying to keep the other rebels away from the stone room. For two weeks, Jun studied with the twelve animal monks.

Ling begged, "Jun, please, tell me what the monks were doing inside the room."

Jun ignored him, so Ling snubbed Bato's requests to help the other monks.

*

After two weeks, Jun sat twitching and sweating next to Bato during supper. With the monks and rebels enjoying the fruits of the monks' gardens, Jun whispered to Bato, "Your Grace, can I talk to you about the fighting systems?"

"Have your eyes been blinded by the monks' moves, Jun?"

"What do you mean, Your Grace?"

"Do you want to study gardening or drawing now?" Bato said, annoyed that Jun did not understand him.

"No, I would like some of the rebels to learn them," Jun replied, not sensing Bato becoming agitated. The leader stood up and moved away from the table. He gestured to Jun to follow him across the marble floor.

Strolling away from the table, Bato snapped in a deep breath and then stated, "We have always used the animal systems for educational purposes."

"Yes, I know."

"No one from outside of this temple has ever touched hands with a monk who has studied them."

"But Your Grace, they are fighting skills which could help us in our quest to defeat the emperor's men." Jun sighed like a man falling in battle, but not wanting to accept defeat, he regained his determination and said, "The soldiers will take everything from our land, and the animal monks can help us stop them. Please let some of the rebels train with them."

Jun followed Bato out of the temple.

"What about the temple?" Bato asked. "How can you protect these secrets?"

"Your Grace, the temple has many wonders and powerful teachings. The monks here are peaceful and warm souls. I would give my life to protect them, but many people in my province need our help. The monks' teachings will protect them and give them hope. If you can't help someone with your teachings, why study them for a hundred years?"

"Well...ah...yes, you may be right, Jun. Everything passed down to us is to help others, and if we don't use it..."

"There would be no point learning it!"

Jun's enthusiasm spun the leader around to face him. Bato answered, "If I allow eleven other rebels to learn the animal systems, you can all study one, but..."

"Thank you, Your Grace," Jun interrupted. "You've always shown your compassion for others."

"Yes, well...but, you will be responsible for choosing the rebels, and if you choose wisely," Bato moved closer to Jun, "you will broaden your wisdom to protect your people. You will fight without fear, and fear is something we all need to face." He placed a hand on Jun's shoulder. "But if you choose with your heart, you may find a greater fear to fight."

In the morning, Jun gathered the rebels in the main hall of the temple and addressed them.

"The monks in the stone building are studying animal movement. I've studied with them and believe we can use these skills to fight back against the emperor's men."

"Animal movement?" Ling said. Shaking his head in disbelief, he laughed, "What do you think of us, Jun? Do you expect us to believe this?"

Jun ignored Ling's laughter. "The leader of the monks has agreed for twelve of us to train with the animal monks. He wants me to choose eleven of you to learn these systems with me."

The room fell silent.

"How can they help us, Jun?" Mea asked in her own voice, as there were no monks nearby.

"The monks move like animals. They train against each other, challenging one another, kicking and pushing. Their fighting skills are like no others."

"I found the monks fighting," Ling bellowed with new-found fervour for the fighting systems. "I should be chosen." He glared at Jun.

"I am struggling to choose so few of you. It's difficult for me. Please forgive me if I do not call out your name."

Ling walked to the front of the rebel group. He stood with a hand clenched into a fist and waited for Jun to call out the eleven names.

"Mea, please come." He beckoned her over. Ling's eyes followed her as she walked towards Jun.

Jun continued to call out the remaining names. One after the other, the chosen rebels accepted his request to join him with a leap across the hall. Then Jun's final choice drew a gasp across the hall.

"Ling."

Later, Jun led the selected rebels to Bato's quarters. When they arrived, Mea banged the metal door knocker with so much excitement it fell off.

Bato opened the door and gestured for them to stand at the back of the room. He stated, "The animal systems you are about to learn are not for combat." He opened his arms towards them. "You must protect these secrets and agree to my conditions to learn them."

Bato moved closer to the rebels, shuffling in his robe, nervous about his decision to let them train with the monks. He knelt down on his prayer mat and wiped his brow, ready to search for guidance for the rebels standing before him.

"An image of the tortured villagers has filled my mind for many days. If you all *feel* the systems you are about to learn, this vision of darkness will fade." Bato then asked the rebels to pray with him.

"Repeat the prayers after me. We will chant them five times."

The rebels studied the prayers engraved in the wooden floor in front of them, and waited for Bato.

"Breathe...breathe for...today." Bato tried to remember the prayers he chanted every day, but he could not read them on the floor. "Touch others without anger. Listen to words. Absorb the...ah...earth. Seek...no, *search* for the compassion in all of life."

The rebels followed, chanting the prayers five times, and each time they were different. When they had finished their prayers, Bato looked up at them and said, "The emperor starving the children of China, has created this day and placed you on my path through life. I will pray each day for our ancestors to guide us. From this day, the elements of this temple will change all of our paths forever."

Bato's words vibrated around the rebels when he said, "Respect the knowledge you are about to learn. Jun believes in you, and I accept his judgement." Bato smiled at Ling, who forced a smile back.

"We won't fail you," Jun said, with the hearts of most of the rebels.

Bato stood up, his mood changed. "The animal systems must only be used for good."

All the rebels nodded in agreement.

"You must protect these secrets, and the monks who will teach you. You must also protect this temple."

The twelve rebels accepted every word Bato said by bowing to him.

Walking to the rebels and placing his hand on each one of them, Bato told them, "Each one of you will train in one of the twelve animal systems." Just as the rebels thought they had taken their final oath, Bato added, "Listen to your animal spirits. Learn from your mistakes, and more importantly, learn from the mistakes of others, too."

"Yes, we will," Jun said.

"You will all be given choices to make, some with your head, other with your heart, and when all seems lost you will need to use both."

Each rebel felt Bato was giving them much more than his approval to study the monks' fighting systems.

Bato moved towards the window and pointed to the stone building where the twelve monks were waiting for them. He said to the rebels, "Please open your left palm and close your right fist. Bring them together and wrap your palm around your fist. If you do not work as one, the systems will work against you."

All of the rebels copied Bato's hand signal.

"Each day you should show this hand signal to your fellow students and the monks who teach you. The palm represents the sun, the fist the moon, and when the hands are brought together, it means 'bright'. This is the first day of a brighter future for your people."

The rebels held the hand signal until Bato opened the door to his quarters. "Remember, you are learning the systems for a brighter future."

The twelve rebels skipped out of the room and ran to the monks waiting in the stone room. That night, Jun and rebels sat watching the monks train. Bato came shuffling into the stone room and approached Jun.

"Did you choose wisely?"

"Yes, Your Grace, I can trust all of them." Jun sensed Bato had doubts about one of them. "We will not let you down."

"Your belief in others may bring you to lose faith in yourself," Bato replied, and then walked around the stone room and watched the monks train. He shouted back to the rebels, "The monks here are studying an element of life known as kung fu."

Ling yelled, "What do you mean, kung fu? They are fighting against each other!"

"Let His Grace speak," Mea growled like a man at Ling.

Bato continued, "The monks learn a kung fu, which means a skill mastered through great dedication. Some of the monks living in the temple study their kung fu in painting or drawing, while others study the garden and growing food." Bato was quick to add, "There is no mystery behind the twelve animal fighting systems. They are used to improve the monks' knowledge of animal movement and meditation."

"We must have a kung fu for beating the cold!" laughed one of the rebels.

Bato's informative review of the monks' training didn't dampen the rebels' fire to learn the animal systems, and he sensed he needed to give a greater explanation.

"For hundreds of years, this temple has studied every aspect of life. Animal movement has been the essence of health and exercise for all of us. You will soon learn the concepts of the animal systems, and they will give you guidance for your kung fu through all the elements of life."

Thinking of the monks' prayers, Jun tried to absorb Bato's insights. He asked, "What elements?"

"Jun...yes, Jun, there are five sacred temples. Each of the temples studies an element of life: water, wood, metal, earth and..." Bato tried to remember the other element.

"Fire?" Jun cried. "Your temple is surrounded by the fire element!"

"Yes...yes, the fire element," Bato said with great relief. "But we will talk about this another time." He stopped pacing between the monks, spun on the spot and walked over to the rebels. He asked the monks to stop training. Each one of the monks moved in front of a rebel, and when they were all standing in front of their new students, they called out the animal system they were about to teach.

"Ox. In our system, we stand calm, strong and rigid. We deflect everything and push opponents to the floor. The ox prayer is 'A strong mind will give your body strength.'"

The ox monk was short, sturdy and the widest monk in the room.

"Monkey. I swing around the room with my arms spinning fast in front of me. The monkey prayer is 'Hands soft and never still.'"

The monkey rebel crouched down and lifted his hands up to his armpits, jumping around the room. Everyone in the room laughed.

"Dog. I move in a balanced way and retrieve everything thrown at me. I send the force back to my opponent. My prayer is 'Receive what comes and follow what goes.'"

"Tiger. Everything I do is about feeling. I search for the gaps in my opponent's defence. My prayer is 'The eyes and mind travel together.'"

"Dragon. I stand strong, and I am the most courageous monk."

The dog monk turned to face the dragon monk and yapped at him.

"I use my arms to sweep my opponent to the ground. My prayer is 'Once you find your centre, connect it to the ground.'"

The dragon monk was taller and stronger than the other monks.

"Pig. I am patient, and use coordination more than the others. I move my hands and feet together. My prayer is 'Everything moves as one.'"

The pig monk was short and his limbs were all the same size.

"Rabbit. I spring at my opponent with my hands burrowing towards them. My prayer is 'Be positive in all you do.'"

"Rooster. I am the most observant, and follow my opponent's every move. I flap my arms and hop around the room. My prayer is 'Move, before you are moved.'"

"Horse. I gallop around my opponent and kick him with every opportunity. I use more energy than any other here. My prayer is 'Alter your position to change another's mind.'"

The horse monk could not stand still for a second.

"Snake. In the snake system, you need to be alert and strike at the right time, straight to your opponent's centre. My prayer is 'Hit straight to the heart, but hold back your head.'"

The snake monk looked along the line of rebels, studying each of them.

"Rat. I use the best system."

The other monks all turned to face him.

"I attack and defend at the same time. My prayer is...." The rat monk glared at the other monks, and then said, "I'm too smart to tell all of you this. I will tell the rebel when we are on our own."

"Goat. The goat system is about being cautious and timing your moves. My prayer is 'Timing is learnt through patience.'"

Until this moment, none of the rebels had realised what animals the monks had been studying or how they fought, but this had not dampened their spirits. The rebels shared Bato's hand signal for a brighter future with the monks, then the rebels walked towards their animal monk. Jun walked to the dragon monk, Ling to the horse monk and Mea to the ox monk.

Within minutes, the monks engaged in hand, foot and body combat with the rebels. The monks' training techniques and powerful fighting skills knocked the rebels around the room. The rebels tried to defend themselves, but gave up when their bruised bodies ached more than walking up a great mountain.

Day after day, the rebels jumped, galloped and swung around the stone room like wild animals in every training session. Jun developed a deep understanding of his dragon system, while some of the other practitioners struggled to keep up with the basic moves of their systems.

Jun's teacher said to him, "You will soon be able to test your skills against the other monks. The dragon system is you, strong and courageous, and will win you many battles."

"What about the others? Some of them are not learning anything from the monks. What do they need to do?"

"I don't know," the dragon monk said as he swept Jun into the wall with his arm. "But you will need to beat me first to find out!"

"What...was...that?" Jun asked, rubbing his head.

"Think like a dragon, Jun. We have wings that sweep our opponents away from us." The monk helped Jun to his feet. "Think...like...a...dragon," he repeated.

Every day, Jun and the other practitioners continued their training with a battlefield passion, unaware of the unrest among the rebels outside the stone room. These rebels continued to help the monks with their painting, gardening and other chores, but were desperate to be taught the animal systems.

One afternoon, as the disgruntled rebels watched the chosen rebels bursting with excitement as they came out of the stone room, one of them moaned, "Why can't we be taught the fighting systems?"

"I am sick of gardening, and I can't even bring myself to eat the vegetables anymore."

Jun walked past them and said, "The monks can't teach all of us."

"Why can't you paint and swap with me?"

"No," Jun snapped back. "Once we've learnt the systems we will teach you."

"Surely it would better for us to learn the systems from the monks." The disgruntled rebels followed Jun and the others around the temple grounds, refusing to give in without a fight. "How long will it take before you can teach us?"

Ling, with an uncharacteristic defence of Jun, said, "We must listen to Bato's request. They may stop teaching us if we don't."

Jun smiled at Ling, acknowledging that he was trying to pacify the discontent, but neither of them was ready for the battle ahead.

# 9

## ZODIAC SECRETS

Jun continued his training with the dragon monk and became more skilled than the other rebels, which fuelled their frustration. Ling galloped around the room trying to learn more about the horse system, furiously kicking, nudging and charging at the horse monk with every opportunity. Mea stood firm, as strong as the ox monk she was learning from, and deflected every push and shove away from her. The three rebels were learning their systems well until one morning when Mea lost her balance and crashed into a wall.

With Mea lying on the stone room's floor, the ox monk walked over to her just as the room stopped spinning around her head.

The ox monk said, "Pang, please let me help you off the floor." Pang, meaning 'plump', was the male name Ling used for Mea when he first entered the temple. "You must be more careful, and not stand too firm. While you were pushing so hard, I moved out of the way and let you go."

The other monks and rebels stopped training and laughed at Mea trying to stand up. She said, "No...no, it's fine... I can..."

The ox monk stood back and said, "Your voice...it... it sounds different. You must have banged your head quite hard."

The other monks continued to laugh, but the rebels held their breath.

Mea wobbled to her feet, quickly trying to remember who and where she was. "I am fine. Let's get back to training," she replied – as Mea, not as Pang.

The ox monk moved closer to Mea, studied her face and rubbed his eyes, believing he had crashed into the wall. He shook his head and looked again, then shrieked, "You are a w…w…woo…man!"

The ox monk ran out of the stone room, and all but one of the other monks scurried after him. The dragon monk stood still beside Jun.

"What are *you* going to do now?" Ling yelled at Jun.

"Why are you asking me?" Jun said. "You haven't listened to me since we entered the temple."

"You encouraged the women to travel with us and enter the temple. Why didn't you tell them to stay under the waterfall?"

"Stop," Mea yelled. "Stop, you can't blame Jun." She looked at the dragon monk and said, "What can I do? Will His Grace speak to me?"

The dragon monk turned to face Jun and said, "What is her real name?"

"Mea," sighed Jun.

The monk stated, "I cannot speak to her. It is forbidden. You asked me when you entered the temple why we shaved our heads. I told you it was a sign of releasing wealth, and the sacrifice of not knowing a family life. We do this to find a true path to enlightenment."

"Yes, I know, but—"

"This is why we do not speak to women, and give everything we have to others."

"I'm sorry," Jun said, "but many of us have sacrificed our

family life too, and given everything to fight for our people's freedom."

The dragon monk walked towards the entrance to the room and said, "You tricked us, and now we've broken our vows to the temple. We will all need hope now."

"This is my fault," Mea sobbed, breaking the silence in the room after the dragon monk had left. "What have we done?" She ran over to Jun and threw herself at him, crying, "Tell me what to do. Please tell me..."

"I will speak to His Grace," Jun said, hugging her. "I will tell him it was my idea for you and the women to disguise yourselves as men."

Ling strolled over to the door and said, "While you are grovelling to Bato," he turned to face the rebels in the room, "we'll start training with the other rebels. It won't be long before the monks ask us to leave." He glared at Mea and tilted his head towards the courtyard, suggesting that the other rebels should follow him.

Jun and Mea ran to find the leader of the monks. Mea fixed her eyes on the ground, not wanting to see the monks' tears falling before her. When they reached Bato's room, they begged him to listen to them, but he told Jun to ask 'the female rebel' and the other rebels to leave the temple. With a pull in her stomach, feeling she had betrayed Bato, Mea ran out of the temple to the waterfall. Jun ordered the rebels to leave the temple, but they refused and then he ran after Mea, not wanting her to be alone.

Over the next few weeks, Jun and Mea trained against each other in the cave, while Ling and the rebels who had trained with the animal monks tried to teach the other rebels. The female rebels inside the temple continued to disguise themselves as men and started to train in the animal systems.

Every day, the rebels jumped, pushed and pulled each other around the temple grounds. Dripping in the hot summer sun, they scorched the grounds with their animal moves and believed they were becoming great kung fu fighters. The monks stayed in their rooms and prayed for the rebels to leave the temple as the fires surrounding the temple diminished.

One morning, Bato tried to sit in silence in his quarters, staring at the prayers engraved on the wooden floor. He searched for forgiveness, blocking out the cries of bones breaking beneath him, rebels drawing blood from each other. He prayed for his insight to come quickly and for the bloody battles swirling around the temple grounds to travel back down the mountain.

"Breathe only for today. Touch others without anger. Listen to words spoken. Absorb the earth. Search for the compassion in all of life." For an hour, Bato sat on the floor, repeating his most meaningful prayers. His mind scrambled through the wisdom of his ancestors, and he questioned his thoughts. Why did I let them stay? he reflected. Why didn't I protect the animal systems?

While Bato was sitting on the floor, the monkey monk came to his room. From the other side of the door, he called softly, "Your Grace, there are more women here. They cannot stay in the temple, it is forbidden."

Bato stood up and walked to the door. He said, "I know, but these are troubled times. We promised to help the rebels, and it's too late to break that promise." He opened the door and worried eyes as red as the monk's ruby robe greeted him.

"You knew?" the monk asked, astonished that Bato was not surprised there were more women in the temple.

Bato sighed. "Can we stop women fighting for their freedom? They are as brave as the men. We should respect them for wanting to fight."

"But Your Grace, we can't speak to them, and the men are—"

"Fighting against each other, I know. Your concerns are shared by all of us, but we promised to help them."

"What about us? The other monks are praying for forgiveness, hiding in their rooms, and they refuse to come out. You must help...it's your duty—"

Bato interrupted the monk. "My duty is to help everyone, not just the monks in the temple. I've lived a life of compassion." The monk stood back as his leader raised his voice for the first time. "Breathe for today. This teaches us to live for today and feel each breath we take, inhaling everything around us. How can we do this when there are children dying in their schools?

"Touch others without anger. This helps us to reach out to people. To be peaceful, but how can someone who has lost their child be told not to fight back?"

"But, Your Grace—"

Bato continued to question his prayers. "Listen to words truly spoken. This tells us not to worry about what we have been told, but how can we when people fill us with lies?"

"Your Grace, the other monks need you. Please stop, you are losing your faith..."

Bato wandered over to the window and stared out. "Absorb the earth. This teaches us to feel the energy around us, but how can we when others use it to bring us so much pain?"

The monk walked over to the window and looked down on the rebels running around the temple grounds, shouting and screaming at each other, looking for another fight. He said, "Search for the compassion in all of life. It's our last prayer, and the most important. You've always told us to look for the good in everything around us, and every person we meet. You did that with Jun and the rebels, and now we must remember the other prayers, all of them. We will need the help of the other monks."

Resting against the window frame, Bato closed his eyes and recited his prayers, trying to fill his spirit with the monks' beliefs.

A few minutes later, he sighed. "You're right. We need to remember our prayers, but time is against us."

Bato and the monk ran out of the room and flew down the corridor with their robes gliding across the floor. When they reached the monks' quarters, Bato walked along the corridors and yelled, "Please don't be upset. You did not betray your vows." He knocked on every door. "The female rebels were heavily disguised. You did not know who they were."

Bato continued to bang on the doors, but after an hour his bleeding hands stopped him. He fell back against the corridor wall and slid down to the floor. Listening to the monks chanting their prayers, Bato closed his eyes and accepted he had failed them.

Then a door opened and disturbed him. A monk cried, "Your Grace, there is a way we can stop this."

"There is nothing more we can do. The women want to learn the animal systems and the rebels will not leave the temple."

"Your Grace, two of us should run to the cave and bring Jun and Pang back to the temple."

"Her name is—"

"I know, Your Grace, but we must not speak of the women, and we should not talk to them. Jun and the men will do that for us."

Every door in the corridor opened. "We've finished our prayers," the goat monk said as he walked out of his room.

"We are ready to bring order back to the temple," the tiger monk added.

Bato pushed himself up the wall and said, "You two should go." He pointed to the dragon and ox monks. "We will try to stop the rebels from killing each other."

Later that day, Ling was laughing in the courtyard at the monks' requests that the rebels stop fighting. Instead, he continued to strut around the temple like the emperor. That night, as Ling and the rebels were eating, the horse monk entered the dining room.

"Ling, the leader does not know I am here. I need your help."

"What is it?" Ling asked, not interested in the answer.

"Please stop training the rebels. I will teach you again, but I need your help to stop the fighting."

"I don't need to listen to you anymore. The rebels are training well."

"It's not...not even training. You are fighting amongst yourselves. Most of the rebels are eating alone, in different rooms in the temple."

"You will do whatever the monk asks," a voice yelled from outside the room. Jun walked in and glared around at the mirror of mistrust sitting before him. "We will respect this temple and the oath we took."

"Where did you run to?" Ling snapped.

"He did not run," Mea snarled as she came into the room. "He came to protect me. We trained every day, and if you want to test my skills, please..." Mea moved behind Ling's chair.

"Calm down, Pang," Ling said without turning to face her. "Bato has told us to stop fighting amongst ourselves. Did you not know that?"

Most of the rebels laughed with Ling, but he did not want to test his skills against her.

Mea moved around the table and stood in front of Ling.

"Sit down, Pang, and eat. You're the size of a goat now, not an ox. What did you feed her with while you were in the cave, Jun?"

"His Grace has asked you to stop training, and you will stop," Jun ordered. "The monks still want to help us, but not if we are fighting amongst ourselves."

Ling thought for a moment and then stated, "I will tell the others to stop training for a few days. This will give Bato time to come back to me with how the monks will help us."

"Thank you, Ling," the horse monk said. Ling ignored him.

"But I will continue to train with *my* warriors." Ling smirked at his old friend, while his followers filled the room with a roar of resentment towards Jun. As Ling stood up and strode past Jun and Mea and out of the room, twenty rebels followed closely behind him. Most of the rebels waited for Bato to announce his decision, but Ling and his followers had continued their training.

Three days later, with most the monks fretting over how to usher the rebels out into the temple grounds, the dragon monk walked over to the rebels.

"Please wait outside for His Grace. He will soon be ready to speak to you."

With the rebels waiting in the grounds and the monks standing on the steps, Bato walked over to deliver his decision.

"This temple is for men to worship, and for hundreds of years women could not enter this sacred place." As the female rebels started to believe they would be going back down to the waterfall, Bato continued, "But the outside world is changing…and we must change too."

"We can stay?" one of the female rebels cried out.

"All the women can stay in the temple grounds. They

are courageous. The people of China are suffering under the emperor's rule, and one day they will need their help to change the villagers' lives." The women's relief wasn't to last too long. Bato stated, "However, I will allow the twelve rebels to continue to train with the animal monks. These rebels can teach the men, but no women can learn the animal systems inside this temple."

"How can we fight back against the emperor's men?" the women cried. "We need to learn the fighting systems!"

"The women are welcome to study other teachings inside the temple." Bato tried to make himself heard over the disgruntled cries pushing him back towards the temple. "Some of the monks will help the women, they just can't talk to them. They will need a man to be with them, and pass the knowledge on to them."

The women held on to their anger. One of them shouted, "Forget the monks. We will travel to the waterfall and find another way to fight. Come on, let's go. I'm not staying to cook for the men!"

Mea moved over to Jun, while the other female rebels walked away from the temple and talked of their battles with the soldiers, believing their fight against them was lost forever. Moments later, when they reached the wall leading to the cave, Mea, Jun and a monk older than Bato came running after them. The monk had come to offer more than just comfort.

He pleaded, while panting for breath, "Jun...tell them... please tell them to come back."

"Please don't go," Mea said. "Listen to him."

"He can't talk to us," one of the female rebels said. "How can we listen to him if he can't talk to us?"

"He has told me," Jun said. "Please come back to the temple."

Some of the female rebels were already standing on top of the wall, while others were standing on the steps.

"You can learn different skills: skills we've not seen before. These skills will win us many battles against the soldiers."

Without waiting for a response, Mea added, "Some of the monks here are studying drawing."

"We know, Mea, but we will not defeat the emperor's men with a picture of Ling!"

"Yes I know, but—"

"Come on, we are wasting time. We need to get to the cave before dark."

"There is another monk who makes farming tools…tools we've never seen before, that can harvest a crop in days rather than weeks." The female rebels continued to walk away from the temple grounds, and Mea followed them. "I asked Jun to ask both monks to help us."

"Why, Mea? You are wasting time. Come with us and teach us what Jun has shown you."

"Stop!" Mea's yell echoed around the grounds. "I believe we can design and build revolutionary weapons that will not be matched by any man. These weapons will help free our people." Her words brought rare smiles to some of the female rebels' troubled faces, and her passion to build the weapons pulled them back to the temple.

Later, Jun split the female rebels into two groups. One group would learn the skills to create farming tools, while the other group would study the most delicately detailed drawings of animals. Jun asked one of the male rebels, Gaun, to stay with the women and pass on the teachings of the two monks, and promised to teach Gaun the dragon system when he was not training with the dragon monk.

During the months of studying with the monks, the

women used their new knowledge to create many weapons. One day, Gaun watched the women working and asked Mea, "Why have you called them butterfly knives?"

"I named this weapon after Wan," Mea said, smiling as she put two swords on the floor. "Look, when you lay the swords across each other they look like a butterfly. They are delicate, beautiful, but very strong, just like Wan." Mea picked up one of the metal knives and held it firmly in her hand. "The blade is no longer than the distance between my hand and elbow. My fingers are protected by this bracket – it's shaped from a horseshoe, which has been moulded to the shaft." She pointed to a piece of metal on top of the sword curling away from her thumb. "This is the best part of the knife. It traps the enemy's sword."

"Yes, it's beautiful, Mea, and you've carved the twelve animals on it. But will it cut through the soldiers' armour?"

Mea pointed the miniature sword at Gaun and said, "The blade facing me is flat and blunt to protect me from cutting myself, but the other side is shaped like the front of a boat. This will cut through the rocks holding back the waterfall!" She picked up the other butterfly knife and swiped the air in front of Gaun, while the other female rebels cheered.

While creating the weapons, the women had an appetite to train in the animal systems again, and begged Jun to teach them his dragon kung fu. In return, they promised to build as many weapons as the rebels could carry back down the mountain. Jun agreed to train the women at night outside the temple, but only if they continued their studying with the monks during the day, and didn't tell the other rebels or the monks. He believed the women had more to give to the rebellion, but did not want to break Bato's trust.

Each night, Jun showed the female rebels how to sweep their opponent away from them with a turning of an arm, like

152

a dragon flipping his wing, spinning his body around from side to side. Mea showed the women how to stand strong, and when to let go. She pushed and pulled them, sometimes even when they were making their weapons.

After months of training with the dragon monk and teaching the women, Jun reached a level of skill not witnessed in the temple before. His dynamic fights with the dragon monk had not gone unnoticed as Ling and the other rebels struggled to learn any more from the monks. Each day, tension was hitting the rebels harder than their fists, and during one training session, Ling screamed at a rebel who was jumping in every direction around the room.

"What are you doing? Why do you keep leaping into me? You're fighting him!" Ling pointed to the tiger monk. "He is holding us back."

Aggressive and agitated, the tiger rebel shouted back at Ling, "What makes you so special?"

"Special? I will teach you." Ling clenched his fists together just as the horse monk moved in between him and the rebel.

One night, Bato walked into the prayer room, and one by one the monks leapt towards him like the tiger rebel training in the stone room.

"I cannot teach the goat rebel anymore," the goat monk said.

"I can't teach mine either," added the monkey monk. "I am using every tried and tested teaching method, but none of them work now."

"The rebels are blaming us, and none of them are learning new fighting skills," barked the dog monk. "My rebel learnt more in the first week than he has in the last few months."

"They sound like wild animals," Bato muttered. "Please ask Jun to come to my room. Bato left the prayer room."

Later that night, the dragon monk searched the temple

grounds for Jun. He could not find him at first, but then heard voices behind the rose bushes and found him teaching Gaun and the female rebels.

When Jun had finished teaching, the dragon monk followed him into the temple. The monk did not tell Jun that he had seen him; instead he asked him to come with him to the leader's room, where Bato stood staring down at the other rebels pushing and shoving each other around the temple grounds.

As soon as Jun and the dragon monk entered the room, Bato asked Jun, "When we first taught the twelve of you, the training went well. Why can't some of the rebels learn anymore?"

"I don't know, Your Grace, but like Ling, I have taught other rebels," Jun said, reluctant to tell Bato he was teaching the women, "and some of them can't remember what they've been taught, while others learn much faster."

"You seem to know a lot about teaching other rebels, Jun." The dragon monk moved away from him.

"Well… I have seen frustration becoming the only fight for a rebel, and when that happens, *he* doesn't improve *his* fighting skills, they fight against *him*."

"How are the female rebels training?" Bato asked. The dragon monk fell back against a wall.

Jun bowed his head in shame and replied, "I am sorry, Your Grace. I did not want to break a promise to you."

"I said the female rebels could not train with the monks." Bato glared at him. "And I asked them not to train inside the temple. Is that how you understood it?"

"Yes, Your Grace, and I never wanted—"

Bato shuffled around the room and stated, "I did not say the women could not help you with your training."

"Are you saying I can continue training them?" Jun's eyes opened wider than the dragon monk's.

"Yes, if it helps *your* training, Jun." Bato smiled back. "Are the women struggling?"

"At first, yes, but I realised my dragon system did not work for some of them, so I taught them what I know of the other animal systems."

"Really?" Bato pondered for a moment. "It would seem we may have a similar problem." Bato and the dragon monk followed each other around the room, thinking about what Jun had said. "Yes," Bato yelled. "I've overlooked something. Bring the other animal monks to the library at once, Jun. Go!"

Jun flew around the temple grounds like a dragon gliding on the winds. Within minutes, he had led the animal monks to the library.

The tiger monk asked Jun, "Why has His Grace asked us to come here?"

"He said—"

"I had forgotten something!" Bato laughed louder than the monks as he jumped out from behind a bookshelf and interrupted Jun. "Thank you, Jun. Please go to the rebels and tell them there will be no training tomorrow."

Jun bowed and walked out of the library. When the monks had settled, Bato stated, "I believe Jun has given me a solution to a problem." He took a sharp breath as he clutched a leather book he had picked up. "We pray deeply every day, but we are ignoring the wisdom of our predecessors." He gestured for the monks to sit down with him as his eyes wandered over the books gathering dust on the wooden shelves. "We should always embrace the knowledge held in this room. That's why we light the fires." Bato tapped the leather book. "This book will help you train your practitioners with far greater success."

Before anyone had time to ask how, Bato closed his eyes

and asked the monks to join him in a prayer. He asked them to repeat, "Breathe only for today. Touch others without anger. Listen to words truly spoken. Absorb the earth. Search for the compassion in all of life."

The twelve monks repeated the prayers five times, and then held their thoughts in silence. Bato looked up with a smile.

"Oh... I forgot about the cymbal. Never mind," Bato muttered. "This holy book, which holds some of our most mystical knowledge, will help us train an army in the animal systems."

The monks sat still, taking in every word from their leader. They had never seen the book before.

Bato continued, "Each one of the fighting systems is also based on animal spirits, not just their movement. When we first studied these systems, we moved like animals, slowly at first, to exercise and be connected to the ground, just like our prayer 'absorb the earth'."

The monks laughed with Bato.

"Then we mastered their movements, and this is how we started to train against each other."

Puzzled as to how Jun had helped Bato, the snake monk asked, "Your Grace, what did Jun do?"

"Ah...he brought me back to this room. This book holds the zodiac secrets. These secrets are as ancient as this sacred temple, and more powerful than any knowledge learnt in it." Bato passed the book to the rat monk. "A monk who travelled to all the sacred temples brought this knowledge to me. He asked me to learn these teachings, and protect this book."

The rat monk passed the book to the tiger monk.

"He told me these secrets could change the course of history. I laughed at him then, but now I realise they can."

"Your Grace, this book feels alive!" the tiger monk gasped.

He passed the book to the rabbit monk, who jumped and said, "My fingers...they are tingling."

"For many years, the leader of this temple would randomly choose a monk to study each of the animal systems," Bato said with a warm smile. "Two years ago, I used the zodiac knowledge to choose the best systems for you to train in."

The monks' mouths opened wider than the book.

"This changed everything we know about the animal systems."

The snake monk asked, "How did you choose us, Your Grace?"

Bato lit up with laughter. "I never imagined my observations of your personalities would be so accurate." He laughed again. "We all have different characteristics, but I never thought for a minute that this would have such a dramatic effect on how each of you would learn the animal systems."

The monks passed the book amongst themselves and listened to Bato's every word, as he explained the zodiac secrets and how they had helped to train the monks in their animal systems.

"If we know our characteristics, which the book calls animal spirits, we can fly along our path through life and walk up a mountain to fulfil our destiny. Our prayers remind us of this."

"Why did you not remember this before we started training the rebels?" the snake monk asked.

"Oh...ah... I forgot about it," Bato sighed. "My memory isn't what it used to be, that's why I carved our prayers on to the floor in my room."

"And now you remember everything from the zodiac book?"

"Yes, I do," Bato chuckled. "As soon as I picked it up, everything came back to me."

"Your Grace, why are you laughing?" hissed the snake monk.

"There isn't time for you to read the entire book, but I knew you would ask me the most questions. That is what I find so amusing."

Bato stopped laughing and asked the dog monk to pass the book back to him. With the book in his hand, he stared deeper into the pages and then held it open and showed the monks the centre pages.

"Look at your spirits," he said. "This is why you learnt so well. You each have an animal spirit, and when it is matched to an animal system, something magical happens."

The twelve monks scanned the book for their secrets, and Bato realised he would not be able to close it again. The monks fell into the zodiac book, and now Bato had opened its secrets to the temple, the passion for the fighting systems would soon become more powerful than the secrets themselves.

# 10

## REBEL RIVALRY

"What are we waiting for? Why can't you train with me?" Ling asked the horse monk in the courtyard.

"You must wait. We are not ready to teach you," said the horse monk. "His Grace wants to make sure you are all training in the appropriate animal style."

Ling moved closer to the horse monk and growled, "We are already training in the right systems." He spun away from the horse monk, not wanting to believe he had wasted months of his training, and ran towards the temple where he spotted the dragon monk.

Ling said, "I need to speak to Bato. Where can I find him?"

"I cannot help you," replied the dragon monk. "His Grace wants more time..."

"More time for what? We've been waiting for days. What is he doing?"

"We must all wait," Jun ordered as he ran to the dragon monk.

"I wasn't asking you," Ling snapped. "Go and train with the women."

The dragon monk jumped in between Jun and Ling and held his arms out to keep both men apart. "Please be patient. You must show your strength in other ways."

Ling stormed off, searching for Bato. When he was out of

sight, the dragon monk said to Jun, "Please follow me, I need to take you to His Grace. We need your help."

"With what?" Jun asked as they walked through the maze of corridors leading to the library.

"Keep up," the dragon monk said. "We are wasting time and the other rebels will not wait forever." He sped up and guided Jun into the library.

With the animal monks sitting around the oval library and Bato sitting in the middle of them, Jun and the dragon monk walked in.

"Your Grace, I brought Jun here. He can help us. We cannot do this without him."

"I am sorry but he can't – his friendship with the others has affected his judgement. He doesn't have a clear mind to help us," Bato said, not looking at Jun. "Anyhow, we cannot talk to him about the book."

"What book, Your Gra—"

Bato interrupted Jun and asked, "Why did you choose Ling?"

"Your Grace," the dragon monk said, "Jun is an outstanding practitioner. He leads by example, and he has trained the female rebels well."

The other monks gasped as one.

"He knows the rebels better than any of us."

Jun held his head and sighed. "I chose Ling because I did not want to lose him as a friend, not because he would teach others well. I'm sorry... I thought he would turn against me..." Jun turned away from the monks and walked towards the door. "He did anyway," he sighed. No one replied.

Just as Jun had walked out of the room, Bato sprung to his feet and said, "Your honesty is in your spirit. Please come back in and sit down." He waited for Jun to come back into the room, and then stated, "Yes, you are right. He is ready now."

Regaining his seat and composure, Bato said to the monks, "Jun understands his animal spirit, and does not fight against it anymore. We can take hope from this. It has taken time, but he has learnt from his mistakes."

"I *am* willing to learn from my mistakes," Jun said.

"Yes, I know, and this is something only the bravest of souls will do. He is also trying to be strong in other ways."

"I *am* trying to be strong, not just with my body, but with my mind," Jun said, with great determination, "and I *am* learning from the mistakes of other people too. This is the path my father spoke of."

"Yes, Jun, yes!" Bato yelled. "I always believed you were ready to help us." The dragon monk smiled at his leader's latest insight. "I must point out that he is not *training* the female rebels. He is merely using them to assist him with his own training."

All the monks smiled.

"What do you need me to do?" Jun asked.

Bato beckoned Jun to move closer to him and then said, "Jun, I am going to show you some insights into the magical teachings of the zodiac, but I must warn you, if these secrets fall into the emperor's hands, it will lead us down a path we will not be able to walk up again."

Jun and the monks laughed.

"The…zodiac," Jun said. He muttered, "I'm sure I have seen that before…"

No one heard him.

"You must keep this information to yourself," Bato said. "Please do not share it with anyone."

"Oh… I promise."

Bato stood up and walked over to a bookshelf and stated, "Last week, after speaking with you, Jun, I realised that I had overlooked the zodiac knowledge. When I picked up the book," Bato held up the zodiac book, "I remembered that the snake practitioner would be the first person to ask me a question about anything, because of his inquisitive nature – it's what he was born with." Bato sat down in the middle of the monks.

The snake monk slithered in silence over to Bato, this latest piece of the zodiac knowledge pulling him towards the book. Bato laughed.

"Some time ago, I learnt the best practitioner for the ox system," he pointed at the ox monk, "was someone who had a stubborn personality."

A crooked frown crept across the ox monk's face.

"His stubbornness matched the fighting skills of the ox system."

Everyone laughed, except the ox monk, who refused to.

"You could say...he was as strong as an ox." Only Bato laughed.

Over the next few hours, Bato showed Jun how he had used the zodiac book to choose the best fighting system for each of the monks. He chuckled as he explained, "This is how I used the book. I studied the monks for six months, and when they were ready for an animal system, I matched them using the knowledge I had gained from the zodiac book."

"I could not see the others' animal spirits because I could not see mine," Jun said.

"Yes, Jun, yes! Now you are ready for the secrets of the zodiac!" Bato stood up and shuffled back over to the bookshelves and presented Jun and the monks with crisp, cream paper, then opened the first few pages of the zodiac book. "Please copy these pages in a way that no one else but you will understand."

Jun and the monks copied the page.

*Ox*: Those born with an ox spirit will be resolute and honest. Hardworking and strong, their stubbornness will never weaken. They take comfort in trusting others, and inspire confidence from all those around them. They must remember: strength without wisdom leads to emptiness. On their life journey, they will never give up the fight, but this may work against them.

*Strength: strong as an ox in all situations.*
*Weakness: their stubbornness can be used against them.*

*Dog*: Those born with a dog spirit are determined and loyal spirits. They will attract allies like no other, but will only befriend spirits who follow a steady path. They must remember: balance without speed leads to rigidity. On their life journey, they will observe everything falling before them.

*Strength: methodical in all they do.*
*Weakness: will not take risks.*

*Dragon*: Those born with a dragon spirit will be most courageous. They will be the first to protect others, and they live with a sense of duty. They will thrive in dangerous situations. They must remember: power without flexibility leads to rupture. On their life journey, they will lead others.

*Strength: brave in all they do, and will never hold back.*
*Weakness: they will not listen to advice from others, until they have seen it for themselves.*

*Rabbit*: Those born with a rabbit spirit will want to be surrounded by family and friends. Compassionate and sincere, the rabbit spirit is intuitive and will avoid conflict.

They live life to the full and strive for their surroundings to be harmonious. They must remember: caution without courage leads to weakness. On their life journey, their sensitivity will surround them.

*Strength: always positive.*
*Weakness: they will not let negative thoughts in.*

*Goat*: Those born with a goat spirit will want to be alone in their thoughts. They are wanderers, and insecure. A goat spirit will seek daily reassurance from other spirits and will do anything to please them. They must remember: harmony without speed leads to stagnation. On their life journey, they will be full of worry if they allow themselves to be.

*Strength: gentle and generous.*
*Weakness: they can be timid, and dislike change.*

*Horse*: Those born with a horse spirit will want to roam wild and free. They are loyal, and this will lead them to become allies with other spirits. The horse spirit will always want to seek praise. They must remember: speed without harmony leads to abandonment. On their life journey, they will drift and keep moving.

*Strength: full of energy, and always loyal.*
*Weakness: they will not know when to stop moving.*

*Pig*: Those born with a pig spirit will be easily gulled into ideas of the other spirits. They are loyal until they believe they have been crossed. They must remember: rigidity without wisdom leads to fracture. On their life journey, they will always seek more knowledge.

*Strength: patient and loyal.*
*Weakness: they will only work at their own pace.*

*Monkey:* Those born with a monkey spirit will thrive on fun. They are good listeners, but will listen to what they want to hear. Always active, and will be the quickest thinkers. They must remember: flexibility without persistence leads to foolishness. On their life journey, they will overcome trouble, but they can look for it.

*Strength: the greatest problem-solver.*
*Weakness: they will sometimes miss the obvious.*

*Tiger:* Those born with a tiger spirit will be strong leaders. They are ambitious, and are always ready to pounce. No other spirit will match their instincts. They must remember: courage without caution leads to carelessness. On their life journey, they will be fast and furious. They will battle against their enhanced sensitivity.

*Strength: sensitive and sympathetic.*
*Weakness: will rely too much on their instincts.*

*Rooster:* Those born with a rooster spirit are practical and resourceful. Perfectionists who will leave nothing to chance, the rooster spirit will want to be at the centre of the spirits.

They must remember: persistence without flexibility leads to stiffness. On their life journey, they will attract new knowledge, but it will not stay with them unless it is written down.

*Strength: more practical than any other spirit.*
*Weakness: they will always blame other spirits for their failings.*

*Snake*: Those born with a snake spirit will be seductive and charming. Snake spirits need to know what others are thinking, and if they don't, they will be the first to ask. They will do all they can to gain other spirits' insights. They must remember: flexibility without strength leads to compromise. On their life journey, they will be intuitive, with a burning need to learn new knowledge before other spirits.

*Strength: more intuitive than any other.*
*Weakness: they will be reluctant to share their wisdom with other spirits.*

*Rat*: Those born with a rat spirit are smart thinkers. They are only loyal to others they consider part of their pack. They seek knowledge and welcome challenges which will test them. When challenged, the rat spirit can be dangerous and will use their mind to control others. They must remember: wisdom without sincerity leads to conflict. On their life journey, they will welcome new challenges, but will have a desire to stop others experiencing them.

*Strength: learning as fast as any animal spirit.*
*Weakness: they will only learn what challenges them.*

When they had finished copying the pages from the book, Bato stated, "This is the core of the zodiac teachings. There is a lot more to learn, and I'm lead to believe that there are more books.

"I'm sure I've seen one," Jun muttered to himself.

"The zodiac's secrets are more powerful than all the knowledge in this temple. They could bring you many unwelcome friends."

Jun studied what he had written on the paper then said, "Ling is not a horse spirit."

"Yes, we know," Bato said. "We've been trying to find the best animal system for him and the other rebels. We do not know the others like you, and this is the reason we need your help."

"Ling will not change his group," said Jun. "He believes he is better than the horse monk, but I believe in these teachings. My family has spoken of knowledge like this for generations." Jun took a deep breath and filled his spirit with thoughts of his father. "My father believed I would find them. He told me that. He said he felt this on the first day he held me."

"Your father, what else did he say?" asked the snake monk.

Jun did not answer. He closed his eyes for a moment and thought of his father and his village. Then he leapt off the ground like a rabbit and yelled with excitement, "Ling's sword!"

Bato fell the floor and stuttered, "W...wha...what about the sword?"

"You know about it?" Jun screeched, hoping it was true.

"Well...um..."

"Does the zodiac book mention the sword?" Jun asked, like a child waiting for a teacher to turn the next page of a book.

"Ah...well...maybe," Bato said with a stern voice. He stood up, and his demeanour cooled Jun's excitement.

"Ling has a sword with the splendour of a thousand stars melted into it. It has the strength of a hundred men, but is as elegant as a young woman."

Each of the holy men jumped to their feet and edged towards him.

"There are five symbols on it."

"F...five," Bato said. "It can't be...the sacred sword? How?"

"An elderly couple gave it to Ling. They brought him up as their son. His parents died when he was young."

"Where is the sword?" asked Bato with a sense of urgency. "He did not bring the sword into the temple. Where did he hide it?"

"I believe he hid the sword in the valley, near the stone wall." Jun turned to Bato. "What is the power of the sword? What do the symbols mean?"

Fidgeting with his robe, Bato stated, "It is written in the sacred book that once the sword is placed in the heart of this land, it will show its powers. I did read something in the book, about how only a guardian's spirit would...shock the ground... or something like that, whatever that means."

"How do we get the sword? Where is the heart of this land?" Again the snake monk was the first to ask.

Closing the sacred book, Bato ordered Jun and the holy men not to talk about the sword with anyone else. "Keep Ling close to you, but out of harm's way. Do everything you can to protect the zodiac knowledge." Walking away from them, he acknowledged, "We do not know the actual power of the sword, and there will be danger ahead if this too falls into dark and dangerous hands."

Concerned Ling would not change his animal system, Jun

asked Bato, "Can the monks teach all the rebels now?"

Rattled by Jun's question, the goat monk said, "No, we can't. How can we train them when we've struggled to teach twelve?"

"I will help. I know how to teach larger groups," Jun said with great enthusiasm. "Some of them must be already training in the right system."

"And we could use the zodiac book to choose the best system for the rebels to train in," said the rabbit monk. "If we help them build an army then the temple will be safe."

Bato stood still in the middle of the room while the monks waited for his response.

Jun, holding in his excitement at the prospect of building an army to send back the emperor's men, could not stand still. He spun in between the bookshelves, yelling, "Our people will be free again!"

Bato walked through the bookshelves and stopped Jun from darting in between them. "I will allow the men to train with the monks, but not the women, you can train them. You must never speak about the zodiac secrets."

"Thank you, Your Grace. We will all remember this day."

Over the next few days, Jun and the twelve animal monks analysed the men and matched them with an animal system. Within a week, the rebels had jostled into their new animal groups, but Ling refused to change his group, ignoring the animal monks' belief that he had the spirit of a rat, and their pleas for him to be more sincere to the other rebels. Because the monks could not tell him why they wanted him to change to the rat system, he insisted on training with the horse monk.

The twelve monks and their rebels spread out through the temple grounds and the zodiac knowledge had a dramatic effect on how quickly the rebels learnt, and each of the animal groups thrived beyond the monks' expectations. As the weeks passed, the rebels became more skilled, but also more detached from each other. They started to eat, sleep and speak with only their animal group.

A few months after the twelve animal groups had been formed, the rebels believed they had learnt enough from the monks to defeat the emperor's men. They paraded around the temple grounds, acting like animals and calling themselves 'animal warriors'.

One morning, outside the temple, Jun was training with the women. Mea stopped for a moment and asked, "What is a beimo fight?"

Jun pulled Mea away from the other female rebels and replied, "A duel to the death."

"I overheard some of the rebels talking of midnight duels, these beimo fights, scattered throughout the temple."

"I know. The monks are doing everything they can to stop them, but every night they are chasing empty shadows trying to find the challenge fights."

In the afternoon, when the monks were sitting in the prayer room, Bato fidgeted with the fright of the beimo fights. He asked the monks to gather the animal groups in the courtyard.

"Please, be strong," Bato said with fear in his voice. "There are greater battles ahead for them, and we must stop them from killing each other."

The monks acknowledged their leader without speaking, and went to each of their groups.

Later that day, when the last group had marched into the courtyard, Bato stared at the warriors who had proudly assembled themselves behind their animal masters. The leader stood with the goat monk, who whispered to him, "Your

Grace, be careful. We cannot trust these warriors, or let them stay any longer."

"My friend, you are forever cautious," Bato said as he turned to face the goat monk. "I feel your animal spirit next to me." Turning back to the warrior groups, he ordered, "There will be no more beimo fights in this temple. We did not teach you the animal systems so you could kill each other."

The courtyard was silent as the animal warriors glared at each other.

Bato continued, "You must train together and test your skills against one another, or your fighting skills will work against you."

His words rebounded off two hundred stubborn souls. The silence was disturbed when Ling shouted, "Why should we listen to you? We've learnt more than enough to continue teaching ourselves." His words were greeted with a screech of neighs from the horse warriors.

"Be quiet, Ling," Jun shouted across the courtyard. "We must listen to His Grace."

"Or you will…?"

"Stop," Bato shouted, "or you will leave this temple today." He squeezed his head with his hands for a minute and then moved closer to the animal groups. With the spirits of his predecessors surrounding him, he bellowed across the courtyard, "You must leave this temple before our holiest of days. You can stay six more nights. Please prepare for your journey down the mountain." He then muttered to the goat monk, "We gave them everything, and look at what this has created."

Jun ran to Bato and said, "Your Grace, my warriors also want to train without the dragon monk. I fear for us when we leave the temple. We're not ready for the battle with the emperor's men."

With each warrior group marching to different areas of the temple grounds, Bato sighed. "You are a true dragon master, Jun, and a most courageous person." Tears filled his worried eyes. "I will pray that the other masters live through their zodiac strengths, but I fear they will follow their weaknesses."

The monkey monk led Bato away from the courtyard and said, "Your Grace, we must now think of the temple."

As they moved into the temple, the rabbit monk bounced over to them and said, "We should be proud of what we did for them. We can do no more."

Smiling at his holy friends, Bato said, "You are both showing your animal spirits. We should be proud that we tried to help, but now we need to protect the temple." The holy men comforted Bato as he reminded them of his dog spirit. "I showed them loyalty, but my kindness has caused this bitter, bragging rivalry."

As the days passed, the monks continued to pray. As the animal chants grew louder inside the temple walls, the monks listened to the female rebels seizing their chance to train with an animal master. Jun tried to cool the other masters' burning passion for fighting the soldiers, but they believed they were ready to go into battle with the emperor's men. Each day a furnace of fighting engulfed the temple, and this was igniting their animal spirits more and more. Now with the women training with them, the inferno intensified within the animal groups.

On the last night of the rebels' stay in the temple, Bato sat next to the dragon monk at supper and asked, "Did some of the animal groups change their masters?"

"Yes, Your Grace. The rebels who first learnt the systems had become the masters, but they were not the most skilled practitioners and some of the female rebels challenged them."

"So they…"

"Yes, Your Grace, but some of the challengers refused to fight to the death, and the masters accepted defeat. There are now six male and six female masters."

"What about Jun?" Bato asked.

"No one challenged him."

"And Mea?"

"She is now the ox master. She did refuse to finish the fight."

Pausing for a moment, Bato then said, "She is as strong as an ox, in more ways than one."

That night, Mea asked Jun to come with her to find the ox monk. They found him in the stone training room. She asked Jun to say, "Please accept this animal shield from Mea. She made the shield from the ruby trees in the valley below, as a sign of respect to the ox system."

"Please thank her," the monk said, placing the shield resembling an ox on the window sill.

"She has asked me to say that she will think of you when she trains near their ox flags."

The ox monk said, "Tell her that I will do the same."

Not wanting to be outwitted by the ox master, the other animal masters created their own shields through the night and gave them to the monks who had trained them. These shields were crafted from wood and metal, and when the last one was nailed to the stone walls, the rebels were ready to leave the temple.

Sitting at the dining table, Bato addressed the dog monk. "Please help me detail twelve maps, one for each of the masters to follow back down the mountain," he said, showing the dog monk where he was sending the rebel groups.

\*

In the morning, just before the sun rose, the monks gave the animal masters the maps which would lead them to base camps scattered across the mountain range. When the ox monk gave Mea her map, she said to him, "Thank you. I will fly my ox flags high and recruit many more warriors to fight back against the emperor's men."

"Mea," the ox monk said, surprising her, "you will need to use your strength wisely. Just remember, ox warriors may become more stubborn than you think. This may bring you danger."

"I will fight with Jun and his dragon warriors," Mea stated. "But I am aware of the battles ahead." She put her right fist into her left palm and said, "I will lead my warriors with this sign of hope."

Mea and the ox monk followed the monks and warriors who were assembling in the courtyard, where they waited for the leader of the temple. Jun walked towards the monks, who were all standing in a line leading out of the temple grounds, and bowed his head.

"I'm sorry."

Bato walked along the line of monks. He said, "You could not have done any more, Jun, but I need you to promise me that you will never return to the temple. If you do, it will bring grave danger to all of us."

"I promise, Your Grace, and thank you for believing in me." Jun embraced Bato, then walked back to his warriors and led them along the wall of holy robes, steering them away from the temple. The warrior masters held their animal flags high, some without a murmur to the monks. For the first time in months, peace descended across the temple, delicately disturbed by the snapping of the flags as the warriors marched out of the temple grounds.

With the summer sun rising over the temple, Bato's troubled eyes followed the warriors winding down and around the mountain. When the warriors had marched to the edge of a blooming forest, he wandered back into the grounds, while the animal monks waited until the last warriors had marched out of sight.

A few minutes later, Bato stopped walking when he heard a flurry of footsteps crunching on the grass behind him.

A voice cried, "Our problems are now behind us."

Bato turned around and acknowledged the rabbit monk with a smile. "You may be right," he said, "but if they do not fight together, there will be a greater danger in front of us because they will not defeat the emperor's soldiers. Then the emperor will order his men to march to the corners of Asia, to find out who trained them."

# 11

## GULLIBLE GENERAL

The animal warriors marched down a narrow rock path cut into the face of the mountain. Most of the twelve groups kept their distance from one another, eager to find the trails the leader of the temple had mapped out for them. These trails would lead them to their own camps, scattered throughout the base of the mountain in forests, caves and behind waterfalls.

Some of the animal groups moved in their animal styles. The dragon warriors spread their arms out like dragons and glided over the mountain trails, dressed in dark robes. The snake warriors slithered through the forests, sliding over the grass as the monkey warriors swung from branches high above the ground with the sun piercing through the trees.

When they reached an open plain at the base of the mountain, Ling ordered two warriors to hide under a black blanket and to disguise themselves as a horse. Hours later, they captured many wild horses and tamed them, ready to be ridden to their base camp. Some of the warrior groups spent days chasing the horses around the plain, capturing just a few.

Jun tamed a white horse which almost every warrior had tried to capture, and then rode it to Ling and shouted, "Ling, before I lose sight of you again, please tell me where you are going."

Spinning around on his horse, Ling snarled, "I will defeat

the emperor's men with my warriors, and I trust you will do the same."

"But one day we will need to fight together."

Ling ignored Jun and rode away with his warriors.

Jun and Mea were the only masters who wanted to share their base camps' locations, and none of the other masters would listen to Jun's pleas. He rode with Mea to them and begged, "Please remember what the leader of the temple asked of us: to protect the systems and fight as one."

Still the masters refused to tell Jun where they were travelling. None of them feared the battles ahead.

"Jun, they are not listening to us," sighed Mea. "We're running out of time, we need to lead our warriors to our base camps – the emperor's men could be close by. Where are you travelling to?" Mea rode alongside him, their warriors behind them.

"South, further away from the mountain range. My map shows a cave hidden in the stone valley by some fallen rocks. If you need to find me, just look for dragon markings carved into the rock paths. I will carve them myself."

"My map is taking me north through a barren plain surrounded and protected by a crystal clay valley."

"How will I find you?" Jun asked.

"I will see you, Jun," Mea said, laughing at her map, "but you might not see me."

The two animal masters pulled their horses closer and wrapped their arms around each other. Not wanting to let go, Mea squeezed Jun until one of his dragon warriors shouted that he had seen the trail to their camp.

Jun lifted his arms out of Mea's embrace and held her face and said, "Keep safe, Mea, and please remember where to find me." His kissed her forehead and then pulled his horse towards his dragon warriors.

"You too, Jun. I will look out for you," yelled Mea.

After months of travelling through the mountain ranges, the animal groups found their camps, and once safely inside, they started to create what they called 'animal kingdoms'.

The leader of the temple had written the camps' locations in his zodiac book.

Rat: north. Waterfall beyond the hollow woods.
Ox: north. Surrounded by the crystal clay valley.
Tiger: north. Caves before the hollow woods.
Snake: south. Woodland in the golden forest.
Horse: south. Trees opposite a grand lake.
Dragon: south. Caves hidden in the stone valley.
Goat: east. Canyon before the desert.
Monkey: east. Woods flowing to the desert.
Rabbit: east. Caves before the deep desert dunes.
Rooster: west. Land before the hot springs.
Dog: west. Trees surrounding the hot springs.
Pig: west. Mud beyond the hot springs.

The rat camp could only be reached by swimming under a waterfall with lime green water pouring from it. At night, and without a leaf in the forest that the water flowed into, the trees looked like warriors running through the water.

Beyond the hollow woods, the tiger camp was hidden in small caves dotted around a steep rock face. The camp was cool in the summer and warm in the snow, and the tiger warriors snuggled into the caves and hid from sight.

The snake camp stood tall out of marshlands in trees with golden leaves. The snake warriors slithered down the tree trunks and wiggled through the marshland without being seen.

Nestled between mounds of mud, the pig camp piled high off the ground. With hot springs warming the mud, the pig warriors rolled in it for hours.

The monkey camp sat high off the ground in a forest. The trees sloped towards the edge of a desert, and provoked by the warmth of the sand, every tree had fruit falling to the ground.

Alongside a great lake, the horse camp lay deep in a forest, protected by the trees. The horse warriors roamed around the camp, wild and free.

Hidden in a valley with a river running through it, the goat camp was tucked away in the rock of the canyon.

Dug deep into the desert, the rabbit warriors hid in burrows as wide as a hundred of them.

Protected by many hot springs spraying a mist of boiling water, the rooster camp cut into the rock of the springs.

Surrounded by a valley of rock, the hot springs trickled into the trees hiding the dog camp.

With the animal kingdoms built and hidden from sight, the warriors spread across the mountain, scouting for more willing rebels. They swarmed through the mountain ranges, sending out battle cries to every village in the southern provinces.

"We will train you to be warriors," they promised to the peasants.

Talk of the 'kung fu fighters' spread infectiously throughout the provinces as the peasants ran through their villages, shouting, "The masters will send back the emperor's men!"

The voices in the villages grew louder and roared along the rugged roads to the emperor's palace like a summer sandstorm. Peasants from the southern provinces listened to the calling from the 'magical masters' about how they had built animal kingdoms around Heng Mountain. Thousands of willing souls travelled for months, with little food or rest, and followed the cries of the warriors. They searched for the animal kingdoms, and as they got closer to Heng Mountain, the warriors eagerly gathered their new recruits and led them to their masters.

A year after leaving the Heavenly Temple, each of the twelve animal groups had assembled an army of warriors to engage in battles with the emperor's men. The warriors started to behave more like animals with each passing day. Some moved, scoffed their food and conversed with each other like animals. 'War' was the word on every warrior's lips.

General Wu laughed at the 'tiger talk' of his men. He ridiculed the rumours, chuckling like a child.

"Where are they? Should we hunt them down like wild beasts?"

"But sir, the peasants are saying—"

"They will send us back to the emperor?" Wu cried. "Soon you will tell me that these warriors are the rebels we chased to their deaths coming back to haunt us!"

"Where *did* they come from?"

"They are pathetic peasants who hide from us," yelled the general, blindly believing that the rebels had fallen to the perils of the mountain.

One afternoon, when the villagers had been celebrating the last day of summer, Wu paraded the latest victims of his ruthless rule outside their homes. General Wu had thrived on the victory against Jun and the rebels when he had 'broken the brittle bones' of the rebels on the mountain, but now a surge of dragon warriors swept towards him with fire and venom.

"Save the villagers," Jun ordered as he rode towards the peasants.

"I will kill the general," Gaun, Jun's most trusted warrior, cried.

When the warriors burst into the village, Wu freaked with fright, fell from his horse and ran into the nearest house, hiding from the dragons outside. Peering through a gap in the wooden walls, with his heart beating faster than the dragons chasing his men through the village, he wracked his brains. Where have these creatures come from?

Crouching in a bedroom, fearing how he would explain his cowardly hiding place to his men, Wu listened to the warriors circling around the house. Gaun stopped outside the front door and kicked it open. He barged into the house, unaware that Wu was now hiding there under a child's bedcovers.

As Gaun walked into the bedroom, Jun shouted to his warriors, "We must go. The soldiers have gone, and the general is running back to his command post."

"But Jun, he might be hiding in the village," Gaun shouted back from inside the house.

"We must leave now," Jun yelled, pulling a villager on to his horse, "and take the men back to our kingdom."

Gaun picked up a pillow off the bed and crushed it. With Wu sweating under the covers, he threw the pillow on top of him and yelled, "We've won with just a pillow fight!" He ran out of the house.

An hour later, Wu wrapped himself in the bedcovers and came out of the house to roars of laughter from the children holding dragon flags.

A child yelled, "He's been crying like a baby!"

"Are you going to tell your father about the *scary* dragons?"

Running with embarrassment, Wu leapt on to a horse and rode away, still wrapped in the child's blanket. As he rode into his command post, a soldier at the gates yelled, "Stop, you can't come in here! Go home to your parents."

Springing from the horse, Wu screamed like a little boy who had lost his toy. "It's me, you fool! Your general." He threw the blanket on to the ground, and the reins of the horse at the soldier.

The soldier asked, without thinking, "What happened, sir? Where are the other men?"

"What do you think happened?" Wu replied, jumping higher than the horse. "Hundreds of deadly warriors, who fought to the very last man, ambushed us. I killed many of them with my bare hands, but my soldiers ran like rats and left me with no choice but to camouflage myself. If I hadn't done this, I wouldn't have been able to retreat, and all would have been lost." He ignored any further questions and marched to his quarters.

The soldiers had laughed with the general at the rumours of the animal warriors, but after Wu had returned to the post, they talked of nothing else but him running from the 'scary dragons'. Wu hid from them and licked his wounds like a beaten dog while the soldiers laughed at the 'gullible general's' tales.

The next morning, when a rage of embarrassment dragged Wu out of his room, he screamed at anyone in sight. "Get me three hundred men. We will march back to the village and grind the peasants into the ground unless they tell me where the warriors are."

Two hours later, Wu and the soldiers rode out of the command post towards the village. With the warriors gone and no one to protect them, the villagers hid in their homes. When Wu reached the centre of the village, he sat proudly on his horse, trying to prove to his men that he was as brave as his story had suggested. Dismounting his horse, he scanned the village, hoping none of the fleeing soldiers had hidden there.

"Where are the animals?" he screamed.

A voice shouted, "General, they flew through the village like dragons sweeping across the mountain."

"Really?" Wu said with a smug smile.

"Yes, General. They've taken our men and left us with the old and young."

"Captured the men?" Wu said, with a curious frown. "And they've taken them into the mountain?" He walked through the village, waiting for a reply. He didn't get one, so he yelled, "Do not worry, we will find them."

"General, be careful – they fight with fists of fury," laughed a villager from inside his house. Wu quickly realised that the warriors' fighting skills had dazzled the villagers.

As the taste of freedom swirled around the villagers, Wu wasted no time in crushing it.

"Burn the village to the ground."

"No, General, please!" was cried in every home.

The general laughed. "Go to the barn and shape a horse-shoe like a dragon. Bring it to me. I want to make it white -hot from the burning houses and scorch a dragon on to their arms."

Later, the soldiers dragged the elders out of the village, and the women and children followed the ashes from their homes drifting away with them. That night, when they arrived at the next village, the villagers ran out of their homes to help the elders. They bathed their blisters and dried the blood seeping from their dragon burns.

Over the next few weeks, the animal masters stormed through every village in the province like the easterly winds churning the desert dunes. Bruised and beaten by the warriors' fighting skills, the general's men scurried back from the villages with a message for his father tattooed on their arms.

Written in the delicate handwriting taught by the monks, it read: *Order your men to the northern territories before you have no men to order.*

Limping back to the command post, one soldier cried, "General, they fight like wild animals." He crawled inside the command post, covering his arm in shame. "They kick like horses and charge like goats."

Another soldier said, "I beg you not to send us back to the mountain. The warriors are trying to make us lose our minds, because sometimes they camouflage themselves like dogs, and then pigs."

Wu snapped at his men, "They are pathetic disguises."

Another injured soldier asked, "What are you going to do, General?"

"I've already sent word to the emperor requesting more men." The soldiers surrounded the general. "When the battalions arrive, we will destroy them with our military might."

By the time the general's plea for more men had reached the emperor's palace, rumours of the warriors freeing the Hunan villages had engulfed the northern territories. The winter thunderstorms flooded the palace grounds with talk of the kung fu fighters, and soon the emperor was rocking on his throne, fearing another uprising. His advisors bowed before him, agreeing with every outburst, but the only thing the emperor wanted to know was how Wu had failed him.

With darkened eyes, Narchi barked at his advisors to gather his generals in the grand hall. He ordered them to assemble an army greater than ever before for his elder son, Commander Kuen.

The emperor charged through the palace and shouted, "I will give Kuen the freedom to march with his men to the southern territories." Kuen's men were the most brutal Manchu soldiers in Asia. "He *will* crush this rebellion."

Weeks later, with the emperor sat waiting for his son to come to him, Commander Kuen marched into the palace grounds, and when he burst into the place, his presence was echoed in every room. Kuen was twice the size of Wu, with more scars on his face than his father, and he had drawn more blood in one day from his father's enemies than Wu had from the peasants of the Hunan province.

"Your Highness," Kuen announced when he reached the emperor's throne, "I will crush these warriors and bring you back their so-called master."

"Kuen, you are my most decorated commander," the emperor acknowledged, mirroring his son's crooked smile. "I trust you more than anyone and I know you will not fail me..." The emperor and his son stopped smiling. "Show them no mercy, and bring Wu back to the palace."

The next morning, just before sunrise, two thousand soldiers filled the palace grounds. The emperor stood shaking on his balcony, trying not to let his quivering salute turn into a weakening wave. He scanned the palace grounds, staring at the soldiers, then with an edgy smile he ordered his men to listen to his every word.

With his knees knocking and hidden behind the balcony wall, Narchi found the strength to deliver one final order to the army below him.

"You must, at all costs, kill these rebels who disguise themselves as warriors."

The soldiers roared as one.

"And bring me back the peasant who calls himself a 'kung fu master'."

Commander Kuen shouted louder than any man near him, "We will not fail, Your Majesty!"

Narchi glared at Kuen, and not wanting to show his fear of losing the Hunan province, he moved to the edge of the balcony and yelled to him, "Punish the peasants for helping the rebels." The emperor dreamt of a victory, and with the roars from the soldiers ringing across the palace grounds, he believed this glorious army would ease his nightmares.

As the sun rose above the palace walls and into the winter sky, Narchi glanced across the city and watched Kuen leading his army out of the palace grounds, with cherry, jade and sapphire leaves swirling around the soldiers' feet. He waited for a moment and then stepped back into the grand hall and slumped on to his throne. He cupped his hands, held on to his troubled thoughts and closed his eyes for the first time in weeks.


Commander Kuen and his men rode south through thunderstorms and blizzards, hunting for the animal warriors, but failed to find a single ripple of resistance. He laughed with his generals, joking that they had gone into hiding again. With no one to fight, he ordered the soldiers to march further south to Wu's command post. Within weeks of giving this order, Commander Kuen arrived.

When Kuen's army marched to the gates of the post, Wu walked through the snow to his brother. He said warmly, "Commander Kuen, welcome."

With a frosty breath and not the warmth of his brother, Kuen replied, "The emperor has been thinking of you, General."

"Please follow me," Wu said as Kuen dismounted his horse. "I will give you everything you need to grace our emperor with a famous victory fitting of his rule." The pleasantries were just a masquerade. Wu knew the truth of the battle ahead, and had ordered his men to cover their tattoos.

"Now we have enough men, including yours, Wu, to crush these rumours of rebellion."

"Yes, Commander, we will need to surround Heng Mountain and wait for the animals to come out." Wu believed his knowledge of the mountain warriors would help to convince his brother that he was valuable in the battle.

"Wait for them?" Kuen snapped. He stopped walking and turned to face his brother. "What do you mean, wait? The emperor's army will not wait for an enemy to fight!" He laughed. "It's not the first time the whispers of the winter winds have gone to your head."

Wu shrunk into his armour, with Kuen tormenting him about running down the mountain two years before when he had failed to find one rebel.

"Commander, please, I don't mean to be disrespectful, but the animal warriors fight like no other army. It will be best to wait until spring for them to come out of the mountain ranges, or we will fall into their many ambushes again."

"Take me to my quarters, General. I will lead the men in the morning."

The next day, Commander Kuen rode with Wu, as the soldiers marched behind them to the base of the mountain. He ordered his four generals to follow other paths into the mountain range, yelling at them to capture as many warriors as they could drag back to the command post.

Wu tried to reason with his brother. "Commander, we only have a few hundred men. We are marching them away from our post and into the warriors' traps."

"Be quiet, Wu," Kuen snapped. "This is why you failed before, because you forgot *our* blood is running through your veins. We do not run, hide or give in to weakness." Kuen glared at his brother as they continued to ride along the path trailing up Heng Mountain, unaware that the animal groups had ambushed the other generals. Wu kept quiet and rode next to his brother.

After days of travelling through the mountain's deadliest passageways, the soldiers marched towards the warriors' traps. One after the other, the warrior groups pounced and pierced the soldiers' ranks, and chased them back to the borders of the mountain range, teasing them with every weary step. While the generals fled back to the command post with their men, Commander Kuen rode around the mountain for five more days, with blizzards burning the scars on his face, before giving in to the deepening snow.

When the commander arrived back at the post, he burst into his quarters and nailed a map of the mountain range to a wooden desk with his knife. He sunk into a chair and listened to his men weeping in their rooms. Pinned to his seat with the dishonour of his foolish battle plans, Kuen realised he had given the warriors what they had been waiting for.

He grabbed a feather from the pot on his desk and wrote on the map, *How did they travel so fast across the mountain?* Then he shouted to the general in the next room, "Bring Wu and the other generals to me."

Once inside, they stood in front of Kuen, who was scribbling on his map, and waited for their interrogation to begin.

"Where did the warriors strike?"

"I can't remember, Commander?" one of the generals said, holding a bandage to his head.

"Tell me everything," Kuen yelled.

The generals filled his head with tales of where the warriors had ambushed them, but after grilling them for hours, he still hadn't realised that there were twelve animal groups. He ordered them to round up their men and follow him back to the mountain.

Wu asked, with the surprise of the other generals, "Commander Kuen, where will we go?"

Kuen pushed himself out of his seat and moved closer to his brother. "Go?!" he yelled. "Where do you think we are going?" He leapt towards the map on the table. "We need to ride together," he scribbled over the trails on the map, "along the north, east, west and south trails of the mountain range, and kill every last one of these rabbits and snakes."

"Kuen, I'm sorry, but we've lost too many men to do that," Wu said, praying his brother would listen to him.

"Leave me now and prepare your men for battle," Kuen ordered the generals. "Wu, never talk of defeat again. Stay here." When the generals had left the room, Kuen whispered to Wu, "How many men?"

"I don't know," Wu said. "But we must find another way to defeat them or..."

"What should we do?"

"I'm not sure, but each time the warriors burst from the mountain, they disguise themselves as different animals."

With a dismissive suggestion, Kuen said, "They want us to believe they are fighting with ten thousand warriors."

"Yes...yes maybe they do," Wu said, with his head rattling with a plan. "And maybe we should fight like they have."

Wu had learnt many lessons from his brother's failed battle plans. The military brothers locked themselves in Kuen's quarters all night until Wu had finished explaining his plan.

"We must empty the command post and find somewhere to hide our men."

"H...h...hide? What do you mean?" Kuen said, swallowing his pride and trying not to scream.

"Kuen, listen: we must make them believe we are returning north. We will leave the injured soldiers here and wait for the warriors to come and destroy the command post. When they return to their camp, we will follow them and plan our attack against them."

"They wouldn't come here," Kuen said with confidence. "They are brave, but they know they couldn't beat our cannon fire."

"What if they saw us dragging the guns away from the post? Would they come then?"

Bursting with excitement, Kuen said, "The villagers, they would see us retreating and send word to the warriors!"

"Yes, brother, and the warriors will believe their own myths. They will want to show the peasants, who believe in them, that they sent us home. Let them believe it."

"You sound and look different, brother. If I didn't know better, I would think I had an *older* brother standing before me," Kuen remarked.

"I tried to live my life through your footsteps and wasted many opportunities to show you, and our father, the soldier I should have been. This is my last chance to do that."

"I will follow you, General," Kuen stated, "but first we need to send word to the other command posts in the neighbouring provinces that we are sending our men and artillery guns there. I will order them to give me their men when we are ready, and then we will fight back."

Months later, when spring had melted the snow on the mountain's peak, the neighbouring command posts were bulging with the commander's men. General Wu's command post was protected by injured soldiers and a skeleton of empty armour resting on top of the walls. Wu and Kuen had ordered the injured soldiers to stay and hold the command post, but they both believed the warriors would attack before they returned.

Wu had ordered his men to leave behind their armour because he wanted them to "March without a murmur," he said, to make the warriors believe they had run back to the palace.

Kuen had handed over the command to Wu without a fight. While riding in their peasant clothes away from the post, Kuen said, "You are different, Wu."

"Yes," acknowledged Wu. "I've tried to be as brave as you, but I'm not. When I realised this, I had to find another way."

"It is a brave man who can make sense of his own weakness, and a wise one who can make sense of others'. You are showing great wisdom, brother. Our father will be proud of you."

Wu smiled back at the commander, but then sighed. "When Ru returned to the palace, my victory against the rebels was paraded along the palace walls. Our father's followers danced with joy at the news of the crushed rebellion. I was given the Hunan province as my reward, and walked the peasants like dogs through their villages."

"I know, Wu," Kuen said, "but we all thought—"

Wu interrupted Kuen and said with conviction, "The rebellion was over."

"Yes, but it won't be long before the emperor is dancing through the palace gardens and celebrating *our* victory."

"No, it won't," Wu said as he sat deeper in his saddle, ready to ride faster to the mountain. "I hid behind my father's name, but soon the people of China will bellow *mine*."

# 12

## ANIMAL KINGDOMS

Spread throughout the mountain range, the animal warriors delicately camouflaged their kingdoms to protect them from the outside world. They embedded their animal signs throughout their surroundings, and during the day the kingdoms were bursting with warriors training in their kung fu systems. Bonded together by more than just the way they trained, the warriors had a far greater sense of their animal spirits.

With each passing swoop through the villages, the warriors gathered more peasants, swelling their kingdoms with willing recruits. Some of them brought much-needed supplies to the kingdoms. Once inside the kingdoms, the new recruits swore never to leave their animal group. The female warriors who had trained in the temple used their knowledge of tool-making to mass-produce weapons for the new recruits, and when ready for battle, the masters presented each recruit with one.

With the commander's men retreating, the warriors believed the peasants' myths about them. They rode through the villages and the peasants cried, "The soldiers are running scared, crying with their commander, and will never return!" Cheering their liberators, the local people danced in their homes and raised the warriors' flags high above the walls of their villages. Ling and his horse warriors believed they were invincible, with greater fighting skills than any of the other groups, and were blind to any rumour that the commander may be plotting a plan of attack.

In the dragon kingdom, Jun reminded his warriors of what the leader of the monks had told him. "We will need to fight together." He firmly believed that the skirmishes they were having with the soldiers were just a taste of the battles ahead. Jun had tried to send word to the other masters, by carving messages onto trees that the soldiers would not understand, ready to warn them of the perils they were parading towards, but only Mea responded.

She wrote on a tree, *We have sent the soldiers scurrying. I trust that you have done the same, but I am ready if you need me.*

Jun then decided to find the other masters himself. He travelled across the mountain, alone, searching for them. One morning, when he was riding along a trail to the south, the clatter of hoofs in the distance startled his horse. He pulled the horse off the path and hid it behind a bush. Spreading the branches apart, he peeped through them, desperate to see if it was the emperor's men.

When the horses got closer, Jun fell back at the sight of Ling, sitting proudly on his horse, bragging about his greatest victory with two hundred horse warriors. He listened to the warriors' laughter as Ling jested with them that he had freed his people from the 'evil emperor'. Jun kept his head down and pulled his horse closer to him.

Ling laughed again, and then said, "Jun, please come out. You can't hide a white horse behind a twig!"

Jun emerged from the bushes and cautiously approached Ling. He smiled at him and said, "I'm happy you are safe and well."

"I am pleased you are safe too, Jun," Ling said, to the surprise of his warriors. "Where are your warriors?"

"I'm travelling alone," Jun replied as he went back to fetch his horse.

"Alone?" Ling yelled, and the horse warriors laughed with him. "You are fearless, Jun. I know we've sent the soldiers back to the emperor, but even I wouldn't travel on my own through the mountain."

"Ling, please listen," Jun said. "No one has troubled the emperor's men more than you, and your horse warriors are as brave as you, but—"

"There are no buts, Jun," Ling interrupted as he jumped off his horse and raised his sword. "Don't worry, the war is over. We've just burnt down the general's command post and their last soldier fell to my sword."

Jun walked behind Ling as he waved his sword. "Why did you go there?" Ling's horse jumped at Jun's fury.

"Don't question me," Ling snapped back. "My horse warriors are the bravest kung fu fighters on the mountain, and that alone scared most of the soldiers into running from the province."

Jun looked up to the sky and sighed. "We agreed not to attack the command posts. There are too dangerous and—"

"Stop!" Ling plunged his sword into the ground. "I agreed nothing with you, but I promised to lead my men to glory, and I did. The soldiers fell like sheep in a slaughterhouse."

Jun sighed softly. "You will lead us all to the slaughterhouse."

"My warriors know where I am leading them," Ling barked. "The other masters are barely wrapping bandages on the soldiers' wounds. Why aren't you offering them your help?" Ling leapt on to his horse and circled his old friend. "All of my life, I've listened to you and your belief that you are the chosen one, but you are nothing to me. Not anymore."

"Ling, I can't stop you from hating me for trying to help, but just remember what His Grace asked of us."

"Look at you!" yelled Ling. "You are more pathetic than the general. He pretended he had more soldiers guarding his command post."

With the horse warriors surrounding Jun, he spun around with them and begged, "Will you listen?"

Ling glared at Jun for daring to speak to his warriors.

"The soldiers will come back with more men, and if we don't fight together, we'll be dragged back to the emperor's palace."

"They won't listen to you." Ling laughed. "They only listen to me, their grand master."

"Please, His Grace said—"

"Bato said nothing to *me*. He spoke to *you*, Jun, just you." Ling yanked his horse to brush against Jun.

Stepping away, Jun asked, "What are you talking about?"

One of the horse warriors yelled, "He's right. Bato was not interested in speaking to us."

"He was talking to all of us, but none of you were listening," Jun said as he remembered the battles he'd had with Ling inside the temple.

With Jun trying to break through the horse warriors, Ling painted a picture of his own legacy in his head, recalling how the soldiers in the command post had fallen to his sword. Despite his ego burning brighter than the fires at the Heavenly Temple, he still feared that, because of Jun, his bravery would not be bellowed across the great mountain. Ling twisted deeper into his saddle and remembered how Jun had been hailed in glory after the battle in the forest three years before.

"Don't listen to him!" Ling said to the horse warriors. "It's not the first time he's lost the will to fight." One after the other, the warriors peeled off from the group circling Jun and rode away.

As Ling's horse pulled away to follow the other horses, he turned back to face Jun. "May the spirits of our ancestors be with you, and if you really believe we are beaten, you will need them!"

"Ling, stop. Please," Jun yelled. "You are like a brother to me, and my father treated you like a son." Ling continued riding away, so Jun shouted louder. "The leader of the temple told me that this day would come, but I won't let our friendship fall."

Ling pulled his horse up and trotted back to Jun. "I've walked with you to the top of this mountain and back down it. No one has given you more than me, but this is my time now. I will lead my warriors to glory, and I pray that you will not try to stop me."

Ling tugged the horse's reins away from Jun and then kicked his horse with all the anger of a broken friendship.

As the months passed, and with winter heaping the rain on to the northern mountain trail, Jun pushed his horse over puddles which were as wide as the trail. After months of riding, he reached a clay valley covered in crimson crystals. Exhausted and drenched from the rain, Jun slumped off his horse and dragged it through the mud, following ox signs carved into the clay until he reached a wall of earth no man could climb.

Jun stopped at the mound of mud, the rain fell harder, like a waterfall pushing him to the ground. Within minutes, he was lying face down in a pool of water gushing around his head, he heard a voice call from beyond the muddy wall.

"Jun, get up!"

Jun held on to his horse's reins and pulled his head out of

the squelching mud until the voice showed her face.

"You found us," Mea cried as she fell down to hold up his head.

"Mea..." Jun gasped, "I... I..." He fell back to the ground.

"Help me!" Mea shouted towards the wall of mud. "I need help." With Mea holding Jun's head just above the muddy water, four ox warriors came rushing out of the clay wall. The warriors lifted Jun off the ground and carried him towards the wall.

Mea squeezed in between the walls and led the warriors into the heart of a crimson crystal kingdom. Jun studied the clay walls, set back from one another, while Mea held on to his hand.

After resting for a while, with Mea still holding his hand, Jun sat up and turned to face the entrance to the kingdom. He rubbed the mud from his eyes and slumped, shivering at the sight of the sodden plains before him, and fell back down to the ground.

"H...how can..."

"Yes, Jun, crystal clay," Mea said, smiling as the rain pounded the plain. "The clay from the top of this cave has for centuries fallen over the entrance, and it's so thin that we can see the outside world, but it cannot see us."

Jun sat up again to see through the crystal clay wall protecting the kingdom. Mea held him up for a moment and then ordered her warriors to bring him some food. She slowly removed most of his drenched clothes and took off her fur coat to wrap it around him.

"Light a fire...here," she ordered, pointing to a small crater next to Jun. "Rest in my arms," she said to Jun. "You must find the strength to eat."

Two hours later, with the fire curling the fur on the coat, Jun said to Mea, "We need your help."

"Shh..." Mea whispered, hugging the fur coat. "You need to rest."

Jun shuffled away from Mea and turned to face the kingdom's walls. He peered at the puddles being pelted by the rain and said, "I found Ling, but he believes he can beat the emperor's men on his own." He turned back to Mea. "The other masters hide from me."

Staring back at Jun's eyes, which were as pink as the crimson cave, Mea said, "When I first saw your face, I knew the other masters were not going to fight with us."

Jun sighed. "Ling rode his warriors to the general's command post. He's a fool. He believes he's the emperor, filling himself with one final day of glory. They burnt down the command post...and the emperor will never let that day pass."

Jun covered his head with the fur coat and tried to hide his tears, which were falling faster than the rain.

Mea touched his back. "I knew Ling would not fight with us, but I prayed the other masters would."

"Where is the commander?" Jun asked, pushing his head out of the coat.

"Jun... You don't..."

Without listening to Mea, Jun continued, "I don't know why, but the command post fell without a fight."

Mea muttered, "You don't know, do you?"

"What's his plan? The horse warriors are brave, but how could they defeat the commander's cannon fire?"

"Jun, stop!" Mea cried. "The horse kingdom has fallen!"

"But Ling said—"

"The commander ordered the injured soldiers to guard the post. He hid his men...they followed Ling back to his kingdom and destroyed it."

"They might have followed me here."

Mea and Jun looked at the plain, and scanned for the soldiers.

"My horse...they will find my horse!" He stood up, but quickly fell back down to the floor.

"You," Mea said, pointing to one of her warriors, "fetch Jun's horse. Take it to the cave with the other horses. Go now!"

An ox warrior whispered, "Mea, look!" He pointed to the plain, grabbed his weapon and moved closer to the entrance of the cave. Mea helped Jun to his feet as they watched General Wu and his men slog through the mud towards Jun's horse.

"Can they see us?" Jun asked.

Mea whispered, "No, but they can hear us."

The horse was standing on a path leading to the cave, but the rain had washed away Jun's steps. With the rain pouring off the muddy mound and pushing the general and his men away from the entrance to the cave, Wu yelled to his men, "The lone warrior has lost his horse...he's dead. Grab hold of its reins and take it to our horses."

Two soldiers grabbed the horse's reins and tried to pull it away from the mound. The horse fell to the ground and on to its side. Mud and water splattered over the soldiers.

Wu yelled, "What are you doing, you fools?"

"Sir...the horse...it won't move!" A soldier tried to pull the horse to its feet with the reins.

"Leave it there," Wu ordered. "If it wants to die like its warrior, then let it." He trudged over to the horse, lifting each boot out of the sodden ground. When he got closer to the horse, he yanked his knife out of his armour.

Inside the ox kingdom, Jun, Mea and the ox warriors stood still, watching the general standing over the horse.

"Don't," Jun muttered to himself. "Don't kill it."

"Shh," Mea whispered. "The horse is dying."

"My horse will not gallop for the emperor's men. It's free, like my people used to be." Jun hobbled towards the entrance of the kingdom.

"Stop," Mea whispered. "If we fight for a horse, they will have found another kingdom."

Jun moved closer to the crimson walls, but just as he was about to charge at the general, the horse jumped up, kicking the general high off the ground and into his men. The soldiers dived out of the way of the flying general, and the horse galloped through the mud and out of sight.

Two soldiers helped General Wu to his feet and carried him back to his horse.

"They are going," Mea said. "I pray that they won't come back."

"Maybe they won't," Jun said. "But they will search for every warrior hiding on the mountain."

Weeks later, when the rainy season had ended, Jun, Mea and the ox warriors came out of the kingdom and rounded up their horses. Mea brought Jun a horse, but just before he climbed on to it, his own horse galloped towards him from behind the mound.

Jun and the ox warriors rode for days to the southern forest and towards the valley of rocks. One morning, just as the sun broke through the winter sky, Jun leapt from his horse and asked Mea and her warriors to tie their horses to rocks that were hidden from sight in the woods. He walked along a tiny trail of stones, engraved with the dragon signs, leading him to an opening in the woods surrounded by rocks that had fallen from the mountain.

Jun bellowed a dragon cry to the mountain. With the sun lighting up the rocks, one of them rolled to the right and a dragon warrior appeared. Jun held out the sign of hope to the warrior and climbed the rocks, Mea and her warriors following him.

When they were inside the dragon kingdom, Mea walked past dungeons tucked inside the inner rock face of the mountain. Jun walked into a cave and was greeted by Gaun, whom he had left in command. Jun had asked Gaun to calm the warriors' burning desire to fight, but instead he had been rallying some of them to fight against the emperor's men.

"What happened to the horse kingdom?" Jun asked.

"The soldiers burnt it to the ground, but there are many horse warriors hiding on the mountain. We found two, but only the female warrior survived."

"Take me to her."

Gaun led Jun and Mea through hundreds of dragon warriors sharpening their spears to a cave where the horse warrior was resting. Jun stepped into the cave and knelt down next to her. He peeled away the bandages covering her face, exposing her brutal battle scars, deeper than the dragons' spearheads.

Softly, Jun asked, "Did Ling survive?"

The horse warrior sighed. "You must be Jun. He spoke of you, but I do not know if he is alive."

Jun held a cup of water to her mouth. He asked, "Please, tell me how the soldiers found your kingdom?"

The warrior sipped the water and then said, "After Ling attacked the command post, the general and his men must have followed the cries of 'freedom' along the trails back to our kingdom." Jun helped her to lie back down on the ground. "It was a trap. The commander placed armour on the walls of the post to fool us into believing there were more men inside. Ling wouldn't listen. Some of the warriors tried to tell him…"

"How did the kingdom fall?" Jun asked.

"We tried to fight back, but we were outnumbered." The horse warrior held on to Jun's hand. "They blasted a hole in the kingdom wall with a cannon bigger than this cave. They stormed into the kingdom, not like soldiers, but like wild animals."

"How did they bring a cannon up into the mountain?" Jun asked in disbelief, but the horse warrior closed her eyes and smiled as her ancestors welcomed her.

"No!" Mea cried.

Jun covered the warrior's face with a bandage, then stood up and said, "She is living in peace now." He asked Gaun, "What about the other kingdoms?"

"I don't know, Jun, but the soldiers are killing their warriors across the mountain." Gaun followed Jun to the centre of the kingdom and said, "The other horse warrior we found was injured and alone. He was on the trail to the cave behind the waterfall. He remembered the waterfall and wanted to see it one more time."

"We must find the other kingdoms before it's too late," Jun said.

"I will come with you," Gaun said. "We will ride together and pick off the soldiers one by one."

"No!" Jun said. "I need you to protect the kingdom. I will ride with Mea and search for the other masters. They will listen to her."

Gaun turned his back on Jun and walked into a cave.

As the months passed, General Wu continued to order his men to draw battle lines along the trails of Heng Mountain. Each day they cut through any resistance from the masters and Wu tortured captured warriors with his bare hands, trying to find out why they disguised themselves as animals,

202

but none of them spoke. Instead, they accepted the general's knife as their last request.

Jun and Mea travelled along the trails, searching for the other kingdoms, but only found warriors lying in pools of blood on the ground. They carved endless dragon signs on trees, rocks and pebbles leading back to Jun's kingdom, praying the masters would come. With each day, more terrifying tales of fallen warriors filtered across the mountain.

When early summer had settled on the mountain, Jun and Mea returned to the dragon kingdom. They had ordered their warriors not to fight and to stay in the kingdom, because they believed they could not defeat the emperor's men without the other masters. The ox warriors had accepted Mea's command, but some of the dragon warriors were grinding their teeth as fast as they had sharpened their spears. Their resentment increased when Jun reached the dragon kingdom, shadowing him inside the cave, watching his every move.

One morning, Gaun was ready for a fight. He barked at Jun, "Why are we listening to you? There are many fires burning in our kingdom because we want to fight. We can crush the soldiers. We've enough warriors to do it."

Jun ignored him and continued to walk through the cave. He ordered two warriors to roll back the rock covering the entrance, but as he reached them they both stood still, waiting for another order.

Gaun followed Jun. "You have not answered me. Why should we listen to you when you betrayed our fellow warriors?"

Jun stared at the fear in the faces of the two warriors standing in front of him. He turned to face his new enemy.

"Gaun, I always believed you would be the first to challenge me." Jun moved closer to him. "We cannot fight amongst ourselves. We must help the retreating warriors."

"You are frightened to fight!" Gaun yelled at Jun, while more warriors surrounded him.

"Stop, Gaun!" Mea shouted as she ran into the centre of the cave. "Don't challenge Jun. We must save our battles for the emperor's men."

"I am not frightened to fight, but we need to find the masters and bring them back here. Soon, this will be the only place to hide on the mountain," Jun said.

"Yes, hide," Gaun shouted. "That's what you want to do, but we could have defeated the emperor's men and nobody would now need saving!" He continued to press Jun for answers, pushed forward by some of the other dragon warriors.

"I tried to help them, you know I did," Jun insisted. "I told the masters we needed to fight together, but they wouldn't listen."

"You should have listened to them," Gaun replied with a smirk. "They believed you wanted to lead them all, but now there is nothing to lead."

The circle of warriors surrounding Gaun and Jun moved slightly away from them.

"I didn't want to lead them," Jun said calmly, not wanting to rise to any further challenges. "The leader of the monks told us this would happen."

"Some of us believe you have forgotten how to fight!" At Gaun's reply, the warriors behind him backed away again.

"If you believe I was wrong not to fight the emperor's men and fall into their trap, then I will step down as your master, but I will never turn my back on a fight."

Jun and Gaun stood facing each other in the centre of the cave, ready to fight to the death, while Mea and the ox and dragon warriors circled them.

Gaun charged at Jun with venom and fury, and knocked

him to the ground. Jun pushed himself up, then, ran to Gaun with fists of dragon fire, and blasted him around the wall of warriors. Gaun fell to the floor and waited for Jun to walk over to him.

With blood pouring from his hands, Jun asked, "Do you accept me as your master?"

Gaun wiped the blood from his face and yelled, "Not yet!" Then he kicked Jun high off the ground, like Jun's horse hurling the general into his men. Jun clasped on to a rock and crawled to his feet, holding his head. Gaun laughed at him and leapt across the cave, but just before he pounced, Jun stepped to the right and swung his arm up like the wing of a dragon. He swept Gaun away from him with a deadly deflection and sent his challenger crashing against the entrance to the cave.

Some of the dragon warriors marched over to Jun and shouted his name, waiting for the fatal strike. Jun stood over Gaun, clenching his fists, ready to hit. The warriors yelled his name louder.

Jun held up his hand and shouted, "Animal warriors are dying on the mountain. We cannot fight against each other. No more warrior blood will be spilt on this mountain." He moved away from Gaun and tilted his bleeding head, indicating to a warrior to help Gaun. Then he ordered the two warriors standing guard to the kingdom to open the cave.

He looked back to the warriors in the cave and shouted, "We must wait for the masters to find us."

Over the next few weeks, hundreds of injured warriors followed the dragon signs to Jun's kingdom. Snake, rabbit and rooster warriors retreated to the dragon kingdom. Jun questioned every one of them, hoping they would tell him where to find their masters, but none of them did.

One summer night, feeling he was losing the battle against the emperor's men and the other masters, Jun entered the cave where the injured rebels were resting. He woke some of them and asked again where he could find their kingdoms. None of them would talk of their kingdoms, but they said that the general had shown his knife to many warriors who had died protecting their locations.

Jun sat in the middle of the cave, closed his eyes and tried to recall the monks' prayers. One of the snake warriors got up and moved closer to him. Jun opened his eyes and studied the warrior, camouflaged by the jade soil of the forest.

He said, "You hold on to your kingdom's location because your master has ordered you to, but soon you will have no kingdom to return to."

With his eyes fixed on the ground, the snake warrior whispered, "She said that you were the bravest warrior on the mountain, and if we could not reach our kingdom we should come to you."

"Will *she* fight with us?" Jun asked with hope in his voice.

But the snake warrior's words struck Jun deeper than the blade of the general's knife when he replied, "It's too late, the battle is lost. That's why a band of warriors are heading for the Heavenly Temple. We passed them on the way to your kingdom, and they refused to come with us."

"Horse warriors?"

The warrior flipped his head like a snake bearing down on its prey. "Yes, horse warriors. You cannot trust them. They are blinded by their loyalty to Ling."

"But what if the soldiers follow them to the temple? Why did they refuse to come here?"

"Running to you would be worse than being captured by the soldiers. They believe it would be a betrayal of Ling."

Jun jumped up off the ground and ran to find Gaun. When

he found him resting in a small cave, he shook him and said, "Now, you're the dragon master. Lead them bravely, but you must not fight with just your heart."

"What...why?" Mea asked as she ran to the cave.

"Mea, please help Gaun to protect the kingdom. The injured warriors cannot leave here and it's too dangerous for us both to travel."

"Where?" Gaun asked as he rolled out of the cave.

"To the Heavenly Temple. I need to save the monks."

# 13

## BROKEN PROMISES

With the summer sun burning brighter than the fires surrounding the Heavenly Temple, the leader of the monks paced the temple grounds with a troubling vision of the emperor and his men in his head. The image of the soldiers hunting down the warriors and searching for the temple had troubled the leader ever since he'd seen a blazing forest fire many months before. Bato walked around the temple grounds for months, worrying about the temple's secrets, and the soldiers interrogating the monks.

"If the emperor's men have found one of the warriors' camps, it will only be a matter of time before the other camps fall," Bato said, wandering through the courtyard.

Rushing around the temple, many of the monks were concerned for the months ahead. "Your Grace, we don't know if they have found one," the dog monk cried as he passed Bato in the courtyard. "But we should be safe here, even if they have, they will not storm into the temple grounds."

Bato stopped in the middle of the courtyard, turned to face the monk and said, "They will rattle the mountain just like the cannon blasts we heard, until they find out who taught them their animal kung fu." He raised his voice and shouted to all the monks, "The soldiers will march along every trail on the mountain to find us. We must protect the temple's secrets."

The dog monk walked back to Bato and said, "But how, Your Grace? How can we document our knowledge if there is so little time?"

"I don't know," Bato said with a heavy heart. He left the courtyard and shuffled over to the vegetable garden, where he knelt down next to a bamboo basket and filled it with carrots. He stood up, turning back to the temple, and then threw the basket of carrots up into the air as he spotted Jun walking towards him.

"Jon!"

"Your Grace, I came as quickly as I could. I've not eaten for days, and—"

"Why did you come back?" snapped Bato.

"I… I…" Jun was shaken by Bato's angry response. He explained, "I wanted to protect the temple."

Bato cried, "*Protect* the temple? You are putting us in *danger* by coming here." He picked up the carrots and threw them back into the basket. "Why, Jon? Why did you not listen to me?"

"Your Grace, I did. I tried to get the other masters to fight together, but they ignored my cries for help. Now the emperor has sent more men, enough to catch every animal on the mountain and—"

"Why are there fires on the mountain?" the dragon monk asked as he approached Jun and Bato.

"The soldiers, they are hunting for warriors," Jun said. "And this led them to the horse kingdom."

"Kingdoms! What kingdoms?" Bato dropped the basket.

"Your Grace, we built kingdoms across the mountain range, we had no choice. Thousands of peasants came searching for us."

"Ling!" Bato sighed. "I warned you. I always believed he would bring you pain." He walked towards the temple.

Jun smiled at the dragon monk and said, "Please, let me explain why I am here." He collected his thoughts, trying to pull together the questions running through his mind as to why Bato had not welcomed him back. "I came here through the cave, hidden by the waterfall. I wanted to get here first—"

"First?" interrupted the dragon monk, his forehead now dripping with sweat.

"Yes, first," Jun replied. "There is a group of horse warriors searching for the temple. They could be following the trail that His Grace gave to Ling."

"Why are they coming here?"

"Only Mea and her ox warriors agreed to fight with me. Ling refused, and the other masters refused too." Jun's eyes mirrored the sadness of the monk's eyes. "I carved dragon signs on every trail on the mountain. Hundreds of warriors came, from all the warrior groups, except the horse warriors. That's why they are coming here."

The dragon monk muttered, "I always believed Ling would fight against his spirit. Come, Jun, we must go to the prayer room. We need to tell His Grace."

When Jun and the dragon monk reached the prayer room, the monk opened the door and moved inside, closing the door behind him. Jun waited outside the door and tried to listen to Bato and the monks talking about him. Five minutes later the dragon monk opened the door and beckoned Jun to come inside.

"Your Grace, I am sorry for coming back to the temple," Jun said. "I came back to help you." He walked into the middle of the room and stood in front of the monks kneeling before him.

"Yes, *Jun*," Bato said. The dragon monk had reminded Bato of his name. "We have just been told about the horse warriors. They should have accepted your help and not brought the fight back to the temple."

"We are all guilty of betraying your trust, Your Grace. We took everything you had to give and only brought you sorrow." Jun knelt before the monks.

"You cannot be blamed for the spirit of others, but *you* broke a promise. I asked you not to return here."

"But Your Grace, the temple..."

"Yes, the temple. Now you are here, we have no choice but to protect it." Bato's voice shuddered through the monks in the room.

"How can I help?" Jun asked.

"Help?" Bato repeated. "If the emperor finds the secrets of the animal systems, he will create an army that will be unbeatable. He took a deep breath. "All we can do is pray – pray for a miracle. That's what we need, a miracle." He stood up and shuffled out of the room.

"But we must do something!" Jun yelled as Bato closed the door behind him. "We cannot just wait for the soldiers to come here. You said that they would build an unbeatable army!"

Bato did not reply, and the prayer room fell silent.

"Jun, pray with us," the snake monk said. "This will help us. We need to seek guidance from our ancestors."

Jun moved in between the dragon and snake monk. Throughout the night, he and the monks stayed in the room and prayed for guidance.

In the morning, Jun followed the monks to the dining room where he dropped into a chair and rested his head on the table. Exhausted from the endless prayers the night before, he listened to the monks as they spoke fondly of the animal warriors. The monks' forgiving natures briefly took Jun away from the battle on the mountain. Their peaceful way of life breathed a sense of calm into him.

After resting for a while, Jun pushed himself away from the table and stood up. He looked along the line of monks chatting to each other and tried to find the dragon monk, but he was not sitting at the table. Jun walked out of the dining room and searched for the dragon monk in the courtyard. Passing the stone room where he had first seen the animal systems, he noticed the door was slightly ajar. Jun pushed the door open and found the dragon monk standing in the middle of the room, staring at the animal shields hanging on the training room wall.

Jun moved closer to him and asked, "How can the monks forgive the warriors? They talk about them with such compassion and—"

"This is our way of life," interrupted the dragon monk. "We don't just study and learn teachings, we embrace them too. Forgiveness is part of our studying. We see the good in everything."

Jun moved closer to the dragon shield. "How can you learn from what Ling has done?" he asked, reaching out to the shield, only to pull his hand back quickly. "What was that?"

"You are becoming more aware of yourself, Jun."

"It felt like a bolt of lightning bursting through my hand."

"I can answer your first question," the dragon monk said, ignoring the second one. "When a hornet stings you, it should remind you of the hornet's purpose in life, and yours. It's just protecting itself – we all do it." The monk walked along the line of animal shields hanging on the walls. "You see, we wait for weeks for plants to grow and we talk to them every day with the patience of holy men. But if we are stung by a wasp, we scream to the world."

"I don't understand."

"Jun, we can learn from all of our life's experiences, good and bad. A hornet has to sting to survive."

Jun asked, "What did His Grace learn from us finding the temple?"

"That you are brave and wanted to help protect your families, but some of you are not following the right path to achieving that."

"Am I on the right path?"

"Only you can judge your decisions," the monk said, brushing his hand over the other shields. "Sometimes we lose sight of our path, and this can lead to us finding a greater one."

"Will I do this?" Jun asked. "Will I find a greater path?" He reached out to touch the dragon shield again. "It's vibrating. My hand is tingling with the shield."

"Jun, it is time. You must find His Grace and ask to enter his prayer room."

"But I was in the prayer room last night."

The monk smiled at Jun and said, "*His* prayer room."

Jun ran out of the stone room and followed shuffling footsteps in the trees to the side of the temple. He found Bato drifting among the trees, brushing his fingers against them in a moment of peace.

"Your Grace, I need to go into *your* prayer room, wherever that is!"

Bato jumped away from the trees, startled by Jun's request, and was shaken back to the worries of the temple. He shook his body, trying to stop the demons draining hope from his mind, and stumbled towards Jun.

"Your Grace, the dragon monk sent me to you." Jun spoke faster than a snake catching its prey. "He explained how you learn from everything around you, and when I felt the—"

"Jun, I was drifting through the trees like a summer breeze, searching for guidance." Ignoring Jun's excitement to enter his room, Bato interrupted him, turning away and then walked in between the trees. "I've failed to learn from my mistakes." He touched the trees again and sighed. "The monks are still learning from their journey through life, but I am their leader, and I should have shown more wisdom than a hornet sting…"

"I know about the hornet," Jun yelled, concerned that the horse warriors would reach the temple before Bato had shown him the room. "Please take me to your prayer room."

Bato held his breath, and then said, "All right. It is time. Please come with me."

As they walked through a labyrinth of corridors to heart of the temple, Bato said, "Jun, please tell no one of what you are about to see. This is the holiest place on the mountain."

Bato stopped at a wall in the hub of the temple, with corridors flowing in every direction. He pushed the wall away from him and Jun followed him inside. Bato stood in front of a door with no handle. He placed his hands out in front of him and hovered his palms over the door. He slid the door open, without touching it. Once inside the triangular room, Jun stood still in front of a large tree. With just enough space to walk around the tree, Jun squeezed past the jagged jade vines spiralling up it. His eyes followed the vines up to the wooden roof.

"How did you open the…?"

"Be quiet, Jun. Hold your palms up to the tree," Bato said. "This is the oldest tree in the valley."

Bato and Jun hovered their hands near the tree, not touching it, but for Jun, it felt like he had.

"Holy men built this temple here, around this tree, to protect it. If you are bonded to the tree and stare at, touch or smell it, you may be connected to your ancestors' wisdom."

Jun moved his hands up and down. "I can feel it beating with my heart." He stopped moving them. "My hands, they are tingling, just like when I went to touch the dragon shield."

"The shield?" Bato laughed. "That's why the monk sent you. You are now connecting to all that is living. Your mind was clouded before, by your past no doubt, but now you are ready for greater wisdom."

"What am I connected to?"

"You are connecting with the earth's energy – it is all around us. For thousands of years, hundreds of monks have tried to connect to the energy emitting from the earth, but very few of them were open to receiving it."

"But I can feel it," Jun said, spreading his hands apart, "and when I close my eyes, I feel strong and alive."

"Everything alive has energy flowing through it," Bato said with a warm smile. He took his hands away from the tree and looked at Jun. "Can you remember our prayers?"

"Um...yes, some of them."

"Absorb the earth?" Bato asked.

"Yes...that one," Jun said, nodding his head, trying to convince Bato that he had remembered it.

"This prayer reminds us to fill ourselves with energy from everything around us: food, water and the—"

"Ground?"

"Yes, the ground. During our prayers, gardening or training in the stone room, we connect to the ground."

"Where does the wisdom come from?"

"From you, Jun. From you."

"Me?"

"Yes. When you are truly connected to a flow of energy,

your ancestors' wisdom will come to you, and for some, when they connect this energy to the heavens, the power to heal others."

"Wha...wha...what if I hold on to the tree? Will I find more secrets of the zodiac, and how to protect the temple from the soldiers?"

Bato sighed. "You will need to hold on to the tree for many years."

"But why, Your Grace?"

"I've been wandering around the temple, praying and touching every tree here, but I cannot think of a way to document the temple's secrets. We cannot record them in just a few days, but if we don't, we may need to accept that the animal systems could be lost forever."

Bato and Jun stood still with their palms held out. An hour later, Jun jumped away from the tree like he had been kicked by a horse.

Standing by the door, he stated to Bato, "Your Grace, I made a promise to help you."

Bato turned to face him.

"And I *will* fulfil that promise."

Shaken by the force that had thrown him away from the tree, Jun stumbled out of the room.

Later that night, while the monks were asleep in their quarters, Jun crept along the candlelit corridors of the temple and into the courtyard. With a blanket of darkness falling over the grounds, he walked into the stone room, lit a candle and sat down in front of the animal shields. He studied each shield until he lost his fight with exhaustion, his weary eyes dragging his head to the ground, but just before he fell into a deep sleep, the twelve animal monks tiptoed into the room.

In the morning, as the sun filled the temple rooms, the

sound of hurrying footsteps woke Bato. Startled, lying on his bed, Bato rubbed his eyes in disbelief at the sight of Jun and the twelve animal monks standing in front of him.

"Your Grace, we talked all night about how we can document the animal systems and we believe we've found a solution."

"Jun," Bato said as he sat up, "you must stop talking of documenting the secrets. You must leave the temple for your own safety."

"Please listen, Your Grace. The monks have never documented any of their teachings in a few weeks before—"

"Yes, that is correct," Bato interrupted, believing Jun was stating the obvious.

Jun continued to explain his excitement. "And you said that if the systems are not documented quickly, they would be lost forever…"

Bato waved his hands in the air and yelled, "You've been awake all night to tell me this?"

"Your Grace, we must get someone from outside the temple to document these secrets. Someone we can trust to record them in days." Jun bounced on Bato's bed.

"Out…side? Have you gone mad?" Bato fell back on to his bed.

"I believe we need the help of someone from the village at the bottom of the mountain. That's where I got the map which led us to the temple, and—"

"Did you say you had a map which led you to the temple?" Bato asked.

"Oh…yes, a map." Jun sighed and got off the bed. "It led us to the waterfall, and that's how I found a passage to the temple."

Jun closed his eyes and thought of the three promises he had now broken – promises to the people he cared about the most: his father with a promise to take care of Ling; Bato with a promise that he would not return to the temple; and he had promised not to tell anyone about Wan's map. Three promises he had tried and failed to keep.

"Did the young teacher there give you the map?" Bato asked.

Jun opened his eyes and asked, "Yes, but how did you know it was her?"

"What do you know about her?"

"Her name is Wan, and she is beautiful, kind and has the strength—"

"What do you know about her family?"

"Oh, I know very little," Jun sighed. "She, ah…came to the mountain range with someone and then fell in love with the children in the village. That's why she stayed there. I'm sure that's what she said."

"Hmm, you are right," Bato replied quickly, not wanting Jun to ask him any more about his interest in Wan's family. "She can help us. She has done many wonderful things for the children in the school."

"Your Grace, Wan told me she had written many stories from memory for the children." Jun bounced on the bed again, sending Bato flying away from him. "She wanted the children to read as many stories as she could remember. She wrote them down in hours. If you or I had done it, it would have taken weeks."

"Jun, go to the village," Bato ordered. He pointed to the dog monk. "You must go with him. Your animal spirit has taught us that you will be methodical in your approach to documenting the animal systems. This will help Wing, because if she can cope with you, then she will fly through the other systems like a horse running…to a…river."

Jun and the monks laughed.

"Tell Wing—"

"Her name is Wan, Your Grace," Jun stated.

"Yes, I know, *Jun*. That is what I said."

Jun and the monks lifted their eyebrows as one, and smiled at each other.

Bato coughed. "You are fond of this young lady, aren't you?"

"Well, she is a kind person, Your Grace. A soft, gentle soul," Jun stuttered.

"Yes, very kind. Now that your eyes are sparkling like the stars at night, I can see how *kind* she is. Tell *Wan* we will be grateful for her help."

Jun jumped off the bed as the monks smirked with their leader, and shouted, "We will leave now." He then tripped over his feet and fell face down on the floor.

The dog monk chuckled at Bato's forgetfulness and Jun's blushes. "Don't worry, Your Grace, I will protect him."

"Jun, may our ancestors be with you and guide you along a safe passage to the village." Bato climbed out of his bed. "Please wait here." He shuffled out of the room. The monks stood patiently, waiting for him to return.

Five minutes later, while Jun was still dusting himself off, Bato walked back into the room with a holy robe in his hand. He gave the robe to Jun and said, "You will need to disguise yourself as one of us. Keep your hood up so no one can see your face…or your hair."

The monks laughed louder than they had for many months.

"This robe is our gift to you. It will protect you on the mountain. No one from outside the temple has ever been given a holy robe before."

"Thank you, Your Grace." Jun put on the robe and bowed to Bato and the monks. "If the horse warriors do come here, please send them to the dragon kingdom."

Later that morning, dressed as a monk, Jun led the dog monk to the cave hidden behind the waterfall. They scurried down the mountain with the monks' ancestors placing paths at their feet. Rocks rolled out of harm's way, branches of the strongest trees bowed away from them and rivers flowed faster when they were running down the quickest trails to the village.

After a few days, Jun and the dog monk reached Wan's village, and with a silent prayer, they thanked their ancestors for their safe passage down the mountain. Sweltering under the afternoon sun, their thick holy robes dripping with sweat, they walked towards the school.

Once inside the school grounds, they stopped when they heard the gentle laughter of a woman. The young lady was playing with the children on the other side of the building, and as they moved around the school to the front door, they saw Wan spinning a child around her. Jun stood behind her for a moment, studying her every move as she beamed with beauty. He smiled at the warmth of Wan's peaceful way of life, but quickly remembered he was about to change it. He moved closer, almost catching the child who spun around her like a wind chime in a summer breeze.

"Be careful, don't drop him."

Wan spun around to face the voice, and dropped the child on to the floor. She gasped, "Jun, is that you?"

"Yes, Wan. Sorry for startling you," Jun said with a smile wider than the line of children behind Wan.

"I can't believe you are here, safe and well! I've thought of you every day," Wan said, picking up the child. Her beautiful, pale skin suddenly matched the colour of Jun's ruby robe. "Well... I mean... I've been worried about you and the other rebels who travelled into the mountain."

Jun beamed at Wan's blushes. Laughing nervously, he said, "I *am* here, Wan, safe and well."

While the two of them chuckled at each other, Wan's eyes were drawn to Jun's robe. She asked curiously, "Have you joined the monastery?"

"Can we talk? I need to ask you something."

Before Wan answered, an eagle landed in front of Jun. "The eagle flew to you?"

"Yes, I have been taking care of it," Wan said as she knelt down with Jun and stroked the bird's feathers. "When the eagle came back, I thought…"

"We had perished on the mountain?" Jun asked.

"Yes, I did, but I am as pleased as the eagle to see you again."

Jun stroked the bird's feathers and felt the same tingling in his hands as he had felt in Bato's prayer room. "Wan, can we go inside?"

Wan's rosy blush started to fade.

"I really need to talk to you inside the school."

The blush was completely wiped off her face when she realised Jun needed to talk to her away from the children. She asked them to stop pulling at the holy robes and coaxed them into the school.

As Wan reached the top step, she called to Jun, "Come here later tonight. I will cook supper for us. I also want to tell you something. It's about the magical animal masters that the villager elders cannot stop talking about. They say they will win back our province for good."

Jun smiled, acknowledging her kindness. He walked out of the school grounds and through the village, smiling at the men and women who were unaware of the fallen warriors. The holy men accepted the endless cups of water and the villagers' prayers for peace.

Later that night, sitting at the kitchen table during supper, Wan bombarded her guests with her questions in a single breath.

"Why are you dressed in a robe? Have you converted to the monastery? Where are the rebels who followed you into the mountain? What kind of help do you need from me?"

"Wan, please let me explain." Jun moved closer to her. He placed his hands on top of hers and told her almost everything that had happened since he had left the school with the rebels. He did not tell her about the zodiac book. Wan listened for an hour without a word of reply, her jaw hanging down to the table like it was being sucked towards it. Just before Jun had finished explaining why he had arrived back at the school wearing a robe, Wan leapt off her seat.

"So, are you telling me the rebels who went into the mountain are the animal warriors who are now defeating the emperor's men?"

"Yes, Wan, but we need your help to document the monks' fighting systems. Time is against us."

"What can I do?" Wan turned away from Jun. "I am grateful that you believe in me, but I am a teacher, not a monk."

"The secrets need to be documented and His Grace believes in you too."

Bato's belief was not enough to stop Wan's tears. "Will the soldiers come here? What about the children? Will they be safe?"

Jun stood up and moved closer to her. He held on to her hand and said, "I will do all I can to protect you and the children. So will my warriors."

"*Your* warriors?" Wan repeated. "You are a master?"

"Yes, the dragon master."

Wan brushed Jun's hand away and put her hand on her sinking heart. Walking away from the table, she said, "You must rest here tonight. I will make your beds in the classroom at the end of the corridor."

After showing Jun and the monk to their beds, Wan walked back along the hallway and into the school library. She lit the candles, stood in front of the bookshelf and lightly dragged her hands over the books. She pulled a book out and blew the dust off it. She was holding a book with crystals and gemstones painted all over it.

With the candles in the room almost melting into their holders, Wan moved over to a window. As she held the book to the stars, a ray of light reflected from the book on to the roof. She studied the ceiling for a while and intuitively felt that the many colours flickering around the room were a sign that she was destined to help the monks. Placing the book back on to the wooden bookshelf, she went back into the room where Jun and the dog monk were resting.

"Do all the monks need to come here?" Wan asked Jun as she opened the door and popped her head into the room. "Because I cannot leave the school, there will be no one else to teach the children."

"Yes, of course," the dog monk replied, sitting up. "They will come when you are ready."

"Oh…you're allowed to talk to me," Wan gasped.

"Yes, Wan," the monk replied. "Many things have changed since the rebels found our temple."

"For all of us," Wan said closing the door. "We will start after school tomorrow."

Over the next few nights, Wan listened to the dog monk as he explained the dog system to her. With Jun's help, the monk showed Wan all the secrets of the system. Within a week of

Jun and the dog monk arriving at the school, Wan was ready for the next monk.

However, when Jun and the dog monk were about to leave the village, one of the village elders ran into the school grounds.

"Wan, I have news about the animal masters," the elder cried. "We knew they had burnt down the soldiers' command post, but never in our wildest dreams did we believe the soldiers would run back to the emperor!"

"Every village is talking about the kung fu fighters." Wan tried to smile at the elder's old news.

"Our people are free!"

Jun held on to the elder's hope for freedom for his journey back to the temple. As he walked away from the school, he turned back to Wan and shouted, "I will hold your prayers until I return with another monk. Tell the villagers that we must all keep praying for a brighter future."

# 14

## CANNON CLOUDS

Before the horse kingdom had fallen, General Wu had personally enlightened each one of his soldiers with his master plan. He laughed with his men, "I want to give the warriors one final day of glory." And then yelled, "Let's tease them with a fortress protected by empty suits of armour. After the command post has fallen to the warriors, we will follow their victory parade back to their kingdom."

The temptation to attack the command post had been too great for Ling. He had blindly led his warriors there and ordered, "Burn down the barracks and let the soldiers' spirits carry its ashes to the emperor!" The horse warriors shared Ling's untouchable belief when he cried, "This will be the greatest victory of our people, and our names will be bellowed across the mountain for a thousand years." But Ling only wanted one name yelled across the mountain, and this led his enemies to the gates of the horse kingdom.

Commander Kuen ordered Wu to wait there with his men until he returned with reinforcements. General Wu waited for three weeks, listening to the horse warriors' victorious battle cries from inside the kingdom, but no more warriors came. Finally, Wu ordered his men to hide in the trees until he returned with more men.

The general rode down the mountain to find his brother,

bouncing on his saddle with excitement, ready to tell Kuen that he had found a kingdom and that victory was in sight. Days later, in the early hours of the morning, Wu reached the valley at the bottom of the mountain and found the commander's men. He slid down in his saddle at the sight of the military might marching before him: artillerymen, infantrymen and archers held their banners high above the ground, flooding the plains with the emperor's colours. Wu sprinted through the yellow, red and blue flags as he searched for his brother.

He spotted Kuen strutting along a line of artillery guns. The general rode over to the commander, and just before he reached his brother he jumped off his horse.

"Commander, why did you bring the guns here?" Wu ignored his brother's greeting and moved closer to the artillerymen. He kicked one of the large guns and snapped, "They can't be carried up into the mountain. The terrain will tear them apart."

"Wu, what are you talking about. We don't have to pull them anywhere," Kuen replied with an arrogant smile as wide as one of the guns.

"You've brought more artillerymen than the other banner troops," Wu said, frustrated with his brother's pompous parading. "How are they going to help us fight against the warriors?"

Pulling his horse away from the cannon colours surrounding him, Kuen cursed his brother. "Don't make me look a fool again. I brought the artillerymen to blast the warriors into the rabbit holes they came from. We will fight them here, in the centre of the valley, and end this war for good."

"Kuen, listen. The warriors fight without fear, and with the strength of the mountain. They move with more energy than our horses and the speed of snakes. If we entice them out of the mountain again, they will defeat us."

"No, General," Kuen shouted back, "I am the commander and I'm giving *you* a direct order. We are fighting them here!"

"I found their kingdom!" Wu cried. "We should take the fight to them. They will not be ready for us."

"Don't be weak," Kuen replied. "Just remember who you are. These warriors use pathetic flags to dishonour the banners of our great army. They don't have ten thousand warriors, do they? How many did you see entering their kingdom?"

"Well...two hundred, but we don't know how many warriors there are inside the kingdom. My plan was always to—"

"I know what your plan was, but when we arrived at the other command posts, I realised that sadly we had forgotten who we are, and what has won us many bloody battles."

"Did you also forget what happened to the young lieutenant who marched his men to death in the Emerald Forest?"

Kuen had not forgotten about the young lieutenant. He said, "Come with me." He moved away from the guns. Wu walked with his horse behind him. "Wu, please do not disrespect my command," Kuen ordered with a grimace as he looked down at his brother. "I am *your* commander: a commander who has won more battles than any other.

"How are you going to use the guns," Wu asked.

"We will lure the warriors out of the mountain, just like we did with your post, and engage them in combat with our troops. They will believe that we do not have enough men to defeat them, and when they charge towards us, we will launch the cannonballs from behind those bushes," Kuen pointed to a row of bushes his men had planted in the middle of the plain, "just like the spears our men rode into in the forest."

"But Commander…" Wu tried to tell his brother that the guns were bigger than the bushes.

"No, Wu," Kuen snapped. "Tell me what you have learnt from the kingdom." Neither Kuen nor Wu had realised there were twelve kingdoms. "There must be something, you've been hiding from the warriors for weeks."

"Commander," Wu said softly, "They behave like animals inside the kingdom."

"I knew it," Kuen said sarcastically. "They disguise themselves as animals to fool us…tricking us into believing there are more of them. This is an insult to our emperor."

Wu waited for the commander to finish belittling the warriors and then chose his words wisely. "Commander, we've seen other animal signs carved into trees and chiselled into rocks. I don't know why the warriors disguise themselves, but I do not believe it is to dishonour our army."

"I know I am right. We use a banner for each of our regiments, and I believe they are merely mimicking us." The commander pulled his horse towards the mountain. "Ride with me."

Wu climbed on to his horse and the two brothers rode without speaking for a while, then Wu said, "Kuen, I'm sorry. I do not want to disrespect your command, but I need you to trust me." He pulled his horse closer to Kuen's. "There may be other kingdoms. I don't know how many or where they are, but the horse warriors never changed their camouflage. I believe we should destroy the kingdom by the lake and search for the others."

"What are you talking about, Wu," laughed the commander.

"If I am right about there being other kingdoms, and we fight here, they will crush our army and then chase any survivors back to our father."

"Chase us to the palace!" Kuen yelled. "How can I listen to someone who—"

"Has never had a command post with two thousand men? Someone who has never won a battle?"

"No, Wu, I meant—"

Wu interrupted, "Someone whose father has laughed at his every failure?"

Kuen did not reply. Their horses trotted towards a stream trickling over rocks; then dipped their heads into the running water.

Suddenly, Wu shouted, "That's it! I know what to do." He pointed to the water. "We must build rafts."

"Rafts?" Kuen said as he patted his horse on its neck. "What good will they do? Shouldn't we be building barricades if you're so worried about there being more warriors?"

"No," Wu said, shaking his head, "rafts. And each one must be strong enough to carry the heavy guns."

"The guns?" Kuen yelled, causing his horse to pull its head out of the water.

"Yes, the guns. We must build rafts and drag them to where the river begins and lift the guns on to them. Then, our men will pull the guns along the river, high into the mountain. I've seen it, Kuen. The river flows from a lake that shields their kingdom. I just hope the cannonballs will reach it."

With excitement, Kuen said, "They *will* reach. I will order the men to pack the guns with enough gunpowder to blast the kingdom across the mountain." He acknowledged his approval of Wu's plan. "I will need fifty men to pull each gun along the river and twenty to pull the gunpowder and cannonballs."

"Let's get back to the men and build the rafts," Wu said, pulling his horse away from the stream.

"It's your plan, brother. You will lead the soldiers into the kingdom, but only after I have blasted their defences into the rock face of the mountain. Put your armour on, Wu, and make sure some of your men take drums with them. I want you to march their leader down the mountain, and I want every peasant in the province to see and hear it."

The commander and general rode their horses back to the soldiers and ordered the infantrymen to gather wood and build five rafts, twice the size of their guns. All day, the soldiers worked tirelessly, chopping and binding tree logs together. When they had finished making the rafts, they carried them deep into the mountain range where the artillerymen had pulled the guns.

Standing proudly by the river, Kuen said to Wu, "I believe in your plan, brother, but we will need to signal to each other, when we are *both* ready to destroy the kingdom."

"It will take a few days to lead the infantrymen there," Wu said, pulling at the ropes on a raft. He moved to another. "I will hide my men in the woods next to the kingdom and then I will send one of them across the lake to you."

"All right. When the guns are ready to fire, I will send him back to you," Kuen said, patting his brother on the back. He then turned away from Wu and ordered ten men to carry one of the heavy guns on to a raft.

"Will it hold them?" Kuen said, smiling back to his brother.

"These rafts could hold a mountain," Wu said, his chest ballooning with pride. One after the other, the commander's men carried five guns on to the rafts and then pushed them into the river.

"Find a safe passage to the kingdom. I will wait for your signal," Kuen said as he marched along the river with his men pulling the guns behind them.

"Seven days, Commander, and then our battle with the warriors begins," Wu said as he marched his men to a path he had carved to lead them back to the horse kingdom.

Days later, and further up the mountain range, the horse warriors rode through their kingdom, yelling their victory to the mountain. Ling had nailed the soldiers' armour he had brought back to the kingdom to a tree, and for hours, he clattered his sword against it. The warriors heckled the metal tree, unaware that the general and his men were hiding nearby. As Wu listened to the cheers of the horse warriors, he was ready to send a signal to destroy their kingdom.

A week after leaving his brother, Wu ordered four soldiers to follow him to the lake beside the horse kingdom. Just as the sun rose, he said, "Find an old tree log, big enough for one of you to hide inside."

Wu's men returned with a rotten tree.

"Dig out a hole in the middle of it, big enough for a head. One of you will need to hide in there, so don't forget to leave a hole at the top for you to breathe."

"Please, sir, I will go," an eager soldier said, as the others kept quiet and hollowed out the rotten log.

"You will need to float across the lake inside the log. Once there, you must inform Commander Kuen that we will be ready to fight in the morning."

"Yes, sir, I will paddle as fast as I can."

"Good, come back swiftly," Wu ordered as he placed his foot on the log. "We'll swipe the laughter from their faces, covered with mud and horse hair."

Wu and his men carried the log to the lake. Bobbing up and down, the soldier held on inside the log and kicked his legs to push it to the other side of the lake. Hours later, he reached the commander and his men waiting for the signal from the general. He fell at the feet of the commander and whimpered, "S...sir, the gen...ral is ready."

Later that day, the commander ordered the soldier back across the lake with a message for his brother: "I will light up the kingdom tonight, just after the sun has set."

The soldier asked the commander if he could rest for a little longer, but the commander refused.

"But sir, the general said he wanted you to fire the guns in the morning when the sun rose above the trees."

"Don't tell me what to do," the commander ordered. "I am blasting the kingdom tonight, as soon as the sun is out of sight. Now go tell the general!"

The weary soldier pulled the log back to the water by himself and pushed it away from the bank.

A few hours later, Wu stood by the lake and caught sight of the log drifting back to him, but then it floated for a while in the middle of the lake and got swept away by the current of the river. Too exhausted to swim back to the general, the commander's orders stayed with the soldier and he drifted away with the log.

With the sun dropping behind the forest trees, Wu ordered his men to rest for the night, believing that the soldier had been swimming back with the commander's acknowledgement of his plan to fight in the morning. Minutes later, with the soldiers and horse warriors resting, bellowing blasts of cannon fire shook the mountain, lifting the general and his men off the ground.

When the last blast had settled deep into the horse kingdom, soft cannon clouds engulfed the soldiers. While the clouds swirled above the trees, with the taste of gunpowder drying the soldiers' bloodthirsty lips, they charged towards the kingdom.

Running through the burning woods, Wu yelled at his men, "I want their leader alive."

Hundreds of soldiers stormed into the kingdom through the crater created by the commander's cannon blasts. Wu ran behind his men into the kingdom, desperate to find the master, but found only his gloating soldiers standing over wounded warriors dying on the ground. Brutally beaten by the cannon balls, the surviving warriors had no will to fight back, but under the cover of darkness some of the horse warriors had escaped.

Inside the kingdom, with a swipe of his knife Wu gave the surviving warriors slow executions, but only after interrogating them about their leader, deepening their wounds to end their silence.

"Tell me! Where is he? Where is your leader?"

"We don't have a leader," a warrior muttered before Wu ended his pain.

"Why won't they tell me?" Wu yelled at his men.

As the cannon clouds drifted towards the lake, the general's eyes fell to a sword sparkling with the stars above, trapped by a mass of burnt bodies.

"One of these warriors must have been their leader." Wu knelt down next to the sword. "Who else would fight with this? Look at these markings engraved on it!" he yelled to the men approaching him.

Wu grabbed hold of the sword and tried to yank it from under the warrior lying on it. He tugged with one hand and then two, but he could not pull it out. Holding the sword with both hands, Wu jumped to his feet. He leant back as far as he could and tried to slide the weapon from under the warrior, but just as the sword moved, the warrior grabbed hold of the handle and pulled himself to his feet. Falling forward with the sword in his hand, the warrior pushed Wu to the ground and prodded the sword into his throat.

The general's men ran towards him, only to be halted by Wu's shaking hand.

"He's…their leader," Wu gulped, fearing the sword would be pressed harder into his throat. "Go back. Let him live."

The soldiers threw their weapons to the ground and reluctantly obeyed their general's order.

Ling held his sword to the general's throat, his eyes trying to find a way out of the kingdom alive.

As his ears cleared from the ringing of the cannon blasts, a deep voice from outside the kingdom walls declared, "Let him live and I will give you my word that I will not kill you."

Commander Kuen strutted over to Ling through the entrance his cannon blasts had created. Kuen had crossed the lake with one of the rafts his men had used to pull the guns up the river.

Ling pressed his sword harder into the general's throat, and Wu held his breath. Ling knew the commander wanted to keep him alive, but only so he could parade him along the palace walls as a symbol of his victory. He also knew that if he killed the general, his dream of leading a great army would be lost forever.

With his head pounding with fear and his heart beating like one of the soldier's broken drums, Ling eased his sword away from Wu, releasing the general's blood, which trickled down his neck.

"How can I trust you?" Ling yelled, still searching for hope.

"You can't, but you might live, which makes it a wise choice."

Ling inhaled his last free breath and pulled Wu to his feet. He held his sword to Wu's back, pushed him in front of the commander and his men, and ran to the lake at the edge of the kingdom. When he reached it, he hurled his sword into the water and fell to his knees, watching the sacred sword spinning and sinking out of sight.

When the soldiers reached the lake, they stood behind Ling for a moment as he held his head in his bloodstained hands. Then they grabbed hold of him and dragged him along the ground, back to the commander. When they reached Kuen, they threw him face down on to the ashen ground. Scrutinising the defeated man before him, the commander leant over him.

"I should kill you, but your emperor will be thrilled to meet you." Kuen's mouth curled into a satisfied smile.

"I will take him to the emperor," Wu suggested.

"No, Wu," Kuen snapped back, quicker than a cannon blast.

"Kuen, you said I—"

"Listen to *your* commander," Kuen shouted. "I found a warrior scurrying into the mountain. She refused to speak about her master, but with her last breath she told me about a magical training camp that one day would send us running back to our emperor."

"There are female warriors?"

"Yes, and you failed to see them and a warrior riding on a white horse along every trail on the mountain. Now take your men and find him!"

"But, Commander," Wu insisted, "I found the master and I should take him to our father."

"That's an order, General. Find this warrior. He might lead you to the training camp, if it exists, and whoever trained these warriors." As Kuen walked away from Wu, he yelled, "General, I know you will not fail me, but be careful – this warrior has killed many of my men."

Wu's resentment towards his brother boiled over his

armour, just like the blood seeping from his throat. Kuen's orders niggled and nipped him deeper than Ling's sword, but he was determined to show his father that he was as brave as his brother. Wu ordered his men to round up the surviving horses and rode out of the kingdom without speaking again to the commander.

The general yelled to his men, "If we find the warriors' training camp, I want to bring the master who taught them back to my father." He pushed them up the mountain trails, searching for the mystical training camp and the lone warrior who could lead him to it. Wu believed he had learnt from the many battles with the warriors, but his newfound judgement was soon to be tested again.

Weeks after storming the horse kingdom, Wu and his men caught a glimpse of Jun on the mountain and followed him along the northern trail, but lost him in rainstorm. When he found Jun's horse without its warrior, Wu was unaware of how close he was to finding Jun and the ox kingdom.

Several months later, Wu and his men tracked thirty horse warriors walking along a narrow trail on the mountain. They followed the warriors until they rested for the night under a ledge of trees hanging over the path. Wu and his men settled further back, and Wu whispered, "They were walking with a purpose." Unable to contain his excitement, he added, "We will not capture them. They may lead us to the training camp the warrior spoke of before the commander silenced her."

The next day, with the late summer sun warming the ground beneath their feet, the weary warriors hiked along a grass path up the mountain. Wu and the soldiers pursued them until they stopped at a canyon. The warriors crossed a bridge of broken pieces of wood, held together by twining ropes, which splintered with every step. Wu waited until the warriors had crossed the canyon; then, concerned about what might be ahead, he ordered two of his men to go over the bridge.

The two soldiers tiptoed over the fragile bridge and followed the warriors to a ruby forest which led to a path spiralling up and around the mountain. The soldiers continued their pursuit of the warriors up the steps. Hours later, after counting a thousand steps, the soldiers stood in awe of the radiant beauty before them. The warriors had brought them to the Heavenly Temple.

The soldiers watched the warriors helping each other up the last step, and when they reached the temple gates, the soldiers retraced their tracks back down to the general. Startled by their glimpse of the holy temple, the two soldiers did not speak until they had crossed the bridge over the canyon.

"General, we followed the warriors through a forest and along a path that led them to the holy temple."

"Holy temple?" Wu repeated. "Why are they going there?" Confusion had now replaced his arrogance. "They are trying to use the monks as a human shield. They must be holding them against their will..."

"We need to help the monks," cried a soldier.

"Yes...but wait...we must not jump to any conclusions," Wu ordered, concerned by the thought of hundreds of warriors hiding in the temple. "The monks...they are in great danger, but we need to go back to the commander and return with more men."

"But sir, there may be no more than thirty warriors inside," another soldier said. "We should help the monks."

"Yes...we should...no, we *are* going back to the commander," Wu stuttered, his judgement clouding as he recalled how his brother had taken the glory of finding the animal master. "Do not question my orders again, or I will send you to the temple alone."

Ignoring any further questioning by his men, Wu ordered the two soldiers who had travelled to the holy temple to wait on the other side of the canyon. He said, "It will take many days for us to return. If the warriors leave the temple, you must burn the bridge."

"Burn the bridge?" one of the soldiers repeated.

"Yes, I want them trapped on that side. And I will leave men along the trails leading to the temple. They will ambush any warriors who try to come here." As he was unaware of the secret passage behind the waterfall, Wu's orders were flawed.

Wu and his men travelled briskly down the mountain. They did not pass or find any warriors, but encountered holy monks travelling near the small village at the base of the mountain. When they reached the valley, they rode to report the plight of the monks to the commander.

After riding for a few days, Wu arrived at the command post Kuen was building. "Commander, I didn't capture the lone warrior, but I killed many others."

"You didn't find him?" Kuen asked, confused. "But you've been gone for months."

"Yes, I did, but—"

"What about the training camp?"

"I haven't found that either, but we followed some warriors who led us to a holy temple."

"A holy temple?" Kuen said. "What good is that?" He laughed. "It's too late for us to pray to the heavens."

"Commander," Wu replied in a stern voice, "the warriors are making their last stance there. I believe they are using the monks as human shields. We need to help them."

"Protect the monks, why? Anyway, how did the warriors know where the temple was?"

"I don't know." Wu had not considered that. "But I need to go back with more men."

"How can they enter such a place?" Kuen asked, not listening to his brother.

"They must have...stormed the holy temple," snapped Wu, "or threatened the monks to let them in." His brother's arrogance was testing his tolerance.

"All right, General," Kuen said slyly. "I will take my men to the holy temple." Then, sensing his brother shaking with rage at him, for wanting to go to the temple, Kuen yelled at his men, "We will travel to the temple with the vehemence and fury of the general."

Wu stood silent. It appeared his brother was now giving him the glory of dragging the animal master to the emperor. Confused and simmering with anger, he said, "Commander, you wanted to take their master to the palace. Why are you now asking me to?"

Kuen moved closer to his brother and whispered, "There are no masters. Just rebels dressed as animals." He laughed at his brother's belief in the animal masters. "Look at him." Kuen pointed at Ling squatting on the ground in the middle of the command post. "Where are his magical powers that the peasants speak of? He hasn't even tried to fight back, or spoken a word since you left. Do you think I'm going to make a fool of myself and bring him to our father?"

"What about the sword? It had..." Wu tried to explain the symbols he had seen on the sword.

"Stop," Kuen yelled, so loudly that every soldier stood still, "acting like a fool! We've destroyed their kingdom and ended the rebellion. Now take the prisoner to the palace and tell the emperor, if you dare, about his *magical* powers."

"You said you believed in me." Wu sighed. "And I…"

"Believed me? The only thing I believe in is winning every battle, even those with my brother."

Kuen walked away from Wu and faced the horsemen. "The general has courageously found a sacred temple and we will travel there with frightening speed."

The three hundred soldiers mounted their horses.

"We will rescue the monks from their captors and we will not be bringing any warriors back to our emperor."

A unanimous cheer from the soldiers bellowed towards the mountain.

Kuen walked back to his brother and said, "General Wu, I hope you appreciate the day of glory I am giving *you* with our father."

"I should be grateful to you, Commander, that you honour me in this way, but I know I am right about the animal masters. There are others, I am sure of it, and they were taught somewhere on the mountain."

Kuen smiled at his brother's blind belief and shook laughter from his head, then mounted his horse and rode out of the command post, standing taller than ever in his stirrups.

He bellowed at a soldier who had returned with the general, "Take me to the temple!"; then sat down on his saddle and rode in between his men, muttering to himself, "We must hurry. We have a training camp to destroy…"

# 15

## ROOM IN THE ROOF

One morning, with the autumn leaves falling in the forests of the mountain, the commander and his men stopped at the canyon and studied the missing planks on the bridge. Kuen dismounted his horse and pointed to the smallest soldier.

"We will wait here behind these rocks, and you will cross the bridge and find the soldiers the general left here. Be quick, I need to know if it is safe to travel to the temple."

With his armour rattling with fear, the soldier crept up to the grass path taking him to the bridge. When he reached the edge of the canyon, he knelt down on the ground and called out to the soldiers on the other side, "Is it safe to pass?"

No one answered.

The commander banged his fist on the helmet of a soldier sitting in front of him and shouted to the quivering soldier kneeling at the bridge, "You fool. Walk across the bridge and find the soldiers."

The shivering soldier stood up and gripped the ropes so hard that they crumbled in his hands. He crept over the bridge, placing one foot at a time on the wooden planks while staring at the rumbling river beneath him. Halfway over the bridge, he wobbled, and the bridge swayed from side to side. The ropes holding the planks in line pinged and popped until a voice from the other side of the canyon shouted, "General, is that you?"

"N...no," the soldier cried, holding the fragile ropes tighter. "The...commander is here. Is it safe to cross?"

"Yes, if the bridge doesn't fall into the river. No one has come here since the general left us."

Wobbling on the bridge, the soldier turned back to the commander. "Com...mander, p...please come. It's safe," he said as pieces of the planks fell into the river below.

Commander Kuen strutted over to the bridge. With his men holding back, not wanting to be next to cross the canyon, Kuen looked back at them, waiting for them to follow him, but they wouldn't look at him. Not wanting to show any weakness in front of his men, Kuen tiptoed across the bridge as it crumbled and moaned with every step. Once on the other side, he ordered his men to follow him, sending the smallest soldiers over first. One after the other, the soldiers crossed over the bridge, those waiting to cross unable to take their eyes off the debris of wood flowing down the river.

With fifty men left to cross, a soldier who was as wide as the bridge trembled over to the edge. He thumped on the bridge like the commander had hit the soldier's head as he moved across it, and when he was three steps away from the other side, he pushed his foot through a plank of wood. Twisting himself out of the splintering steps, he held on to the ropes only for them to give way, sending him and the bridge plunging into the river below.

Kuen ran back to the canyon and watched the soldier bobbing up and down in the river until he was washed up on to a rock. Minutes later, when the soldier was safely out of the water, Kuen shouted to his men on the other side of the canyon, "Go down to him. Try to find another way to the temple, but if you can't, march back to the post."

Relieved that they did not have to cross the bridge, the soldiers ran down the path towards the debris being swept up on to the riverbank and the drenched soldier. Meanwhile, Kuen and his men followed the two soldiers Wu had left at the bridge to the temple.

The commander and his men marched through the forest filled with fallen leaves as ruddy as the morning sun. Later, when he reached the top of the steps leading to the temple, he said, "We must hide in these trees. Then during the night, we will creep up to the temple gates and wait there until morning."

Just as the sun rose, with the hummingbirds swooping through the temple grounds, the grand temple doors opened with a spinning thud, Commander Kuen signalled to his men to be ready. The doors opened and two monks walked out. The soldiers brushed them aside and stormed into the temple, searching and screaming for the warriors' blood. Kuen followed behind his men.

The soldiers flew through the temple like birds migrating in the summer, and swarmed through every corridor, but they found no warriors. Frustrated, Kuen ordered his men to round up the monks and march them to the courtyard. While the soldiers were doing this, he walked through the empty temple and studied the many wooden statues inside it.

With the monks lined up in the courtyard, Kuen strolled up to them and demanded to know which one of them was the leader. The monks stood still and none of them answered him, but with a quick shuffle of robes from inside the stone room, Bato strolled into the courtyard with thirteen monks behind him.

"I am the leader here. What brings you to this holy temple?"

"Where are the warriors?"

"We are not warriors, General." Bato laughed. "We are humble monks and seek—"

"I am a *commander* in His Majesty's army," Kuen said, biting his lip at Bato's humour. "And my men have seen warriors entering this temple. I need to know where they are." His patience was dwindling as his temper grew louder. Knowing that the leader of the monks could not lie to him, Kuen yelled, "Every time I have to ask you where they are hiding, I will set fire to one of your statues, then the temple."

Bato had to tell the commander the truth. "Oh...ah... I will tell you everything, but please promise not to destroy the temple."

Kuen bowed his head and accepted the leader's plea.

The monks stretched their hands out and held on to one another. Bato muttered, "The rebels who first entered this temple learnt their fighting skills from the monks studying here."

"Speak up!" Kuen shouted.

Staring at the floor, and waiting for the monks to be punished for helping the rebels, Bato said, "We taught the rebels how to fight."

"*You* taught them?" The commander erupted with laughter, filling every corner of the courtyard while his men cringed at Bato's compassion for the warriors. After five minutes of unstoppable laughter, Kuen composed himself. He said, "These animals must have frightened you." He laughed again and skipped in between the monks, breaking their holy chain. "Or did you feel sorry for them?" Again he jumped in between the monks. "But you should not feel either. We will protect you now."

Realising the commander did not believe him, Bato said,

"There are no warriors here, just men walking a path of destiny."

"So there are no warriors here?" Kuen asked, glaring at Bato. "Can you promise me this?"

"Yes...no warriors," Bato replied, with Jun standing next to the commander disguised as a monk, his hair covered by the hood of his robe. Bato had not broken his vow to tell the truth because he believed Jun was searching for wisdom and peace. He had also sent the horse warriors to the dragon kingdom, following the path to the cave behind the waterfall.

Jun watched Kuen strolling around the courtyard, still laughing at the thought of the monks training the warriors. As the commander mimicked the animal warriors' moves, one of his men shouted to him, "Sir, come here, quickly!"

Kuen ran to the echoing voice bellowing in the stone room. Bato and some of the monks ran behind him.

Once inside the room, the soldier pointed to several faded animal patterns marked on the stone walls. Jun moved closer to the monks. Bato stood still, a sudden glow of moisture trickling down his forehead. He frowned at the monks, fearing the animal markings would convince Kuen that he had been telling the truth.

Kuen stood in front of the markings and nonchalantly studied them until once again he rattled with laughter inside his armour. He shook his head until he was dizzy.

"You painted these markings to convince me you trained the warriors! That's what you were doing when we stormed the temple." Kuen's arrogance had blinded him from seeing the picture puzzle waiting to be solved.

Later, when the commander had become agitated with the monks for trying to protect the warriors, he barked at his men, "I want you to turn every room upside down and find me something leading to a warrior. If they're not here, find out where they are hiding."

The soldiers ran from sight in search of something to pacify the commander's simmering temper, while the monks dispersed throughout the temple grounds.

Two hours later, as Kuen threw wooden statues around the temple rooms, he reluctantly accepted that his men could not find anything. The commander strutted out of the temple and ordered the monks, "Feed my men. We are staying here until the morning."

Bato and the monks ran round the temple and prepared a meal big enough to feed a battalion of men. Jun sneaked off to Bato's prayer room in the centre of the temple, which none of the soldiers had noticed. Bato had hidden the twelve animal shields there. When he reached the prayer room, Jun tried to slide the hidden door open, but it would not move. He closed his eyes, held his palms out to the door and waited for his hands to tingle. Minutes later, his hands vibrant just like the tree inside the prayer room, Jun moved them to the left, and the door opened. Once inside the room, he wrapped the animal shields in a blanket, ready to take to the cave behind the waterfall.

Later that night, with the commander and his men snoring like pigs in their rooms, Jun sent word to Bato to meet him in the vegetable garden. Carrying the shields over his shoulder, Jun crept through the temple grounds and waited next to the stone wall for Bato to come to him.

With the moon lighting the steps, Bato shuffled his way over to Jun and helped him carry the shields up on to the wall.

Jun whispered, "Thank you, Your Grace. I'm sorry for everything we have brought upon you." His voice broke with shame when he said, "Forgive us – we used your kindness against you."

"I don't blame you, Jun," Bato said, looking deep into Jun's spirit as the two men stood on top of the wall. "You gave your people a taste of freedom."

"Freedom?" Jun sighed, picking up a shield. "Did we? Or did we bring greater suffering to them? The commander and his men will surely punish us again for fighting back. My father, he told me that I would lead my people to a brighter future, and I was foolish enough to believe him."

Bato picked up another shield and gave it to Jun. "Hope can be found in many forms. If the other masters refuse to fight together, your people may suffer cruelty and contempt, but their sacrifices will show their children that there *can* be a brighter future."

Jun carried two shields down the trees and then climbed back up for more. With two left to take, he wrapped them in the blanket and placed them on the ground. He smiled warmly at Bato, who gave him the sign of hope. Jun did the same to him and picked up the blanket; then Bato moved closer to Jun and gave him a bracelet.

"Please take this with you. It has five wooden beads, and a prayer is carved into each one. Every day, if it helps, please recite and try to remember them."

"I have seen them before," Jun said, moving closer to Bato. "The travelling monk...he had the same bracelet."

"Yes, he did," replied Bato. "When we are young and take our first step along the path to becoming a holy man, we are given a bracelet. We are told to use it to help us remember our prayers, and then pass the bracelet to someone else who will embrace them. With my memory leaving me faster than I can learn new teachings, I have held on to it, but now is the right time to let go."

"But, Your Grace," Jun said, handing the bracelet back, "you must keep it for—"

"Please take it." Bato moved away from him. "I know you will embrace the prayers more than anyone else I have ever met." He climbed down the wall and returned to the temple, while Jun held on to the bracelet and then climbed down the trees.

In the morning, a crashing of falling trees woke Bato and the monks. They moved to their windows and witnessed the chopping of wood around the temple grounds. Bato ran outside and fell over the piles of wood scattered in front of the temple doors. Kneeling on the ground, his heart pulling him back inside the temple, Bato stared at the soldiers' eager eyes, ready to light the wood.

The other monks ran out of the temple and one of them helped Bato to his feet. Bato tried to run back inside, but the commander jumped over the wood and stood in front of him.

"We will take you down the mountain," Kuen stated.

"But, Commander, you..." Bato tried to reason with the commander.

"You will seek refuge in the village there." Kuen smirked, ignoring the monks' pleas to stay in the temple. "The warriors may return here and we won't be here to protect you."

"We can't leave the temple," Bato cried. "It's our place of worship, please..."

"You cannot stay here," interrupted Kuen. He moved away from the monks and yelled to his men, "Torch the temple!"

"No! Stop! Please, Commander," the monks cried.

Kuen walked away from the monks and ordered his men to take them out of the temple grounds. "We cannot allow the warriors a fortress to hide in. They can scurry like wild animals through the mountain, and we will hunt them down until we have killed every last one of them."

Bato ran to Kuen. "Please, Commander, I told you…"

"Stop your lies," Kuen shouted.

"You promised not to destroy the temple!" Bato fell at the commander's feet. "I told you the truth, we *did* help the rebels."

"Stop! You are a man of faith," Kuen said, pulling Bato up off the ground. "You took an oath not to lie. Stop trying to protect the warriors. You should fear me more than anyone because I blasted their kingdom into the heavens and ended the rebellion."

Kuen signalled to his men to light the piles of wood surrounding the temple. The monks ran with Bato, and once outside the temple gates, they turned back and held on to each other. Aching at the sight of the wood surrounding the temple flaming into life, their eyes followed the fires swirling along the walls and scorching the morning sky.

Within minutes, the raging fires pushed the monks away from the temple. Turning their backs and pulling their hoods over their faces to protect them from the blistering ash, the monks denied the commander the pleasure of seeing them witnessing their holy place of worship crumbling into a mountain of flaming wood. But as they moved further away, they could hear the tree in the heart of the temple crying out to the heavens.

With ash drifting to the valleys below, the commander ordered his men to march the monks down the mountain. With a blazing smile glowing across his face, he shouted to the monks, "We cannot take the path to the canyon because the bridge has crumbled away, just like your temple. Find another trail to the village at the base of the mountain."

A few hours later, trying to think of a way to document the animal systems, Bato walked in between the monks and listened to their concerns. He whispered, "We need to lead them along the longest path. This will give Jun time to reach his warriors."

"Has he taken…?" A soldier moved closer to the monks.

Staring at the monkey monk, Bato said, "Do not be concerned. Our prayers and faith will *shield* us from pain and give hope to the Hunan people."

Bato's words painted a half-smile on to the monks' faces. They now knew Jun had escaped with the animal shields.

After travelling for many days, the commander and his men were weakening with every step. Bato and the monks were leading them down a trail that passed no rivers, no trees and no animals to catch for food. Each year, for a month, the monks had abstained from eating food and this left them with the strength to walk every trail on the mountain.

Two months after leaving the temple, the soldiers were all thinner than the first one who had crossed over the canyon, but they somehow found the will to march the monks into Wan's village. Staggering through the village, the commander and his men fell to the ground just after elders had greeted them. An eagle landed in front of the monks as they walked towards the village elders.

Bato asked the elders, "Can we please pray alone in the school? We couldn't pray for a few days because the commander wanted to reach the village quicker than a—"

"No," croaked the commander. "Pray in there." He pointed to the smallest house in the village.

Once the monks had squeezed inside the house, they prayed for the soldiers to let them stay in the village so they could finish documenting the animal systems.

After resting for a while and drinking a thousand cups of water, Kuen and his men brushed the villagers aside and ordered the peasants to feed them. The commander and his men stayed in the village for three weeks, consuming more food than the villagers had eaten in three months. With their stomachs bursting against their armour, the soldiers chuckled with bellyaching laughter at the monks' tales of training the warriors.

When the soldiers left the village and rode to the command post, full of food and still laughing at the monks, none of them had realised that a monk had escaped from the temple and was searching for the horse kingdom.

A few minutes after the commander left the village, Bato shuffled over to the school. When he opened the door, a wall of children falling at his feet greeted him.

"Please tell us about the Heavenly Temple."

"Did you see them? Did you see the kung fu masters on the mountain?"

"Oh…the masters. Yes, of course." Bato stuttered at the children's excitement. "But I need to speak to your teacher first."

"They will not let you talk to me until they hear stories of the magical masters," Wan said, trying not to laugh at the children pulling at Bato's robe.

Bato followed her inside a classroom, pursued by the children, and for the next two hours he lifted them high into the mountain with his tales of the temple and the warriors. When he could not think of any more stories, Wan asked the children to tidy their desks.

"Please can you tell us one more story?" a child begged, excited to hear of more mysteries and magic on the mountain.

Smiling at the beaming faces sitting in front of her, Wan

said, "One more, and then I'm going to lock the school doors, with or without you sitting inside."

The classroom pictures hanging on the walls flapped with the shrieks of laughter from the children. Bato rustled up one last story, but the only one he could think of was about a rebel who had fallen in love with a young teacher.

After the children had gone home and Wan's blushes had died down, Bato walked with her to the kitchen.

She said, "Why didn't you send another monk? Did the dog monk say that I didn't understand his secrets?"

Bato sighed. "No, Wan, it's not that. I'm sorry, but we could not send another monk here because so much has happened since…"

"Since what, Your Grace?" Wan asked, concerned at the sight of the single tear trickling down Bato's saddened face.

"We haven't told the other villagers. I asked the monks not to. They still believe the commander is running scared to his command post."

"What is it, Your Grace?" Wan asked, holding back her own tears.

"After the horse kingdom had fallen, the soldiers hunted for every warrior on the mountain. This led them to the temple, and because they believed more warriors would retreat there, they burnt it to the ground."

Wan's tears stopped her from asking how the soldiers had found the temple.

"I'm sorry, Your Grace," she sobbed. "But…what about Jun?" she asked, falling down on to a chair. "I haven't seen him in the village."

"When the soldiers came, I asked him to hide the twelve animal shields the masters had made for us. I pray he found a safe place on the mountain for them."

"Then where will he go?"

"The horse kingdom. He wanted to know what happened to Ling."

Wan dropped her head on to the table. Bato moved closer to her and placed his hand on her head. "Please be strong. Jun told me you were, and I believe in his faith in you. I'm sorry to put you in more danger, but we need your help again, and we don't have much time before the commander realises that we made a fool of him. I told him that the monks trained the warriors, but he just laughed at me."

"Your Grace, I will help," Wan said, lifting her head up, "but it will take weeks to document all the animal systems, and we will have to be more careful because the soldiers will guard the village. The commander said he was sending more men to protect us from the warriors."

"Thank you, Wan," Bato said with a smile. "Jun was right about you, and not just because he is fond of you. You are as warm as the children, and as wise as a monk."

Wan's tears dried as she blushed and smiled.

Sitting down next to her, Bato said, "The commander told us to stay here, but if he finds out we've helped the warriors, it won't be safe for us to stay. We will need to leave the village and travel to another temple."

"The other temples." Wan sighed as if she had been thinking of them.

"You know of them?"

"Yes, there are four more."

"Oh...well, most of them will welcome us, but the most important thing now is that we do not put *you* in any more danger."

"Why won't they welcome you?" Wan asked.

"Ah...some of the monks believe that the element teachings in their temple are greater than others."

"What are the elements?"

"A way of life," Bato sighed. "Our element was fire, the other elements are water, wood, metal and..."

"Earth," Wan said, to the surprise of the Bato."

"Yes, it is," he replied, startled by Wan's wisdom.

Over the next two months, the monks visited the school and told the children more mesmerising stories of the mountain. Each evening, after the children had gone home, Wan continued to document the kung fu systems. This became the daily routine for the monks and the children.

One night, when a group of soldiers was patrolling through the village, the rat monk trudged over the first snow-fall of winter and entered the school grounds. Not realising the monks had been going to the school to show Wan their fighting systems, a soldier joked, "Have you found a new training camp?"

"Maybe you're training the children in your deadly fighting skills," laughed another.

"No, I am helping the teacher to paint something," replied the monk.

Meanwhile, high in the mountain, Jun had followed the scent of gunpowder drifting through the forests. He had swum across lakes and climbed steep rock faces until he stumbled on a path with horse-warrior camouflage scattered along it. After travelling for many weeks, he found the entrance to the horse kingdom which the commander had created. Exhausted after his journey and with night falling, he fell into the smouldering ruins of the kingdom.

In the morning, he woke up with his face covered in the black ash piled on the ground. He walked through the bodies lying throughout the kingdom and dug out a grave for the warriors. After carrying each of them to their place of rest, he buried his anger at Ling and prayed he would find him alive.

When Jun had eased the last body into the ground, he walked to the lake nearby. He knelt down and cupped his hands in the water, washing the ash from his face, with scorched pieces of the horse warriors' flags drifting over his hands.

"Look what we found: a monk with hair as long as a warrior, but he's praying by the warriors' kingdom."

Jun turned to face General Wu.

"Who were you expecting?" Jun asked.

Wu and his men marched over to Jun.

"No one alive, and I certainly didn't expect to find the rebel leader," Wu said in a smug tone. "Now, did the monks give you that robe, or did you steal it from one of them? Because if they gave you the robe, then they trained you, but if you stole it, you must have killed a monk to take it from him." He pulled out a knife from his belt.

Jun moved closer to the edge of the lake and asked, "Where is Ling?"

"Your friend, I assume. Well, he is travelling to the palace with my men. But don't worry, you will be with him soon…" Wu laughed loudly. "I came back for something he had thrown in the lake, but now I have a greater trophy to parade around the palace. You are the lone warrior – the one who started the rebellion."

Throwing his robe to the floor, and with the strength of every soul he had buried, Jun yelled, "You have taken my village, our province and my oldest friend, but you will not take me!" He fell back into the water and swam under the fallen flags for as long as he could hold his breath.

"Stop him!" Wu screamed at his men. "This is the warrior I want."

Two soldiers dived through the flags and followed in Jun's wake through the water. Jun surfaced in less than a minute and swam as fast as the soldiers swimming behind him. The general leapt on to a raft, which Commander Kuen had used to cross the lake, with four men and they paddled to the other side of the lake. The soldiers in the water did not have the strength to cross the lake, so they swam back to the kingdom.

Slowing with every stroke, Jun drifted across the lake to the riverbank, but as he came to rest in the shallow water, he looked up to see the general standing on the bank in front of him. Jun fell back into the deeper water and kicked his legs away from Wu. He held his breath and sank to the bottom of the lake, swaying from side to side in the current until he drifted to a shining ripple of light.

The general and his men remained at the water's edge, resting on a cannon the commander had left after blasting the horse kingdom. When a few minutes had passed, the general shouted, "The water has taken him. One of you will need to search the lake for the sword. You," he pointed to a soldier trying to hold his breath, "take you armour off, and get ready to swim to the bottom of the lake." Wu was eager to find out if his brother had found the training camp, so he yelled to his men, "While he is searching for the sword, I want the rest of you to destroy the other rafts. Then, we will cross the lake and back to the men waiting in the kingdom. Hurry, we need to find the commander."

The soldiers pulled the rafts out of the water, but just as one settled in the shallows, Jun sprang from the lake like a flying fish. The general and the soldiers fell to the ground as he swung Ling's sword towards them. With Wu lying on the ground, Jun cut a crooked scar along his face, mirroring the emperor's.

Jun ran to the raft and dived on to it. The raft glided

over the shingled bay and, using the sword as an oar, Jun dug deep into the stones and pushed the raft away from the shore. He paddled away from the general and his men, concerned for the safety of Wan and the monks. Breathing deeper with every stroke, he knew the general would find the commander and they would punish the monks for helping the warriors. As the soldiers paddled a raft across the lake with their hands, Jun propelled his raft towards the many rivers flowing from it, and as he got closer, he steered his raft to the river that roared the loudest.

One night, back in the village, the ox monk left the school and passed Bato, who was strolling towards the school grounds. The monk smiled and said, "Wan has finished documenting my animal system. It won't be long before she has documented all of them."

"The dog monk said she wrote faster than Jun's heart beating when he was standing next to her," laughed Bato.

He walked into the school and found Wan. "Thank you for helping us." He walked next to her along the school corridor. "You are flying through the secrets like—"

"The children have enjoyed the monks' stories," Wan interrupted, laughing at how Bato described most things by comparing them to something else. She walked into a room at the end of the corridor and moved over to a table placed under a window. Standing in front of the table, she put something in a crystal bowl in the middle of it.

Bato shuffled behind her, and as he reached the table, he said, "We have enjoyed telling the children our stories of the mountain. They have great imaginations."

"So do the monks!" Wan laughed loudly, lighting up the room with a pearl glow radiating out of the crystal bowl.

Bato peered into the bowl and said with amazement,

"How did that happen? One of the stones lit up. They…look familiar." He picked up one of the twelve stones.

"They are gemstones," Wan said, moving her hand over the others. "Twelve of them, each with their own shape, beauty and colour."

"I have seen them before," Bato said, stretching his mind to remember where. Wan span around to face him as he gasped, "The zodiac book!" He let go of the purple stone he was holding with one hand and caught it with the other. "Please, tell me where you got them."

Wan dithered for a moment and then asked Bato to follow her along a corridor to a large cupboard. She asked him to step inside the cupboard, which was just wide enough for both of them, then squeezed in after him and closed the door behind her.

They both stared at an empty bookshelf to the right. "What are we doing in here? Are we hiding from someone?" Bato asked.

"No. Please wait here, Your Grace," Wan said as she pushed the bookshelf away from her. It came to rest against a wall three feet behind it. "Follow me up when I have lit a candle."

Wan climbed up the wooden shelves. "Is that…a room in the roof?" Bato asked as she rummaged around in the room, searching for a candle to light.

He crawled up the bookshelf, and when his eyes had adjusted to the flickering candlelight, he focused on the drawings resting on a table at the back of the room.

"These pictures hold some of the secrets of the zodiac," Wan said, holding one of them up to the light.

"Z-z-zodiac teachings?" Bato stuttered. He rubbed his eyes in disbelief. "Look at the children – they are beaming with the beautiful colours around them." He walked over to the table, the floorboards creaking beneath his feet, and said, "Wan, who told you about the zodiac teachings?"

"Someone I love dearly," Wan sighed, placing the drawings back on the table. "But please, do not ask me about him."

"Jun?"

"No!" Wan said, blowing out a candle.

"Oh," Bato said, relighting the candle. "The zodiac knowledge...it's more powerful than an army of men, and only for—"

"I am blessed with this knowledge," Wan interrupted. "When I first arrived here, there wasn't a school. I offered to teach the children, but they learnt very little. So I used the stones to make up for lost time."

"What? How?" Bato asked as he picked up a drawing. "What did you do to the children?"

"How did you use them?" Wan asked at the same time.

"I used the zodiac teachings to choose the best fighting systems for the monks to study, but I foolishly did the same thing with the warriors too."

"You used the zodiac secrets on the warriors?" Wan whispered, even though they were alone in the school.

"Yes, but everything got out of control. The travelling monk who brought me these teachings did not warn me about this."

"But, Your Grace, the warriors have won many battles against the emperor's men."

"It's my fault," Bato sighed. "The twelve warrior groups would not train together. They elected masters and became over-protective of their own systems..." He sank his head into his arms as he rested against the roof, which was covered with cobwebs in every corner.

"You cannot blame yourself," Wan said, gathering the drawings from the table. "I experienced the same thing."

"You did? Where?"

"Here, but I made a promise…"

"What is it, Wan?" Bato asked.

"I promised not to tell anyone about my findings."

"Do you know why the warrior groups fought against each other?" Bato pressed her for an answer. "You can tell me."

"We must go down to the school. The candles will not last much longer." Wan gestured to Bato to go down the bookshelf. After he had climbed down, she blew out the candles and followed him.

When they reached the front door of the school, Wan said, "You are right, I can trust you. The man who gave me the stones, he said I would know when to tell someone, and—"

"Your Grace," the horse monk yelled from outside the school, "the general is coming back to the village!"

Bato and Wan ran out of the school. Bato asked the monk running towards them, "Who told you?"

"I don't have time to explain, but hundreds of soldiers are riding here," the horse monk said as the other monks came running into the school grounds.

"We must go back inside the school."

Once inside, Bato stood in a classroom and gazed at the mountain. He said to the monks standing alongside him, "Teaching the rebels was the right decision. We've seen why they wanted to fight just by spending time with the children in the school. Now *we* must fight back." He turned to Wan. "You must come with us, for your own safety."

Shaking her head in disbelief, Wan tried to hide her tears. Abandoning the children was her greatest fear. She drifted out of the classroom, her delicate face flowing with tears. With her eyes fixed firmly on the floor, she stumbled into the library.

Bato and the monks stepped quietly into the room. Holding one of the stories she had written for the children, Wan said, "I will leave for a while, but someone will need to stay with the children and read one of these stories to them every day. I won't leave unless someone is going to teach them, and I'll come back to them as soon as it is safe."

The dog monk said, "I will stay. You have already documented my system."

"No, I will," insisted the ox monk. "You have documented mine too."

A tender smile from Wan held back the monks' tears. She said, "The children have warmed to you, as much as you have warmed to them."

"No, I will stay," a voice cried from behind the wall of animal monks. The old monk who had taught the female warriors how to make their weapons squeezed through them.

"But you must come with us," Bato said, surprised by the suggestion.

"I'm too old to travel," the monk sighed. "And the soldiers won't realise that I am a monk, I don't need to shave my head anymore, because I have no hair."

The other monks smiled at him.

"If the soldiers ask me about the animal systems, I will not need to lie, because I never learnt them. I will be safe here."

Wan gave the book to the monk, then she moved over to another row of books and picked up one with drawings of gemstones on the front of it and said, "I will take this one with me."

Later that night, after saying goodbye to the monk staying in the village, Wan and the other monks walked towards the village gates. They passed one of the elders, who said, "Where are you going? It's late. Come back in from the cold."

"I need to take care of my father," Wan said, not looking at the elder. "It will be safer for me to travel with the monks. One of them has kindly agreed to stay and teach the children. If the soldiers come, please don't tell them that he is a man of faith." Her voice fading with her heart being pulled back to the school, she said, "Tell the children I will return. I promise I will."

Then, just after Wan and the monks stepped out of the village gates, she wrapped herself in a robe that the monk who was staying in the village had given her to shield her from the cold, and sighed, "My heart will ache every night for them."

"The children will miss you too," Bato said, comforting her. "But, you've brightened their lives, and one day they will brighten yours..."

As Wan and the monks trekked away from the village, the eagle was flying above them.

# 16

## ETERNAL SPRING

With a wall of wind and sleet pushing them away from the village, Wan and the monks travelled until the morning sun lit up the forest they were walking through. Filled with towering trees, the forest's muddy trails weaved in between them and led them to the heart of the woods. Once there, they hid and waited until it was safe to travel at night.

Wan stood next to Bato and said, "The man who came to your temple, the one who gave you the zodiac teachings..."

"Yes, what about him?" Bato said, ready to find somewhere to sleep.

"He was not a monk..."

"What? Yes, of course he was," laughed Bato. "Wan, I think you are tired and need to rest. Please lie here." He put his robe on the muddy ground for her to lie down on, believing she was dizzy with exhaustion. "He told me he had travelled to the other holy temples, so he must be a person of faith. He said he went there to share his knowledge of the world."

"He said..." Wan slid down on to the robe as she closed her eyes.

"You need to rest," Bato said, now more concerned about Wan than the emperor's men finding them.

Wan lifted her head slightly and sighed. "I'm all right,

Your Grace. I'm tired, but I've not lost my mind. The stones – they could have…" She drifted off into a deep sleep.

Later, after Wan and most of the monks had slept, she sat up and smiled at Bato.

"Wan," Bato said, shuffling closer to her, "Do you think the crystals…?"

"Yes," Wan replied. "Yes…they could have stopped the warriors from fighting against each other. I was going to tell you, but the horse monk came to warn us about the soldiers. I'm not supposed to talk to anyone about it, but he did say I would know when to tell someone."

"Do you believe it is now?" Bato asked, hoping it was.

"If I can't trust you, Your Grace, then who can I trust?" She whispered in his ear. "I used the gemstones on the children."

"The stones?" Bato repeated.

"Yes, the twelve stones. Each one of them has its own beauty and powers."

"How did they help you with the children?"

"When the stones were given to me, I was told they would light up when 'held by a pure spirit', but only if the spirit could feel the connection—"

"There is no purer spirit than a child," Bato interrupted.

"Yes, the children at the school show their true spirits. As we get older, our life experiences can change who we think we are. The zodiac teachings will help your true spirit, but a man or woman might forget who they are. You used the zodiac knowledge on adults, but the stones will show us the spirits we are born with."

Bato fidgeted with this knowledge as the sun set behind him. "How did you do it? Did they laugh near them?"

"No, they did not laugh near them," Wan said, smiling. "I remember telling Mea—"

"The ox master?"

"She's a master?" gasped Wan. "She is strong, but I never thought she would be a master. She has the warmth of the sun."

"Jun is fond of her too."

"Oh...he is? Well, I told her when she came to the school that we are all given a birth name: a name wrapped around us when we are born, from our parents. Our names will show us how we should live our lives, but as we get older, most of us forget."

"So did the stones light up when you laughed?"

"No." Wan smiled. "Not at first. That has just started to happen."

"Just started?"

"Yes, when you arrived in the village."

"So how did you...?"

"Use the stones?" Wan asked. "Well, I needed more help to understand the children. I didn't have much time, and I wanted to teach them the wonders of the province..."

"And?" Bato prompted, bouncing quietly on the ground.

"The stones...they are created in mountains, oceans and valleys throughout our land, and we are connected to the powers held within them. When the children held the stone connected to them, it lit up in their hands. That's when I saw the spirits inside them."

"And you think the stones would have helped us with the warriors?"

"The gemstones would have shown you their true spirits. You chose an animal system for them because of how they were behaving. This book warned me of this." Wan pulled a book out of her robe.

"Ling!" Bato cried.

"What is it, Your Grace?" the tiger monk asked as he jumped to his feet.

"Err...ah, sorry. I was just thinking of the horse king-dom."

"Yes, Ling," Wan whispered as the tiger monk sat down. "His inner spirit is not the one he shows."

"He has not only been fighting the soldiers, he has also been fighting Jun and his inner spirit, just like many of the warriors. That's why the animal groups fought against each other."

"They were fighting against themselves, and tried to hide this with a conflict against others."

"And... Ling, fought so hard against Jun because he saw Jun grow into his true spirit while he did not know his own. But why didn't the travelling monk warn me that this would happen?"

"Maybe he did, in his own way."

"He did? Did he? He might have...but I can't even remember what he looked like." Bato tried to recall the trav-elling monk to see if this would help his memory. "And even if he had told me, I probably wouldn't have remembered it anyway."

Wan laughed with Bato.

"But I *do* remember seeing stones in the book, but I'm sure he never mentioned *them* to me...or did he?"

"He has given pieces of the zodiac knowledge to many people because he wants to protect its secrets. He said that whoever he passed this knowledge to would be destined to experience it before they could fully understand it." Bato marvelled at her wisdom.

"Do you know where the travelling monk is?" he asked. "We need to find him and tell him about the warriors, the horse kingdom falling, the temple being burnt to the ground and that we are now being hunted by the soldiers. Not to mention the glowing stones."

Wan laughed and said, "If I know him at all, he already knows this."

"He does? I really don't know much anymore. My memory is fading like..."

"Shh," Wan whispered, putting a finger to her lips. "We need to find the horse monk. He wanted to take us somewhere, but he is not here." She scanned the monks sitting nearby.

"I'm here," said the horse monk as he walked over to Wan through the trees behind her. "We must go. The soldiers are close by and we must leave as soon as night falls."

An hour later, the horse monk led Wan and the monks out of the forest. They followed him throughout the night, continuing on the trail alongside the river which carried them away from Wan's village. With the rain washing the mud off the monks' robes, they travelled in darkness until the morning.

Just before sunrise, with Wan wobbling from side to side with exhaustion, they reached a flour mill next to the river. The dragon monk helped to carry her to the mill, and when they were all standing in front of it, the horse monk asked them to wait outside. He knocked twelve times on the door and then went inside. A few seconds later, he popped his head around the door and beckoned to them.

"Jun! You're safe," Wan cried as she fell into the mill and threw her arms around him.

"Yes, Wan, I am now," Jun said as he embraced her.

"Did you find the horse kingdom?" Bato asked quickly.

"Yes, I found the kingdom."

"Did you find Ling?" Bato asked.

"No, but I found this." Jun pulled the sword out of his coat. "It's tingling in my hand." He beamed as the sword lit up the room, reflecting the light from the burning candles.

"The general went back to the kingdom searching for this."

"The general?" Wan said.

"Yes, he was shaking with excitement when he found me there. He is desperate to prove to his brother that there is another kingdom. He wants to find you, to interrogate you, and find out if you gave me my robe or whether I stole it from one of you."

"Where is he now?" Bato asked.

"Riding to the village. He will not stop until he finds out the truth, and he will show you no mercy when he does."

"How did you escape from the general *and* his men?"

"I swam across the lake, away from the kingdom and the general, but he was waiting there for me. I dived, away from him, and I found Ling's sword at the bottom of the lake," Jun said, putting the sword back into his belt. "When I touched it, I didn't need to come up for air, so I waited, and then I leapt on to the general and his men and threw them to the ground. Then I jumped on to a raft and rowed away from them."

"You're so brave," Wan said, hugging him again.

"Yes…very brave," Bato said, blushing as Wan held on to Jun. "And so are we," he added, trying to ease the monks' concerns, "for helping the rebels, protecting the animal secrets, not eating for weeks and walking for two nights with no sleep."

"Yes, you are too," Wan said, trying not to laugh at Bato's blushes. "Very brave, all of you."

The monks smiled back at her.

"So after defeating the general's entire army, how did you get here?" Bato asked.

"I paddled to a river that screamed like my warriors when charging into battle," Jun said with a smile, lifting the monks' spirits. "It surged into the heart of the mountain, through caves and tunnels. Then, as the river twisted and turned through a valley of stone, I knocked my head on a rock. When I woke up, I was lying on the raft by the mill."

"And the soldiers?" Wan asked. "Did they follow you here?"

"No, they stopped at the edge of the lake," Jun said in a more serious tone.

"There are soldiers everywhere," warned the horse monk.

"I know," Jun said. "When I woke on the raft, I crept through the forest for two nights and came to the village. I wanted to warn you about the general – he is building an army to find the people who trained the warriors and me."

The monks stopped smiling. "You came to the village?" Bato asked.

"Yes, I spotted the horse monk at the allotment, and startled him while he was talking to his plants."

Wan and the monks laughed at Jun's description of the monk attending to his garden.

"When he *finally* stopped shaking, I asked him to warn you about the soldiers, and to bring you here."

"I'm happy you are safe," Wan said, trying not to think of the children she had left behind.

"I promised I would come back to you," Jun replied.

"Where are you going to hide, Jun?" Bato asked.

"I will find somewhere, but I am more concerned about you," Jun said to Bato and the monks. "Where will you go?"

"To another temple, but we do not know where they are," Bato said, glancing at Wan and sighing. "And if we find one, they won't let Wan enter."

"Jun, you must go with them and live your life in the sanctuary of a temple," Wan said in a second. "The general has seen you and—"

"No," Jun said sharply. "I am not leaving you." He held

on to Wan's hand and smiled at the monks.

"But how will we finish documenting the animal systems?" the snake monk asked.

"Gaun, the dragon master, and his warriors, will guide you to a temple," Jun said, letting go of Wan's hand. He walked around the room and stated, "I will stay with Wan and wait until you are safe, then we will find a village nearby." He walked over to Wan. "They can come to us in the village, and you can document their secrets there."

Bato moved closer to them, placed his hand on top of Jun's and Wan's and said, "We will find you, when it is safe for all of us." He looked at Wan. "Jun is right: we will need the other animal secrets documenting, but now we must be guided by the dragon warriors."

"But we can travel together, can't we, Your Grace?" sobbed Wan. "And then we can—"

"I won't put you in any more danger," Bato said, with the sadness of all the monks. "One day we will be together. It's not safe for you to travel with us."

Wan fell into his arms. The tiger monk gasped, "Wan, no!"

Bato held her tight and said to the monks, "Yes, we took a vow never to talk to or touch a woman, but many things have changed since we helped the rebels. The rebels coming to the temple has shown all of you that you can talk to women without falling from your path. Getting to know Wan and all her wisdom has taught me how to embrace my faith, and to love another." He held her again, tighter than before. Jun smiled, then walked into a room at the back of the mill, asking Wan and the monks to follow him.

Bato wiped his tears on his robe as they all followed Jun. Once they had settled in a circle on the stone floor, Jun lifted a basket over their heads and placed it in front of them. The basket was bursting with roasted fish that Jun had taken out of the oven. He cut a fish in half and gave a piece each to Wan and Bato. He then passed the basket to the monks, but before eating his own piece, he went to the window and looked out at the watermill churning with the river. Then he threw a piece of raw fish out of the window for the eagle resting outside.

Jun sat down next to Wan and said to Bato, "We need to find Dao, the monk who sent us to the waterfall. I know he can help us to protect the monks' secrets."

Bato opened his eyes as wide as the basket of fish and said, "Yes, he can. We don't know where he is, but I have a feeling he will find us."

Wan almost smiled at his reply.

"Find us?" Jun repeated.

"Yes, he will." Wan sighed.

"Do you know him?" Jun asked her.

"Yes, but I've not seen him for many years. He has given his life to protecting our country's most precious secrets, and his family still cries for his many sacrifices."

The sorrow in Wan's voice was all Bato needed to hear to realise that the travelling monk was her father.


Later that day, Wan, Jun and the monks walked out of the mill with the cries of fifty dragon warriors calling out to them. Led by Gaun, the warriors signalled from the forest that they were ready to ride with the monks. Jun had ordered Gaun to lead the monks to the safety of the woods running alongside the river.

Standing outside the mill, Wan held on to Bato. Then the monks, one after the other, walked up to her and kissed her hands. No one spoke. Jun turned to face the monks and placed his hands together, showing them the sign of hope.

Bato and the monks returned the sign and then pulled their hoods over their heads and walked towards the forest.

With the sun breaking through the clouds above, and the eagle circling around them, Wan and Jun watched them walk away.

Several years later, in a village in the western province of China, a fourteen-year-old girl read a story to the youngest children in the school.

"Children, please sit down. My mother has asked me to read to you because she has had to rush off to find my father," the girl, Wing, said.

With the children sitting in a curved line on the floor, Wing walked over to the bookshelf and picked up a book, opening it at the page she had marked.

"All right, last week, if you can remember, Jon and Wen watched the monks ride away from the mill with the dragon warriors. And it said in the book that Wen's gemstone lit up with her heart breaking at the thought of not seeing the monks again, sending a ray of pearl light drifting towards them."

The children's eyes opened wider than the book Wing was about to read to them.

"Three months after the monks had ridden away with the dragon warriors, Jon ran inside the mill, shouting to Wen to hurry to the raft resting on the riverbank.

'Why, Jon?' Wen cried as she ran out of the mill.

'The general,' Jon shouted, 'is riding here with his men. I can see them charging towards us.'

"Wen ran to the raft and waited for Jon, as he ran inside the mill to find his sword. When he reached the raft, he pushed it off the bank and jumped into the water, swimming with the raft and holding on to it as it spun around, floating down the river.

"Minutes after he'd left the mill, the general and his men kicked the door open. They searched inside the mill, while others rode further down the river, and one of them shouted back to the general, warning him that Jon and Wen were getting away. The general and his men burst out of the mill and charged along the riverbank, and within minutes, they had caught up with the raft.

"Riding alongside the river, the general and his men jumped over fallen trees, keeping up with the raft and laughing at Jon slipping off the raft. General Wu ordered his men to be ready to pull Jon's body out of the water.

"Wen held on to the raft as it spun around, faster and faster. She lunged at Jon and held on to him with both hands, trying to stop him from drifting away. With his face bobbing in and out of the water, Jon cried in between breaths, 'They – are – stopping.'

"Wen turned to see why the soldiers were pulling up their horses. 'Jon, look – there!' she cried, pointing down the river. 'A…waterfall!' The raft spun faster as it got closer to the river's edge, which was a hundred feet above the rocks below. The waterfall hummed like the monks singing their prayers."

With Wing's tears dropping on to the page she was reading, her eyes swelled just like how she had imagined the waterfall. The children sat staring at her. One of them said, "No, Wing, they don't—"

Wing interrupted the boy and continued reading. "Wen closed her eyes and held on to Jon. The raft sank and twisted, but just before it tipped over the ridge of the waterfall, an eagle swept down, grabbed hold of Wen and pulled her off the raft."

"Yes!" one of the children cried. "I knew they would be saved."

Wing continued, "The eagle gripped its claws into Wen, but Jon, the sword and the raft tumbled down on to the rocks below. Flapping its wings as fast as it could, trying to keep Wen off the rocks, the eagle dropped to the water.

"Holding on to Wen's back, the eagle spread its wings as wide as Wen, swept her away from the rocks and carried her to the riverbank. Once safely over the bank, the eagle placed Wen on to the ground and they both scanned the water for Jon.

"Twenty feet down the river, Wen spotted pieces of the raft caught on rocks bulging out of the riverbank. She jumped to her feet, as quickly as her cold and fragile body would allow her, and stumbled along the river to find Jon. When she was opposite the broken pieces of the raft, she fell down on to the riverbank.

"'Wen... I'm here,' wheezed Jon, before falling back into the water, but she could not hear him.

"Believing the water had taken Jon, Wen reached down into the river and cried out, 'Jon... Jon!' Suddenly, sweeping over Wen's head, the eagle flew across the river and dived into the pieces of the raft. Seconds later, the eagle dragged Jon, who was still holding his sword, across the river and pulled him over to Wen and on to the riverbank.

"Once Jon was away from the edge of the water, Wen turned him on to his back, kissed him and held him tight, but Jon lay still in her arms. She shook him when she realised he was not breathing."

The tears from the children in the classroom flowed faster than the river. Wing continued in a soft voice, "Wen then fell down on him and tried to listen for a heartbeat. She couldn't find one.

"Without her realising it, some of Wen's crystals had fallen out of her coat and on to Jon. With a feeling of warmth and light surrounding her, she was thrown off his body as one of the crystals burst into life and glowed brighter than the spring sun.

"The rugged jade stone grew brighter and brighter until Jon lifted his head up and gasped, 'W...Wen, run.'

"'No, Jon, I'm not leaving you,' Wen sobbed. 'The soldiers will be here soon, we must move away from the river.'

"She helped Jon to turn his body to the side as he coughed up some of the water he had swallowed, then pulled him to his feet and they staggered away from the river. They settled down in between bushes, holding on to each other, while listening to the soldiers charging by.

"When the soldiers were out of sight, Jon said, 'The stone...it saved me. How?'

"'One of the gemstones that fell on to you was *your* crystal,' Wen said, placing a hand on his heart.

"'My crystal?'

"'Yes, there are many crystals. All of us can use one to connect us to the energy around us, and when we need it the most, it can bring us back to life, but only if you are a pure spirit.'

"After they had rested for a while, Wen pulled Jon to his feet and they walked until they reached a rock path that led them into a small valley, with grass hills on both sides of its plain and a rainbow in the distance. They travelled for a while, and then Wen and Jon stopped walking and held each other. They had seen Commander Kuen and six hundred of his men riding towards them. As Jon let go of Wen, he turned back to the path leading to the river and saw General Wu and his men charging at them. Both of them fell to their knees, and Jon held Wen's head against his body, shielding her from the emperor's men."

Wing closed the book and said to the children, "It's late,

and we don't have enough time to finish the story today, but I will read it to you next week. I promise."

"No, Wing, please," the children cried as one. "We can't wait. Please tell us now."

Wing took one look at the children's faces, with their eyes dripping with tears and fixed on the book she was holding, and said, "All right, but don't tell my mother. She told me not to read this story. She thinks I'm reading you the story about the animals on a farm."

The children snuggled closer to Wing as she read the book again, but this time her voice was much quieter.

"Kneeling on the ground, Jon and Wen closed their eyes and waited for the soldiers. Minutes later, the commander's cavalry charge turned towards Mea, the ox master, and two hundred ox warriors stampeding over the hill. The warriors swept down as quickly as the commander and his men had changed direction.

"To the east of the valley, bloody battles broke out as Mea ordered her warriors to charge at the soldiers' ranks, but the commander's men brushed them aside. Desperate to reach Jon, who was now being surrounded by the general and his men, Mea jumped off her horse and swung her butterfly swords in front of her. Carving out a path, she charged towards them.

"'Mea, no!' one of her warriors cried. 'There are too many of them, you must wait for—'

"One of the general's men sent him to the ground with his sword. Mea continued to charge towards Jon. Jon watched General Wu slide off his horse and pull his sword out in front of him. Pulling out his own sword, Jon staggered towards the general. The general ran over to him and they crashed their swords together and swung at each other with the might of the mountain, the general's men ready to pounce if the general fell to Jon's sword.

"Then, to the west of the valley, a rumble of horses being ridden down the hill drew the general's men towards them. Gaun and fifty dragon warriors were flying over the valley to save Jon."

Wing again looked up at the children, weeping over the battle described on the page, and sighed. "Jon and the general fought for a while, but Jon's legs, bruised and cut from the waterfall, could not hold him, and with a swipe of the general's sword, he was cut to the floor.

"Wen ran forwards and threw herself at the general's feet, pleading, 'General, please spare him. Take these crystals, they are all I have...'

"She opened her map in front of the general and laid the crystals on the ground. Wu knelt down, picked them up and threw them to one of his men. Waving his sword around his head as a sign of victory, he strutted over to Jon and pushed Wen aside. Standing over Jon as he lay in a pool of blood, he lifted his sword above his head and laughed at the approval he was going to savour from the emperor.

"Just as he was about to thrust his sword into Jon, Mea burst through the wall of soldiers surrounding the general and charged at him. Head down, knocking soldiers off their feet, she charged at the general and launched him into the soldiers behind him. She then stumbled to the ground, with the general's sword piercing her back.

"Seconds later, one of the general's men pulled him to his feet. Wu stepped back, dazed, his head spinning like the raft in the river, and tried to focus on Mea lying face down on the ground. He looked beyond her and glared at the band of monks riding through patches of rain, behind the dragon warriors.

"Wu yelled to his men, 'Leave them, they're dying. Ride to the warriors to the west. I want those monks captured alive. The commander will hold the warriors to the east.'

"The general and his men rode towards the dragon warriors, colliding with them and sending the roar of battle back to Jon.

"Outnumbered, and with their weapons smashing against the soldiers' armour, the ox and dragon warriors' blood spilled into the ground. They were losing more than just the battle.

"As Mea lay still on the floor, Jon stumbled over to her and eased the general's sword out of her back. Wen knelt down next to her. With the battle almost lost and Mea drifting off to her ancestors in his arms, Jon glanced at the monks trying to blast the soldiers across the plain. Bato and the monks were fighting with more deadly skills than any warrior, but they too were losing the battle with the general's men.

"Holding on to Mea, Jon cried to Wen, 'The stones... they might have saved her.' He closed his eyes and felt Mea's pain through his hands. Seconds later, he opened his eyes, kissed Mea on the side of her face and whispered goodbye, then his eyes fell upon a sapphire stone resting on the grass, with a rainbow in the distance reflecting off it.

"Jon shouted to Wen to fetch the stone. Wen picked it up and ran back to Mea, placing the square stone on to her back.

"Oblivious to the cries of the warriors falling all around them, Jon and Wen were mesmerised by the sapphire stone as it lit up with the colours of the ocean, bringing Mea back to the battlefield. Wen slowly slid the stone along Mea's wound and watched in wonder as the deep cut on her back closed and stopped bleeding.

"When the stone stopped glowing, Wen hid it in her coat. 'The warriors,' Jon cried. 'They need my help.'

"Wen stood up sharply and ran to Jon as he staggered towards his sword. 'No, Jon, no,' she cried. 'The battle is lost!'

"Jon stared at the fallen warriors, and then just before he picked the sword up, Wen grabbed hold of it with both hands, and with the blood of every warrior that had seeped into the ground running through her veins, she stabbed the sword into the ground as if the general was lying in front of her. Then, with Wen still holding the sword, the ground shook and a tremor of light rumbled along the ground and lit up the valley, as a beam of light burst through each of the soldiers' armour.

"Minutes later, with most of the soldiers pinned to the ground by a vibrant light, the warriors' spirits lifted off the ground, and then the rays of light spiralled around them and brought them back to the battlefield. Seconds later, they stood up and walked through a rainbow of colours shooting up into the sky. The other soldiers ran to the hills, with the general carrying his brother on his horse. When the light faded, the soldiers lying on the ground wobbled to their feet and ran towards the river.

"As Jon held Mea up and Wen knelt in front of them, Bato and the monks rode over, with Gaun and some of his dragon warriors riding behind. When Bato reached Jon, he said, 'We had been hiding in the forest with Gaun and his warriors, but when we saw the commander and his men riding with so much fury, we knew we had to help.'

"'But Your Grace, you took a vow never to fight...'

"'Yes, we did.'

"'And you lost your temple because of us,' Jon sighed. 'You have given so much...but you shouldn't have broken another vow for...'

"'For you?' Bato said. 'For people who've walked a thousand miles and given their lives to help others?' He climbed off his horse and moved closer to Jon. 'Something we've learnt from you, Jon,' Bato explained, 'is that we can study how we *should* live our lives, but if we cannot use it to change other peoples' lives, then there is little reason to do so.'

"Bato and the monks smiled at Jon. Wen and Mea stood up and smiled back at them.

"'I wish I had an army of warriors for every time I have thanked you,' Jon said.

"'It looks like you have, Jon,' laughed Bato, turning around to the warriors blooming in the spring sun. He turned back to face Jon, and without thinking, he said, 'The emperor's men are running like...'"

Everyone laughed.

"Gaun rode over to Jon and said, 'I knew you couldn't defeat the emperor's men without me.'

"Jon bowed his head to Gaun and said, 'I knew you would become a great dragon master.'

"With the emperor's men scurrying away from the plain, the dragon warriors helped Jon and Wen on to the dragon warriors' horses and they rode away from the valley. They travelled for many months to a village in the western provinces of China, and Jon and Wen settled there with the monks, who disguised themselves as peasants until they found a temple. The two animal masters, Mea and Gaun, rode back to their kingdoms.

"Wen and the monks opened a school in the village and named it Ving Tsun, meaning 'Eternal Spring', after the battle with the emperor's men."

"Yes!" a child cried. "They sent the soldiers back to the evil emperor."

"Yes, they did," Wing sighed.

*

Moments later, Wing's mother ran into the classroom. "Children, it's time for you to go home. Please hurry."

"I'm sorry, Mother, I know it's late, but the children wanted me to finish the story."

When the last child had left the room, Wan took the book from Wing and held her hands. She said, "We must leave the village."

"Are you crying?" Wing said.

"I'm sorry, Wing. I don't have time to tell you everything. We need to find your brother."

"You can't just leave the children."

"We must leave. The emperor...he is sending his men to find your father."

"Father? Why would the emperor send his men here?"

As a tear from Wing's mother dripped on to the *Animal Masters* book, Wing realised why Wan had not wanted her to read it to the children.

# ACKNOWLEDGMENTS

I could not have written *Heng Mountain* without the support and encouragement of my Wing Chun family, especially Alan Gibson, my coach, and Jim Woodcock for their constant belief in my ability to write this story.

I would also like to thank my Reiki family for their support, love, and excitement for me to finish this book. And a special thank you to Debbie Cook for her help and guidance with Jikiden Reiki.

Also, to the friends who never doubted me, gave their time to help and always filled me with the belief I could write such a story; thank you Lisa Smythers and Donna Stroud.

Thank you to Jasmine Stanfield, for being the first teenager brave enough to read, and critique, *Heng Mountain*. Her, name was written into the story in gratitude for her enthusiasm for the ideas behind the story.

Thank you to Dawn Austin for designing the book cover concept – I can't stop looking at it! And to SilverWood Books for their patience with my constant tweaking of the manuscript, and for producing such a professional book.

I also owe a special thank you to Lisa Gill, because without her help, ideas, and understanding of the story, it would not have blossomed into life. Her reward was far less than her effort, and if by luck or chance *Heng Mountain* is successful I promise to change that.

Lastly, I am indebted to my family. My parents have always believed in me and shown me that if you have a dream and work hard enough, you can achieve it.

Joyce, my wife and best friend for over twenty years, understands me better than anyone else; your kind and generous nature has protected me since the first day we met.

And my daughters;

Maddy, my vibrant spirit, for being ten years older than you are and for making me smile every day with your love for living life.

Ella, my compassionate spirit, for your laughter, warmth and constant kisses.

Ava, my gentle spirit, for your hilarious drama and sweet, innocent mind.

# COMING SOON

*Song Mountain*: the story continues...

As a young girl, Wing dreamt about twelve monks coming to her father's barn and her mother studying the monks' deadly kung fu skills. When she was older, Wing would tell the youngest children at her school about her dreams and how the monks had 'magically' appeared in them.

The older children in the school laughed at Wing's stories of the monks, but one afternoon, when she read to the young children in the school, Wing quickly realised that her dreams of the monks were true and her parents were about to live an old nightmare.

On her journey to a great mountain, Wing tries to protect the secrets of her parents' past and lives through her dreams, but she finds out that the *Animal Masters* book was not how the story of the animal warriors ended...

www.songmountain.co.uk

Find out more about the author and his work at
www.hengmountain.co.uk

Lightning Source UK Ltd.
Milton Keynes UK
UKOW03f1216310316

271231UK00002B/55/P